The Third Temptation

Charles Templeton

The Third Temptation

a novel

McCLELLAND AND STEWART

The Canadian Publishers
McClelland and Stewart Limited
25 Hollinger Road, Toronto M4B 3G2

CANADIAN CATALOGUING IN PUBLICATION DATA

Templeton, Charles B., date
  The third temptation

ISBN 0-7710-8544-3

I. Title.

PS8589.E46T55   C813'.54   C80-094573-5
PR9199.3.T42T55

The song on page 78 is from "The Little Irish Girl,"
by Edward Teschemacher.

Typeset by Title Page Inc., Toronto, Canada

Printed and bound in the United States of America
by the Arcata Book Group

to Madeleine

BOOKS BY CHARLES TEMPLETON

Act of God
Jesus
The Kidnapping of the President
The Third Temptation

The last temptation is the greatest treason:
To do the right deed for the wrong reason.
— *T. S. Eliot*

The desire for glory
clings even to the best men
longer than any other passion.
— *Tacitus*

PART ONE

1

In Toronto that mid-March there was the annual lusting for spring. Winter had hung on with its usual tenacity, but a run of temperate days had raised an unreasoning optimism. The streets were awash with runoff or pale with a patina of salt, and the last snowbanks were trickling to death. In the open harbor, ducks foraged in the gray water or hunkered on pans of rotten ice. Above the commuter rails the CN Tower skewered the descending sun. At the city's core, gleaming blocks of glass and concrete reared as though to catch the amber light.

Jimmy Coulter, walking from his hotel on Queen's Quay, felt the sun on his shoulders, knew its promise to be a lie, and recalled those years when he too had permitted hope to discount experience, convincing himself that winter had been routed.

He stopped to look up at the *Tribune* building. How unlike the squat, sooty, Victorian pile that had housed the newspaper when he joined it. Behind a flourish of flags it thrust upward from the center of an open plaza – forty storeys of gold-tinted reflecting glass; a building more appropriate, he thought, as head office of a bank.

He'd come to his appointment alone despite TG's pleas that he be allowed to go along. TG Wheeler was Jimmy Coulter's oldest and closest friend and bore the official title Associate Evangelist. A self-described country boy from Tennessee (who had once addressed the Archbishop of Canterbury as Brother Archbishop) TG had developed a sensitivity to protocol the equal of a Vatican-based Cardinal's. He had been fretting since the invitation had been relayed by the Chairman of the Jimmy Coulter Metropolitan Toronto Campaign.

"Hugh Hoffman wants to see Jimmy."

"What's he want?" TG asked warily.

"No idea. It was his secretary who called."

"She must of said something."

"Just could they get together at his office tomorrow."

"I don't get it. In twenty years, not a word. All of a sudden he wants a meeting. Tell her no. Tell her –"

Coulter's voice broke into the conversation. "Hold it, Tee."

TG jammed the heel of a thumb into the mouthpiece (a reflex; he spent half of his waking hours on telephones) and looked across the room to where Jimmy Coulter was slumped in a chair, feet up, simultaneously reading and keeping in touch with a hockey game on the radio. Although past sixty, his body was flat-bellied and fit. The face – as familiar around the world as any actor's, politician's or pope's – might have been created for television. The skin was fair, the brow was straight, the cheekbones and jawline were square. The extraordinary feature was the eyes. Beneath jutting brows, their color was an enameled blue; even in the shadow of the baseball cap they seemed to glow with intensity.

Not looking up, he asked, "Why are we saying no?"

"Okay, we say yes. But not at his office."

"I used to work at the *Trib*."

"This I know. But better he comes to us."

"It really doesn't matter, Tee."

"Not to you maybe, but to him, yes."

"So, if it matters to him, why not do what he wants?"

"Because," TG said solemnly, "Hugh Hoffman is a very strange-type guy."

Jimmy Coulter entered the private elevator that would take him from the top floor of the *Tribune* building to the penthouse, wondering why he felt apprehensive. The *Tribune*'s support wasn't essential to the success of the Toronto campaign. Gone were those years of anonymity and uncertainty when he'd agonized each night before the service, wondering whether the crowd would come. Even when the weather was foul, even if his preaching lacked inspiration, the banks of seats would be filled and hundreds would throng the aisles as he began the altar call. He had become an institution. No faith was required, no wrestling with God was necessary.

He knew, though, that his early insecurity had simply given way to another: a lurking apprehensiveness that some day, at an unexpected moment, something would happen to destroy all that had been built up over forty years. At times he almost welcomed the thought. There were moments when, emptied by the unremitting demands made on him and heavy with fatigue, he wished that the burden of the fame he'd seized with such eagerness could be sloughed off and he could return to anonymity.

The elevator door slid silently open. Hugh Hoffman rose from behind a massive rosewood desk set dead-center in an office comprising the entire penthouse area and strode, hand outstretched, to greet him. "We'll sit over here," he said, gesturing to an island of low sofas and tables. "Can I buy you a drink?"

"A club soda?"

"I forgot. You don't drink."

"But I do," Coulter said with a slight smile. "Club soda on the rocks."

He studied the man at the bar. He had only faint memories of meeting him in the 1930s when they both worked in the newsroom. He saw a man in his sixties whose skin looked as though it had never seen the sun. The face was expressionless, black-jawed and thin-lipped. Dark eyes glittered behind black-rimmed glasses. Thick black hair was brushed straight back. He was wearing a gray suit and a nondescript tie on a white shirt. Looks like a picture on black-and-white television, Coulter thought.

Hugh Hoffman had come to the *Tribune* shortly after Jimmy Coulter had: an intense 20-year-old whiz-kid with one outdated suit and a set of advanced political beliefs. A dozen years later, in part through a gift for executive infighting (at which, as one report put it, "he demonstrated the ruthlessness of a Mafia don and some of the fanciest footwork in the history of Canadian business"), he took control of what had become the largest newspaper in Canada and began to look south to the United States.

They sat talking, drinks in hand. Coulter was aware that the publisher was studying him. Everyone did. How had *Time* described him? – *Jimmy Coulter, the celebrities' celebrity; the thinking man's Billy Graham. The Man of God in the Hardy Amies suit.* But there was no awe in Hoffman's eyes, and in his voice there was a hint of baiting, a note of challenge. Now he took a long pull at his drink and with some deliberateness prepared to light a cigar.

"Before you arrived, I was thinking about the two of us," Hoffman said, biting the tip from the cigar. "Both setting out to be newspapermen. You a grade ten dropout, I an Amish kid from the wrong side of the tracks. You from a family that wasn't religious and you end up one of the best-known preachers in history. I from a family that saw God in every blade of grass and I end up an agnostic."

"Raised in an Amish community, you must have had some experience of religion," Coulter said, not wanting to move the subject forward but seeing no option.

"Dozens. I was six the first time I was saved – along with every other kid in town."

Coulter felt an irritation yeasting in him. It seemed Hoffman was deliberately trying to provoke; his manner was brusque, almost rude. He decided to yield nothing. "No pleasant memories of God or the church?" he asked.

"None," Hoffman snapped. He took another sip of Scotch, swirling the ice in the glass. "God's like your father. You obey him when you're young because you're afraid not to. Then you grow up and see him differently. For a while you keep in touch because you think you should, but over the years the contacts become fewer and, finally, you forget he ever existed."

He went to the bar to splash more Scotch into his glass. "But never mind that," he said, "let's get to the reason for our meeting. The *Tribune* is prepared to pay fifteen thousand dollars for an exclusive feature we'll call *Jimmy Coulter's Toronto Journal*. A thousand words a day for the fifteen days of your campaign. First-person, but you won't have to write it. We'll have a reporter sit down with you each night after the service. You'll talk about how things went, about people of importance who were there, and he'll put it in shape."

A handsome offer, Coulter thought, but not that princely. The articles would be syndicated through Hoffman Press to the two dozen newspapers in the chain that had made him the most powerful publisher in North America.

Jimmy shook his head. "I couldn't do that."

"Why not?"

14

"I couldn't make an exclusive arrangement with one paper. I'll be glad to talk to your reporter, but if the others want to sit in ..."

"No, that won't do. I want those fifty thousand at the service each night to have to buy the *Tribune* to find out what happened in the afterservice."

"If I start selling exclusive rights to parts of my campaigns, I'll alienate the rest of the media. How would you react if I sold rights to the *Star* or the *Globe*?"

"You don't owe them anything. You do us."

"You're not serious?"

Hoffman returned with his glass and plumped onto the sofa. "Of course, I'm serious. The Hoffman Press made you," he said flatly. "The coverage we gave your Los Angeles campaign back in 1950 – playing up you and your team, that Mafia hood, and that Hollywood broad ... what was her name – the one with the big tits ... ?"

"Helene Marlowe," Coulter supplied, his voice icy.

"You don't think that's what made you?"

"You've left out Bobby Herman. He set a Rose Bowl record for rushing that year."

"Exactly," Hoffman said, his eyes glittering behind his glasses.

The two men looked at each other, eyes locked, the air bristling. Hoffman broke the silence. "How long had you been preaching before Los Angeles?"

"About ten years."

"Same preacher. Same sermons. Crowds no bigger than others in the business. Right? After L.A. you couldn't hire halls big enough. What made the difference? We did. The Hoffman Press. Overnight, the whole country knew about you."

Jimmy Coulter put down his glass and leaned forward. He could smell the Scotch and tobacco on Hoffman's breath. "Let me ask *you* a question," he said, his voice steely. "What would you have built your coverage on if it hadn't been that Helene Marlowe and Bill Virden and Bobby Herman had taken a stand for Christ? It was the Mafia and show business and God, and you were astute enough to recognize it. I'm grateful for what God used you to do, but you weren't out to do me any favors."

"Granted, it was a good story, but somebody had to print it. Without us you'd still be beating the bushes." He drew deeply on his cigar and lofted a great cloud of smoke. "Coulter, I'm going to set you straight. You're a creature of the media like any celebrity. Face it: back there evangelists were on the fringes of the church. Outside the Deep South your followers were the lunatic fringe. Today you hold prayer breakfasts at the White House. You have lunch with the Queen. You're like health food. Once it was for kooks, now it's for the masses. Sure, you're good – you could sell milk to a wino – but don't give me that crap about God using me. We used each other. One hand washes the other."

Coulter got to his feet. "You've got a convenient memory," he said. "What *really* happened? It was the summer dog-days. News was scarce. You used me to sell papers. You did exactly what was done with Jesus. The miracles weren't as important as the parables but they were bigger news. The big-name converts in my meetings weren't as important as what was being preached but they made better copy." His eyes narrowed. "Now, Hoffman, let me set you straight: you may launch politicians and rock stars and new cars, but God doesn't need anybody's backing. Not even the Hoffman Press."

He turned and walked to the elevator. The doors slid silently closed behind him.

2

He was in his hotel room changing for the press conference when TG poked his head past the door.

"Pick up the phone. It's your daughter."

He strode to the telephone. "Julie!"

"I'm in the lobby. May I come up?"

He sensed something in her voice – a distance, a hint of tears. "Is anything the matter?"

"Well, may I come up? I promise not to take much of your time."

Something was wrong. "Of course. Suite 2502."

There were few things from which Jimmy Coulter drew as much satisfaction as from his daughter. After fifteen childless years of marriage, the twins had come: Jonathan, who hadn't spoken to him for almost four years, and Julie, whom he adored.

At the door, beautiful in a simple but elegantly tailored brown suit, auburn hair drawn high, her face was pale. He embraced her then pushed her to arm's length. "Julie, darling, what's the matter?"

She didn't answer but went to the window. The harbor was empty; the winter-gray islands seemed abandoned. When she spoke, her voice was unsure.

"Daddy, if I ask you a question, will you tell me the truth?"

A tiny warning flag went up in Jimmy's mind. "When you're standing with your back to me?"

"Well, will you?"

"If I can."

She turned toward him but remained at the window. "I was at Jonathan's last night. He started in about you –"

17

"Again?"

"Daddy, I'm sorry. But you know how he goes on – about you being an evangelist, about what you believe and ..." Her voice trailed off. "Daddy, I need to know if it's true."

"Is what true?" he said. "Right now I'm trying to understand what's going on."

But he knew what was happening; the alienation between Jonathan and him was threatening his relationship with Julie. During their childhood, Coulter had seen little of the children. More often than not, he was off somewhere, preaching. He hadn't then learned to guard his privacy – hadn't wanted to, in fact. The children had reacted in completely different ways. Jonathan had grown solitary and seemed to guard his emotions. During his university years he'd begun to paint and associated with a small coterie of bookish students who were scornful of religion – the church was a medieval holdover, the clergy were exploiters of the superstitious, and evangelists (My God – evangelists!) were ecclesiastical buffoons. Julie, on the other hand, had delighted in her father's fame, identifying herself by saying, "I'm Dr. Coulter's daughter." She came almost to worship the man who turned heads everywhere and left whispers as a wake when they passed through a crowd.

"What I'm trying to understand," Coulter said, "is why my daughter is standing across the room from me, a million miles away."

"I didn't mean to do that," she said, "but Jon says ..."

"Says what?"

"That you're a ... a hypocrite."

"And what did you say?"

"That I didn't believe it of course."

"Then why are you asking me?"

"Jon says there's a letter ..."

So *that* was it! The letter: written four years ago in a time of despair, a foolhardy attempt to regain contact by making himself vulnerable, by sharing his doubts.

"He read me part of it," she said. Suddenly her voice broke. "Daddy, I don't understand."

He led her to sit facing him on the bed, taking her hands in his. "Julie, I don't remember exactly what was in that letter. It was a bad time in my life. The gulf between Jon and me was widening. Whatever I wrote, it alienated him further. It was a mistake."

She looked at him, eyes wide and worried.

"I was trying to reach Jon," he said. "Perhaps I went too far."

She leaned forward and put her forehead against his. They stayed that way for a moment. He almost asked her if it would be so terrible to know that the beliefs he'd held in earlier years had so changed as to be unrecognizable.

"I suppose I shouldn't have been so upset," she said, straightening up, "but Jon worries me. Then, last night I had this dream. There were these swans on a pond. A pair, with a cygnet. The cygnet was just learning to feed off the bottom. Then, suddenly, it was struggling, flapping frantically, beating its wings, being pulled under. And the water and its feathers were bloody. I couldn't see what it was, but I knew that something that lived in the rushes – some dark thing – had caught it by the neck and was killing it." She shuddered. "It was horrible. I couldn't get back to sleep."

He tried to lighten the moment with a laugh. She smiled wanly and said, "Silly dream. Sorry."

He took her by the hand. "I've got a great idea. Any reason why you couldn't come back with me to Malibu? Shake the winter blahs? See your mother?"

"Daddy," she said, "I'd love to."

3

The sun was bedding down on a mound of cloud. Lights were coming on night duty. In front of the *Tribune* building the row of flags was responding to the freshening wind. Hugh Hoffman stood in the darkness of his office, feet planted, hands on his hips, scowling as he looked out over the city. *His* city, goddam it! He'd made it his over thirty years by pandering to its tastes, by exploiting its needs and by outdoing the opposition in the volume and editorial excellence of the *Tribune*'s coverage. The *Tribune* dominated Toronto, its influence extending to the provincial legislature, to Ottawa, and to the board rooms of the movers and shakers across the nation. He drew pleasure from the exercise of his power and took it as his right. He'd earned it – first as a reporter, by an unremitting commitment to his goals while others were off swapping shoptalk and arguing over bar chits at the Press Club, and later, as editorial director, by developing a gift for detecting the soft underbellies of his associates.

He had been angry – in part at himself – since Jimmy Coulter had turned his back and walked from his office in silence. Coulter! – an *evangelist*, for Christ sake!

He'd had a bellyful of evangelists before he reached his teens. As a boy, deposited by his parents in the front row at the Spring Meeting – there was no refusing when you were a child in a Mennonite town like Brechin; parents had absolute rights; rights to be challenged only when you were alone in your bed at day's end. There, you could hate. Hate evangelists. Those black-garbed, black-browed bullies, thundering their denunciations, venting their own frustrations in the name of God. Hate Eleazar Schmidt! Fury in his eyes, spittle on his beard, veins bulging at his temple – like a hound in full cry after sin.

Sin. You thought a lot about sin. It draped your youth in crepe: the thousand prohibitions, the Thou-shalt-nots, the guilt – all dark companions of your youth.

Honor thy father. Why – when from your father there were nothing but commands, complaints and beatings? Honor thy mother. Toiling from dawn to dark after her husband and eleven children, she had no tenderness left for a boy who longed for it.

Was it a sin to hate the Bible? Filled as it was with "hard sayings" and foreign experiences that had to be committed to memory.

Was it a sin to hate your clothes? – broad-brimmed black hat, hot, chafing black jacket and breeches, identical to every other boy's in the community?

A sin to think black thoughts while pitching hay and horseshit, fighting a bucking plow in a stony field, your thumbs almost disjointed and your forearms and shoulders aflame?

A sin to hate God? – to be so enraged by him at times that you were prepared to risk the lightning bolt, standing in an open field railing against the heavens?

The whoop of a siren in the street drew Hugh Hoffman from his reverie. Jimmy Coulter – what was he but the impeccably clad, prepossessing, public-relationized equivalent of the Eleazar Schmidts of his youth? What had possessed him years ago to have his editors promote the young Canadian evangelist in his ridiculous circus tent?

He'd watched Coulter since on television (there were nights when he seemed almost ubiquitous) and had once shouted at the screen, "You monumental fake!" The gall, to propound to tens of thousands of people such utter drivel! No modern man with two wits could believe it for a moment, much less present it with such thundering earnestness. It was obvious that Coulter wasn't a fool. And was he not part of the society he so resoundingly condemned? It wasn't *possible* that anyone could believe the nonsense he was spouting.

There was a buzz from the telephone console. He strode to the desk. "Yes?" he said, his voice almost inaudible.

"Mrs. Hoffman to see you."

It was always Mrs. Hoffman – never "your wife," that phrase

being reserved for the present Mrs. H. who in the ten years of their marriage seldom came to Toronto and never to the *Tribune*.

"Send her in," he said. "And ask Mr. Rogers to stay on. I'll see him as soon as I'm free. Tell him I'll want to take a look at the first of the Jimmy Coulter articles."

Marlene ... He'd married her when they were eighteen and taken her out of Brechin. She was as aware of the world as Coulter was, yet she believed the things he preached and loved the Christ he professed to love. And there was no hypocrisy in her. It was as a favor to her that he'd promised to promote the Toronto campaign.

He turned up the lights and went to the elevator door. There was an embrace and a touching of cheeks and much warmth in their greeting. Marlene Hoffman was a pleasant-looking woman whose skin lied about her age but whose body affirmed it despite clothes bought at Creeds without troubling to read the price tags. She was on the Coulter Campaign's Executive Committee, and he couldn't resist telling her that "the great man" had just left.

"Oh, Hugh," she said, "why didn't you *tell* me!" Then, puzzled, "What in the world was he doing here?"

"Looking for free publicity."

She made a face. "Seriously?"

"I made him a proposition – that he do a daily column for the *Tribune* during the campaign."

"And?"

"He turned it down."

"Did he say why?"

"I gather he'd like to keep his distance from the Hoffman Press. To God all the glory."

"Now stop that!" she said. A small wariness had crept into her voice; they were edging on an old battleground. "I know you don't believe this, but he really *is* a fine man."

Hoffman's smile had a pasted-on look. "Loves Jesus. Good to his mother. Says his prayers."

"We agreed we wouldn't discuss religion."

"I thought we were discussing a man. Has the Holy Trinity become a quartet?"

"I know why he bothers you," she said. "He makes you feel guilty. He reminds you of Brechin."

Brechin ... where his Amish forebears had settled in the early 1800s, and where he'd lived until he broke with his parents – fled the house of God into the sunlight, as he thought of it – and went off to university. In his memory, the town was slate gray: grass, trees, flowers, houses. And people.

"The last thing Jimmy Coulter reminds me of," he said, "is Brechin. He reminds me of show business and circus tents and pitchmen."

She smiled at him and put out a hand. "Truce?"

He held her hand. "Too bad I had to unmarry you to learn what a nice lady you are."

A gay laugh. "I kept telling you. But never mind that. You *are* coming to dinner? Heidi's coming with the grandchildren."

"I'll be there."

"Seven-thirty," she said. At the elevator she paused with a sly smile. "Don't be unkind to Dr. Coulter," she said. "We all need him." As the door opened, she burlesqued leaving in a great hurry.

4

When the summons came, Clyde Rogers shrugged into a jacket, buttoned the collar of his shirt and tightened his tie. As he entered Hoffman's office he was wearing the usual drawn-pursestring frown at the center of his brow.

Hoffman, at his desk, flipping through a pile of manilla folders filled with newspaper clippings, grunted "Sit down." Rogers lowered himself into a chair and waited. He noticed a slight tremor in the boss's hands.

Clyde Rogers had been Hoffman's last senior editorial appointment at the *Tribune* before he'd gone off to run the chain of American newspapers that formed the core of the Hoffman Press. But the *Tribune* had remained his first love and he kept a heavy hand on its operations. His meddling had cost him two publishers, the latest having gone, after much bloodletting, only a month earlier. Rogers survived not only because he was the best managing editor in the chain but because he remained inconspicuous. Trying to describe him to an associate, Hoffman had once ended up saying, "It's difficult, he's so ... so goddam average!"

And he seemed so. Height and weight average. Fortyish. Brown hair thinning on top. Eyes a medium blue. Off-the-rack suits. Socks with clocks. Laced black shoes. You'd know he was a Canadian by his flat A's and his "Eh?" Meeting him you'd take him for a civil servant or an accountant.

"The Jimmy Coulter series," Hoffman said, looking up.

Rogers passed across a manilla folder, his manner betraying some nervousness. "It's a first draft," he said. "Just came to me yesterday. I was about to forward it to you. It needs work ..." His voice trailed off as Hoffman moved a lined foolscap pad to within reach and began to read. From time to time he made notes.

TO: Hugh H. Hoffman
FROM: Clyde Rogers
SUBJECT: Coulter campaign series (1)

Herewith the first draft of the kick-off article in the five-part series on Dr. Jimmy Coulter. I am not yet clear on exactly what is wanted, and although admittedly the attached needs work, I thought it best to forward it to you for your reaction. With three months to go before the Coulter campaign, there should be no problem in completing the assignment.

Tentative subject areas for the other four articles are: (1) Coulter's personal wealth; (2) the Coulter insiders—his family and friends; (3) Coulter, the friend and confidante of presidents and kings; and (4) Coulter-style evangelism: its effect on a community. Each has been assigned and is in the works.

lead copy—coulter   macdonald-reimer

Jimmy Coulter—with Billy Graham one of the two world-class evangelists—was begotten by an atheist and born of a Roman Catholic. The preacher, who golfs with presidents, dines with royalty and is revered by millions, was born in a city with a population fewer than the fifty thousand expected to greet him next Sunday afternoon at the Canadian National Exhibition stadium when he launches his 15-day Metropolitan Toronto campaign.

Hoffman made a gesture of impatience. "Who are Macdonald and Reimer?"

Rogers had been lacing and unlacing his fingers. "Hal Macdonald and Natalie Reimer. They're both staffers. Macdonald's done a number of features for us. Natalie's a first-rate researcher. Something wrong?"

"'Begotten by an atheist and born of a Roman Catholic'!" Hoffman said acidulously. "This is the lead-off piece about a religious leader, and we begin with an ill-conceived and awkwardly phrased take-off on the biblical account of the virgin birth. It hasn't even the saving grace of wit. Really, Clyde ..." He went back to reading.

The pursestring drew more tightly at the center of Rogers' brow.

The Canadian-born evangelist's life has been a series of paradoxes:

— He is a follower of "the lowly Nazarene," yet he wears $500 suits, heads a multimillion-dollar enterprise, and as the Tribune has learned, owns four houses: in Malibu, California (his principal residence); Puerto Vallarta, Mexico; Penetanguishene, on Georgian Bay, Ontario; and at Cap Ferrat on the French Riviera.

— His supporters include: megamillionaire Texas oilman, Marvin "Wildcat" Wilson; Pulitzer prize-winner, John Gonsalves; Nobel Laureate (chemistry), Cyrus R. Herman; Hollywood cine whiz, Jerry Jackson; rock star, Sammy "Superman" Mann; and not least, the President of the United States; yet he is a grade ten dropout.

— His one-man ecclesiastical empire is larger than some denominations and wealthier than many, yet it pays no taxes.

— The budget for the 15-day Toronto campaign has been set at $410,000; yet when Coulter was a youth living in the Parkdale section of the city, his family was on welfare.

In cities like Los Angeles, London, Brisbane, New Delhi and even behind the Iron Curtain, no sports arena is large enough to accommodate his followers, yet in recent years he has been spending much of his time alone and grows increasingly reclusive.

The Coulter story is a poverty-to-celebrity saga unmatched in the worlds of politics or entertainment. His parents were Irish, coming from Roscree, county Tipperary. They emigrated to Canada during the potato famine, settling in Saskatchewan.

"His parents emigrated to Canada during the potato famine." Hoffman snorted. "Which would make them at least 150 years old. The potato famine was in the 1840s." He looked up from the page. "You were saying that this Reimer woman was a first-class researcher." Before Rogers could respond, he added, "You might ask her to look into what the Coulter family or, at any rate, a family of four – it was four, wasn't it?''

"Yes. Coulter's father walked out on them. There were three children."

"… what a family of four would receive by way of a monthly handout."

"I'll mention it to her."

"And the term, megamillionaire. I'm damned if I know what it means. Whatever it is, Marv Wilson isn't it. The word I get is that he's sold everything that isn't already in hock, trying to keep out of bankruptcy court."

Coulter was an indifferent student. To improve his school grades, his father enrolled him in a private school run by Howard L. Rimmington. At the early age of eighteen he was hired as a columnist in the Toronto Tribune's sports department.

Coulter has maintained his enthusiasm for sport. "Until I was twenty," he says, "my heroes weren't saints or philosophers, but Howie Morenz of the Montreal Canadiens hockey club and Joe Louis, the best heavyweight in the history of boxing."

He still follows sport ("mostly on television these days"), and has been known to refuse preaching engagements when a world series is scheduled.

He also retains his interest in writing and has produced five books (they sell in the millions to the faithful). He has written the screenplays for three motion pictures produced by one of his companies, Coulter Films, Inc.

The evangelist lives in Malibu, California, in a 14-room beach-style house perched on a knoll overlooking the Pacific Ocean. His neighbors are film stars. (Ed note: Names to come.) Coulter's acre of the primest of prime land was a bequest to him by a convert and is estimated to be worth more than one and a half million dollars.

Unlike most of his neighbors, Coulter has been married only once: to Helga Nostrand (a former Miss America), who reportedly gave up a promising movie career when she responded to the then-little-known evangelist's altar call in Sandusky, Ohio, and

b copy next

27

walked the sawdust trail. Six months later she led *him* to the altar.

After almost fifteen years of childless marriage (insiders say children would have kept Mrs. Coulter from traveling with her husband), Jonathan and Julie were born. They have no other children. Coulter called the birth of the twins "a miracle." Now twenty-four, Julie lives in Toronto. She is an actress who has worked mostly in Coulter film productions. Deeply religious, she has refused parts in secular motion pictures. She and her father are said to be very close.

There is evidence that such is not the case with Coulter's only son, Jonathan. According to reports, he is estranged from his famous father. He refuses to be interviewed and little is known about his private life. Dr. Coulter responds to questions about his son by saying, "I'm the public Coulter. Leave my family out of it." The younger Coulter refers to himself as a painter but has yet to have a public showing of his work. Friends say that he and his father split over the son's avant-garde lifestyle.

"Jonathan Coulter," Hoffman said, peering over his glasses. "What's the source of your information?"

"A friend of his. Apparently, the lad is something of a social misfit. Natalie Reimer talked to someone who attends a class in oil painting he's enrolled in at the Hockley Valley School. He simply refuses to talk to reporters. All she's been able to get out of him after a dozen tries on the telephone is something like, 'Look, if you're doing a story on my old man, why bug me? He's the most famous talker in the world, isn't he?'"

"Interesting," Hoffman murmured. He made a few drumrolls with his fingers on the desk top. "That would be worth following, I would think." He reviewed his notes. "You say in your story that Coulter owns four homes but you list the value of only the one in Malibu. Why don't we have the other three?"

"We don't have a stringer in Puerto Vallarta or anywhere near Cap Ferrat, and –"

"Get in touch with a real estate agent. Hire an assessor. Property in Puerto Vallarta has gone sky-high. And Cap Ferrat ... If the place has a view, you're talking about a small fortune. Your readers will want to know Coulter's worth in real property – this, as your story calls him, follower of the lowly Nazarene." There was acid in his tone.

He was about to read on when he raised his head again. "Incidentally, there's an ambiguity in the data on his Malibu house. That million and a half – is that the value of the lot or of the house and land? And why don't we name the so-called convert who made the bequest? Surely such generosity should not go unrecognized."

Rogers' head was down. He was writing furiously.

Dr. Jimmy Coulter is not simply a mass evangelist, he is an industry. His worldwide success has spawned a corporate colossus, the Jimmy Coulter Evangelistic Association, employing some 600 people, with an annual budget in excess of $82 million. Additionally, he controls a separate organization, The Inasmuch Foundation, with assets in stocks, bonds and real estate totaling $30 million. The Foundation funds various Christian enterprises.

On none of this do the Coulter enterprises pay a penny tax. Nor are they accountable to anyone but themselves. While other tax-exempt groups are required to file public financial records, churches are not, and the United States Internal Revenue Service has officially decreed that the Coulter Association is a church. As a consequence, estimates as to the net worth of the Coulter enterprises cannot be confirmed and are based on information provided by Coulter officials.

The enormity of the Coulter empire may be comprehended, however, through a partial listing of its activities:
— A weekly radio broadcast on 950 stations around the world.
— The televising in 325 metropolitan areas of half a dozen campaigns each year (the Toronto campaign will be videotaped for later release), exposing Coulter to a potential audience of 90 per cent of all TV viewers. The average cost of airing each program is in excess of $1.2 million.
— The publishing of a monthly magazine, Outreach, in seven languages and braille, with a circulation of 3.2 million.

c copy next

— The production of two major motion pictures each year. One Coulter film, "All the Lost Children," has taken in $11 million at the box office and has been seen to date by four million patrons.

— The distribution of approximately 100 million pieces of mail each year and the receipt of between sixty and eighty thousand letters each week, most containing contributions, the average gift being $10. The offices in Burbank, California, handling this enormous volume of mail are fully computerized and employ more than 400 full-time workers.

— The syndication of a daily newspaper column of personal advice (in a born-again Ann Landers style) to 160 newspapers in ten countries. It's ghost-written–Coulter hasn't the time or the inclination.

— A variety of other evangelical enterprises ranging from publishing and selling books to training Christian workers and providing scholarships.

Coulter has little involvement in the day-to-day operation of his enterprises. The Association pays him an annual salary of $50,000 a year, modest by any reasonable standard, but he also receives expenses while on the road.

Even his critics admit that Coulter is not given to avarice. He has simple tastes. Away from the platform he dons well-worn clothes and drives a three-year-old Ford LTD. (Mrs. Coulter owns a Mercedes 240-SL sports coupe.) Although he lives by the ocean he doesn't own a boat. His only concessions to the California lifestyle are a battered dune buggy and a swimming pool–not much more than a king-size bathtub by comparison with some of his neighbors.

Hoffman put down his pen and reached for his cigar. "You know that Coulter and I are neighbors?" He seemed in an expansive mood.

"I knew you both lived in Malibu. I had no idea you were neighbors."

"Perhaps not neighbors," Hoffman conceded, sitting back and directing a cloud of smoke at the ceiling vent. "Coulter lives on the beach. I'm on the mountain. Maybe a mile or two away. The real estate agent pointed out his house when he was showing me mine."

30

"That's very interesting," Rogers said vaguely.

"I mention it only because Macdonald makes a great deal here about Coulter's modest salary and his spartan way of life. What was the salary – $50,000? As you might imagine, I have some idea what the taxes are in Malibu, and I can't help wondering how he manages on that kind of salary. Incidentally, where does the $50,000 figure come from?"

"From Coulter's PR people. Coulter won't discuss money. He used to take love offerings at his meetings, but to avoid criticism, he decided to put himself on salary. I can have it checked."

"If memory serves," Hoffman said, placing a hand on the pile of manilla folders, "he also receives royalties from his books. Your story says they sell in the millions. That would be income, would it not? As would the revenue from his newspaper column. And this swimming pool you mention: it happens that it was built by Condor Pools, Inc., the same people who built mine. Condor Pools is owned by John Condoroni, well known in southern California as a member of the board of the Christian Businessmen's Association, and something of a philanthropist. He was proud of having done Coulter's pool. It might be useful to check what Dr. Coulter actually paid. I would estimate that, with the patio, it would run well over a hundred thousand." He butted the cigar, picked up the pen and prepared to return to the article.

Rogers had a dolorous look. "The problem we've run into in checking the finances is that damned ruling by the IRS. Coulter isn't required to file on his holdings."

"Ah, but he is. The Jimmy Coulter Evangelistic Association isn't required to report, but Jimmy Coulter will himself have filed personal income tax returns."

Rogers' frown seemed almost to reflect pain. "But personal income tax files ... There's no way you can get at them. Or is there?"

Hoffman was back at his reading. "Have a word with your counterpart at the Washington *Register*. Bill Lennock. He has a source at the IRS." He read for a moment, then added without looking up, "Be discreet, of course."

It is this complex and controversial servant of the Lord ("The celebrity celebrities celebrate") who brings his traveling gospel

d copy next

roadshow to Toronto beginning Sunday afternoon at three. He
will have the cooperation of most of the city's Protestant churches
and the unofficial blessing of the Roman Catholic Archdiocese.

Monday through Friday of next week, the Tribune will print an
exclusive unofficial biography of the internationally famous evangelist. The series, in pamphlet form, will be available by mail and
through vendors at each campaign service at $2.50 a copy.
Address requests to: Coulter Offer, Box 999, Terminal A, Toronto,
Canada. (Ed note: Each paper to sub its own mailing address.)

"Well," Hoffman said, picking up the manuscript, shuffling it and
jouncing it on the desk top, "there we are. What's your feeling
about the piece?" he asked, his voice gentle, disarming.

Rogers shifted in his chair and gave a small shrug. "It needs
work, of course, but–"

"It reads like an inventory report," Hoffman said. "I would
hope we could get a bit more grace in the prose. And more bite."

"Yes, of course."

"Two or three small points. No mention is made of Coulter's
father. I presume he's retired, but I have a dim memory of his
being a clergyman." He drew deeply on the cigar. "It occurs to me
also that when you're talking to Bill Lennock in Washington you
might have him check on Mrs. Coulter's returns. I note she drives
a Mercedes .... That's about all."

As Rogers gathered his papers, Hoffman glanced across at him.
"Are you a religious man, Clyde?"

"No," Rogers said with a grin, "I'm an Anglican."

"What's your personal opinion of Coulter?"

"Never thought about it, to tell the truth."

"You must have some opinion."

Rogers shrugged noncommittally. "Seems like a decent sort."

What the hell was the boss getting at? He'd known from the
beginning that there would be trouble with the Coulter series.
Hoffman's interference in the operation of the *Tribune* seldom
took the form of requests for specific stories; and when he'd
ordered the Coulter series in a brief telex from Los Angeles, he'd
assumed it stemmed from the fact that the Hoffman papers had

promoted Coulter in the early years; and since both lived in southern California, they may have become friends. But clearly there was more to it.

"My point is," Hoffman was saying, "here's a man who's the intimate of powerful people, who has an influence on government policy, yet very little is known about him."

"He's hardly an unknown quantity. His file is fat as the pope's."

"I have it here. Coverage of his campaigns. Coulter at the White House. Coulter behind the Iron Curtain. Coulter golfing with Bob Hope. Coulter with his family .... You'd think he never had to take a piss. It's time somebody did a first-rate job of investigative reporting on the man. I had hoped it would be the *Tribune*, but judging by our first effort ..."

"You'll forgive me," Rogers said, nettled, "but it hasn't been made clear what's wanted."

"It's very simple. Tell our readers what the real Jimmy Coulter is like."

"That's well-plowed ground."

"Set the plow to go deeper."

Rogers looked off, excavating in an ear with a finger. "Is there a particular angle you'd like looked into? Money? Women? Some skeleton in the closet?"

"Perhaps a series like the one Jenny Wedger did on Senator Brownlee."

"That was an exposé."

"If the good senator hadn't been trading construction contracts for party contributions – not to mention his kinky tastes in bed – he'd have come off looking fine. You don't expect to find that kind of thing with Coulter?"

Rogers said, "Who doesn't have some secret locked in a drawer somewhere?"

"Then there's no problem." Hoffman rose, indicating that the meeting was over.

As Clyde Rogers got to his feet, Hoffman said, "By the way, this business of selling bound copies during the campaign ... I suggest we not do that. I want the people there to have to buy the *Tribune* to read the series. I would remind you, Clyde, that we're in the business of selling newspapers, not books."

5

Jimmy Coulter stood at the window in the darkened living room of his corner suite on the twenty-fifth floor of the Harbour Castle, looking out over the city.

He shouldn't have agreed to the Toronto campaign. He'd known that to return to his home city would be a mistake, though he couldn't pin down his reasons.

Over the past thirty years he had refused perhaps a dozen invitations. Never outright. He'd mumble apologies, feign regrets, never quite closing the door. "I'm fully committed ..." "Sorry, try me next summer ...." Or, "You really don't want me – 'A prophet is not without honor save in his own country ....'" Or, laughing, "Look what they did to Jesus when he went back to Nazareth to preach ... They tried to pitch him off a cliff."

On the closing night of his Chicago Stadium campaign, in a moment of weakness, he'd acquiesced. He'd been waited on by a delegation led by the Metro Chairman himself, bearing with them a motion duly passed and inscribed on parchment, with the official seal of the Corporation of Metropolitan Toronto.

He hadn't known then what the circumstances would be when the time came: his mother ill, intent only on staying alive until her most cherished dream was realized; the rift with his son Jonathan widening; his own sense of foreboding deepening; the struggle with his faith settling into his psyche to such a degree that every day he was beset by spasms in his chest and upper arms.

And the reappearance in his life of Hugh Hoffman.

Off to his right, the *Tribune* building stood against the halation of the city, dark except where the cleaning staff were at work. The light in the penthouse glowed against the night sky. As he watched,

34

he saw a shadow traverse the long rectangle and suddenly the lights went out. He was certain it was Hoffman who had crossed the office to the elevator.

To the north, the Manulife Centre reared high above the cluster of buildings at midtown. Julie would be in her apartment there, packing for the trip to California. He attempted to count to the forty-ninth floor but lost track.

His eyes moved to the Annex. Jonathan! King David's tragic lament for his son Absalom sounded in his mind, and substituting the name, he whispered in the darkness: "O my son Jonathan, my son, my son Jonathan! Would God I had died for thee, O Jonathan, my son, my son ... !"

Off to the west, Parkdale. Days of his youth. A welter of memories crowded forward ... Beatty Avenue. King Street, Dufferin – the houses he'd lived in, now gone. The First Church of the Galilean, gone. There he had preached his first sermon. How many had there been since in how many cities in how many nations of the world? How zealous he had been. The passion with which he'd prayed and preached and witnessed to the miracle that had turned his life inside out. It had all been so simple then: "God says ..." "The Bible says ..." The chairman of the little group of holiness preachers who'd examined him and granted him his first Evangelist's License had smiled at him fondly and said, "Amen, brother. You'll do fine. What you lack in lightnin' you sure make up for in thunder."

Due west, just visible as he leaned forward and pressed his brow against the cold glass, the Canadian National Exhibition stadium. The pods of lights atop their poles were blazing. They must be checking them out for the opening of the baseball season. Earlier, when he and TG had driven out to check the layout, he'd seen the billboard: COMING EVENTS. APRIL 14 – THE BLUE JAYS OPENER. And beneath it – only because the stadium manager had known he was coming – OUR OWN JIMMY COULTER. JUNE 13-28.

6

In Burbank, Jimmy Coulter opened the door to his office and found TG Wheeler at the desk, feet up, the ever-present phone at his ear. Without missing a beat, TG put a finger to his lips and gave him a slow, confidential wink. Jimmy crossed to him silently, took him by the back of the jacket and lifted with forefinger and thumb. TG came up unresisting, adopted the role of a boneless puppet, and let himself seem to be dangled across the floor, to be deposited in another chair.

Jimmy grinned as he stepped over the telephone cord. TG, always the character. Playing to audiences. Keeping it light, as though the world were filled with potential explosions and it was necessary to bleed off pressures.

Jimmy often found himself spent after a few hours with TG. But then, was he not also forever performing, holding himself forward to the world? *Presenting ... Jimmy Coulter, the man you know and love!*

"I appreciate what you're sayin'," TG continued, sliding low in the chair, crossing his long legs. "But it's one thing to schedule a big rally, and somethin' else to see that the bodies show."

He covered the phone with one hand and pointed at it with the other, stage-whispering, "Gerry White at President Scott's office ... the outdoor rally at the Jefferson Memorial." He turned back to the phone. "Martin Luther King drew how many? Fifty thou? We'll want to top that. We won't actually need fifty. The press always overestimates outdoor crowds by a third, but we're dead if we don't pull thirty. Remember, this is the first Salute America Week. The coverage will be total. I mean, everybody – the networks, the wire services, the dailies, *Time*, *Newsweek*. Everybody.

Ger, there's no way you can do it without I send Billy Joe – Billy Joe Harewood, Jimmy's advanceman .... Sure, your people are good, but Billy Joe's an old pro. Believe me, he'll get it laid on. Delegations. Buses. Groups from every town within two hundred miles. Churches. Ministerial associations – you gotta clear it with them, believe me. Union locals. The DAR. Ger, don't forget, the President's got a big stake in this too ...."

At his desk, Coulter drew a black leather folder toward him. He was not in the mood for correspondence but there was no escaping it. Betty, his secretary, would look reproachfully at him with her aqueous gray eyes. He read swiftly with part of his mind, listening to TG's conversation, making brief notations at the upper left-hand corner of the stationery. Betty would build a letter around them.

"... And could you maybe get them to spring for another ten thou for the radio and TV ads? ... Well, then try for five and we'll get somebody here to match it. It'll take at least ten, believe me. Ger, this is the big one this year. We're gonna need every dime."

On a small table beside Coulter's desk there were piles of books neatly stacked, some gleaming and new, others scuffed. He pushed a button on his intercom panel. Betty Anderson entered. She was a woman of about forty, with ash-blond hair drawn back softly into a bun. Her glasses, enormous circles rimmed with silver, enhanced a pleasant face free of makeup. She glanced at the table where the books were piled, and when he nodded, went to open them, extracting a slip of paper from the flyleaf of each.

"To Senator Muldoon," she said, putting an open book before him. Jimmy printed the senator's name and dashed a signature beneath it. The book was immediately replaced by another. "To Karen ... To His Eminence Cardinal Maloney, a brother in Christ ... To Pat and Missy ... To the Centurion Bible Class, Romans 8-28 ..." Her voice was low in deference to TG who was still on the phone.

"Press conference at noon is fine," he was saying. "No desk – he likes to stand. Nothing between him and them. Great. God love you ...."

"... To Pastor Hunnicut on your fiftieth anniversary ..."

TG was shaking the telephone cord, sending ripples along its length. "That was Gerry White at the President's office. Washington's looking good."

"To the winner of the Berean Baptist Scripture Memorization Contest ..."

"The outdoor rally," Jimmy said. "You're sure it's going to work?"

TG nodded vigorously. "No sweat. Billy Joe will whip their asses into line."

"Do you want your phone calls now?" Betty asked.

He looked across at TG. "Anything special on your mind?"

"When you're free."

Betty said, "Tony Rodriguez of the *Journal* called several times."

"That's what I want to talk to you about," TG said.

Coulter shook his head. "No way."

As Betty closed the door behind her, TG said, "I told him tomorrow afternoon at three."

"You did *what?*"

"Out at the house. He wants to know can he bring a photographer."

Coulter was about to speak sharply but drew a deep breath, loosened his tie and began to sort through a batch of photographs, occasionally setting one aside.

"Tee, I will not see him. Not after that run-in with Hoffman in Toronto." He looked up, his anger seeping through. "You've read some of Rodriguez' stuff? You remember the number he did on me after my trip to Cambodia? And still you told him yes?"

TG swung a leg over the arm of the chair. "Jimmy, you're making altogether too much of that hoorah in Toronto. You've been paranoid since we been back. Rodriguez has been after me for the interview for weeks – long before you saw Hoffman."

"Okay, forget Hoffman. Rodriguez is the *Journal*'s hitman."

"Jimmy, look, I had lunch with him yesterday. It's all very simple. The *Trib*'s doing a series to run when we open in Toronto. Friendly stuff: he gave me his word. What he wants to do is a straightforward piece – Jimmy Coulter away from the pressures of the campaign trail. Homey stuff. That's why he wants to come out to the house."

"No go."

TG studied Jimmy as he continued to leaf through the photographs. "You're the resident expert on sport – right?"

Jimmy looked up, puzzled at the sudden change in direction. "Why?"

"Do you remember the Joe Louis, Billy Conn fight?"

"Vaguely. New York City. Around 1942."

"Do you remember what Conn said he was gonna do to Louis and what Louis said?"

"What's it got to do with Rodriguez?"

"Conn said he was gonna stay out of range, and keep stickin' Louis with jabs."

"Okay. And Louis said ... ?"

"Louis said, 'Tell him he can run, but he can't hide.'"

"So?"

"Jimmy, you work with the public, you talk to the press. Occupational hazard. You can't hide. Cancel Rodriguez and he'll put the knife in. He's gonna file a story anyway. Better he gets it firsthand. At least then you got some control."

Jimmy was quiet for a moment. "Okay. When?"

"Tomorrow at three. I emphasized three sharp. You're having lunch with the governor at the Beverly Hills, and you're back here at four-thirty."

"There's one thing I will not bend on, Tee," Jimmy said. "No photographer. Not at the house."

"Agreed."

As he headed for the door, Jimmy asked, "What's the end of the story?"

"What story?"

"Louis and Conn?"

"Oh," TG said, grinning, "he couldn't hide. Louis knocked him out in the thirteenth."

7

Juanita, the teenage housemaid, had whispered in her downcast-eyes way from the door, "*Por favor, señor. Señora Coulter.*"

Going to the phone, Coulter flinched at the thought of an extended litany of his mother's physical woes and spiritual triumphs. He'd been back in Malibu only a week but she'd called collect every day, asking for him or for Julie. He'd decided to bring her back with him for a holiday after the campaign. Have to clear that with Helga, he thought, and grimaced.

He picked up the phone. "How are you, Mom?" he said cheerily.

There was a background of garbled talk and the tinny sound of a public address system. "It's not your Mom. It's your sister."

"Kathy! How in the world are you?"

"Tanned and gorgeous," she shouted. "What else? Can you hear me?"

"Only just. Where are you?"

"At the airport."

Above the noise he was able to piece together that she'd flown in from Hawaii with a friend and would only be in town overnight.

"Where are you staying?"

"The Beverly Hilton."

"My day's shot after noon. How about dinner? Can I meet you at the hotel?"

"Can't. Ken's got a banquet. Very big deal. We're at the head table."

He made a quick decision. "Come out to the house as soon as you check in."

"To the house? You're sure?"

"Yes," he said flatly. "And Julie's here."

He gave her directions, but when he put down the phone he began to worry. Helga was out shopping; he wouldn't be able to prepare her. The two women had only occasionally seen each other in the twenty-four years since that morning Kathryn had brought the babies to the house – two mites bundled in a basinette. He recalled the ugly scene with Helga when Kathryn had last been in Los Angeles. Even with the children visiting their grandmother in Toronto, Helga wouldn't have her in the house. She was common. She had a foul mouth. Let her get a foot in the door and there would be no end to it. A promise is a promise.

But the children were grown now and he hadn't seen his sister in ten years, not since she'd moved to Honolulu with the captain of a grain carrier.

He'd invited her on impulse but now it deepened to resolution. He wanted very much to see her. The family had drifted so far apart: Julie and his mother living three thousand miles away – his mother ill and perhaps dying; his son Jonathan beyond reach; his younger brother in Mexico and seldom seen .... Helga would simply have to accept it. It didn't matter now if she learned that the twins weren't Kathryn's; things between the two of them could hardly get worse.

He heard Helga's heels in the hall. She came through the door, arms filled with packages. She was a strikingly handsome woman, well ahead in the battle with time, the victory having been gained through the expenditure of much effort and many dollars, on surgery and on the latest triumphs of the cosmetician's art. In anticipation of the reporter's visit, she'd gone to the beauty parlor a day earlier than usual and her lacquered hair was a fine-spun golden hive. The blue eyes were shadowed with an identical blue and the coral lipstick exactly matched her sleeveless cotton frock. Jimmy took some of the packages and followed her to the kitchen.

"Kathryn's on the way over," he said. She stiffened but said nothing, continuing to put the contents of a large paper sack in the refrigerator. "She's in town for the day."

"Does she know Julie's here?"

"Yes. I told her."

"Where is Julie?"

"Visiting down the beach."

Helga slammed the door of the refrigerator. "Why the hell's she coming here? Why'd you *let* her?"

"I invited her," he said, his voice quiet but unequivocal. "It's been too long."

He left the kitchen before an argument could flare, went down the stairs to his study and closed the door. He knew it was going to be touch-and-go. Early in their marriage he'd made the mistake of telling Helga something of Kathryn's seamy years – when she'd quarreled with her mother and left home at eighteen to go off to Vancouver. Helga had never let him forget it, embellishing the details with the passage of the years.

When an hour passed and stretched to two, he became concerned. He tried the hotel but she wasn't registered. She wouldn't be, of course, and she hadn't mentioned the last name of her new friend. At 11:30 he found Helga in her dressing room refreshing her makeup. He told her she would have to greet Kathryn – he had a luncheon date and was already late – and went with the sound of a tirade in his ears.

The guard at the gate announced her as "Dr. Coulter's sister." Helga watched unobserved through a window as she got out of a cab. Her clothes bespoke expensive shops. No gray was visible in her hair. Her figure wasn't trim, nor was it dumpy. Skinny legs, Helga noted with satisfaction as Kathryn came up the walk.

She let Juanita answer the door, and after an interval went to say hello and to lead Kathryn to the living room. They'd hardly passed the explanations and small talk when Helga asked, "Jimmy told you that Julie's here?"

"Yes. I'm looking forward to seeing her."

"She's visiting down the beach with some friends."

"Will she be gone long?"

"I have no idea."

"You couldn't call and tell her I'm here?"

"No," Helga said, "I couldn't." She smiled thinly. "It's too bad you came all this way and missed them both. Jimmy should have realized. He had a luncheon date and he knew Julie was down the beach."

"Jesus, Helga!" Kathryn said. "If you think that after all these years I'm about to meddle in your life, you're wrong."

"I'm glad to hear that," Helga said. "In which case I'll have Frank call you a cab." She picked up the telephone and dialed two numbers. "Frank, this is Mrs. Coulter. Would you please call a cab for our guest .... Yes, right away. Thank you."

As she put down the phone, Kathryn said, "Boy! Aren't you the original pain in the ass!"

Helga's smile was icy. "And incidentally, you can skip the Christmas and birthday cards—"

"Oh, hello!"

It was Julie, coming from the hall, a short beach robe over her swimsuit, sandals dangling from a hand. "Sorry," she said, "I didn't know we had company." She was looking closely at Kathryn. Helga, having rummaged in her mind for an alternative and finding none, said, "Julie, this is your aunt Kathryn."

"I thought so!" Julie exclaimed. She went to her, and as Kathryn rose, said, "Aunt Kathy," and embraced her.

"Julie, darling," Kathryn said. Her eyes were tearful but she was smiling. "Such a beautiful young lady."

"Isn't this marvelous!" Julie said. She turned to her mother. "Why didn't somebody tell me?" She turned back to Kathryn. "My one and only aunt and we've never met. *My*, but it's good to see you!" She studied Kathryn's face. "I knew it was you," she said. "The Coulter eyes. Everybody has them but me."

"I'm so glad you got back in time to say hello," Helga said. "She's just leaving."

"You're not really?" Julie said. "Mom, make her stay."

"I've been trying to," Helga said, "but she's in town only for today and ..."

Kathryn said, "To hell with my appointment. It's a big affair. They won't miss me."

"Wonderful!" Julie enthused. "We can catch up on things at lunch. It'll be fun. And you can see what life's like around Daddy. There's a reporter coming this afternoon ..."

8

a copy—coulter   rodriguez

The Reverend Doctor James (Jimmy) Coulter, to put the best face on it, recently saw me off the premises. To state it baldly: I was given the bum's rush.

It came about in this way: An appointment had been made for me to interview the world-famous evangelist at his home in Malibu, the purpose being to discuss his upcoming Toronto campaign. The time arranged was three o'clock on a Saturday afternoon. I arrived half an hour early, partly because I wanted to scout the area in advance and partly (to disclose a trade secret) because I like to arrive ahead of time for an interview so that the subject hasn't had a chance to get his/her public personality all neatly buttoned up.

Let me report that the reverend gentleman lives well. His three-level, 6,000-square-foot home is in an ultra-posh neighborhood in the strung-out city of Malibu some fifteen miles north of Santa Monica on the Pacific Coast highway, an easy half-hour's drive by Cadillac or Ferrari from downtown Hollywood. Not posh like, say, Beverly Hills where the wealth and some of the families are generations old, but posh in that uniquely California fashion where the residents are mostly recent immigrants from the other forty-eight states where the snows fall and the greenbacks may not be so ripe for picking. ("Lift up your eyes and look on the fields; for they are ripe already to harvest.") For all the difference in the two areas, the smell is the same—money and success.

b copy next

It should be understood that Coulter doesn't simply live in Malibu–which, in some sections, is riffraffish–he lives in The Malibu Community, which is as gold is to brass. The Malibu Community is a tiny enclave exclusively populated by escapees from adulation–People magazine subjects who no longer need the puffery. They dwell cheek-by-jowl on a perfect sandy beach, secured from intrusion by a security guard in a gatehouse astride the only entrance. You don't drop in on friends in The Malibu Community; you are cleared and then announced.

The Coulter place is by comparison with some of his neighbors'–but only by that comparison–undistinguished. But then, in this neighborhood, so would your average state governor's mansion be. ("For ye have the poor with you always.") It is set atop a manicured sandy knoll fronting on the ocean.

— Neighbor to the south is Maria Montoya, a two-time Oscar winner and a five-time loser in the divorce courts.

— Neighbor to the north is Daniella Dawning (née Sadie Kiester) who has parlayed a Figueroa Street shampoo-and-set hole in the wall into a worldwide chain of calendar-reversing rejuvenation clinics.

— Across the road, neighbor to the east is Godfather rather than Goddess. There behind an eight-foot-high mortarless stone wall and a massive ornamental iron gate (locked) lurks the fortress home of Manny "The Finger" Bandino who, when he isn't entertaining the like of politicians, high-rollers and assorted photographic models for the FBI's most-wanted list, is at-home near his private mint, better known to Las Vegans as The Diamond Palace. ("In my Father's house are many mansions.")

Having arrived early, I had trouble getting admitted. The guard at the gate, wearing a gun ("They that live by the sword shall die by the sword?"), checked a list on a clipboard, moving his lips as he did, and lit upon my name as though he'd found his number on a lottery winners' sheet. "You're early!" he said in a voice that suggested that promptness was next to ungodliness. Nonetheless, he telephoned the house and minutes later I was escorted to the Coulter home down a set of stairs and along a boardwalk

c copy next

that the Atlantic City Chamber of Commerce would be proud to claim.

To set the scene for you, dear reader: Think of all the open-spaced, high-ceilinged, glass-walled, sumptuously broadloomed contemporary habitats you've lusted for in whichever imitation of Better Homes and Gardens you read. Think of all the modular, spartan-opulent, natural-grain, oatmeal-upholstered furniture that embellishes such structures as inevitably as tongue meets groove, and you have the picture: Jimmy Coulter's "Be it ever so humble." ("For I am meek and lowly of heart.")

I was met at the door by a compatriot, a housemaid tradition-ally attired in black with a white apron and suffering from what I took to be a terminal case of shyness. Wordlessly, she led me through the house and out to a patio on the ocean side at which a post-luncheon party of sorts was going on. Present were: the wife of the Great Man, Helga Coulter; their daughter, Julie; and the evangelist's sister, Kathryn.

Mrs. Coulter is a former beauty queen out of Sandusky, Ohio, who on the evidence (although I didn't get quite close enough to check) must trace her lineage to Ponce de Leon. Either that or she is living proof that it does pay to live right. ("I have looked upon her and she is fair as the morning.") Her hairdresser may know otherwise, but this amateur in things cosmetic has little doubt that her blondness is natural. In her fifties, she has a figure that makes Venus de Milo seem a refugee from a local YWCA fitness class. She was dressed in a long, flowered gown with a distractingly low-cut bodice. Add to the visual impact her conversational charm and you will understand why this reporter, dressed in sandals, jeans, a turtleneck and open leather vest, suddenly felt like sending himself out with the dry cleaning.

It seemed, said the First Lady of Christendom, that Dr. Coulter was having lunch with the governor ("a friend of publicans and sinners") and wasn't due until three. In the meantime, would I have a glass of sangria and meet her guests?

Julie Coulter: Auburn hair, fair of face and skin, and in a shorty beach robe over a swimsuit, enough to make a coronary patient

d copy next

46

reach for his glycerine pills. Visiting from Toronto for a few days, I was informed, and working on her tan. Little if any resemblance to her mother, but as they stood side by side before me, the candlepower generated made me don my sunglasses. Random thought: how beautiful heaven must be!

Kathryn Coulter: Odd-woman-out. Also visiting; in from Hawaii. The famous denim-blue Coulter eyes, but, I fear, losing the battle of the bulge and the battle with the sangria.

Despite the setting, things did not seem to be going all that swimmingly. Kathryn could get work as a gag-writer for Bob Hope to judge by the number of one-liners she dropped–which jests, it was evident despite the fixed smile, were not going down all that well with her hostess. Her language is direct and studded with such biblical words as hell and damn and God Almighty, but not, it may be said, in their customary ecclesiastical context. As we (they) made conversation, Kathryn kept insisting that she simply had to go, but didn't budge despite pointed encouragement from Mrs. C.

At which point there was a "Haloo" from the balcony, and there was Himself beckoning me to join him. Reluctantly, I took my leave of the ladies.

I'd never seen Coulter when he wasn't surrounded by a flock of the Faithful, so I hardly recognized what has been called "the best-known face in the Universe" when its owner strode, hand outstretched, across the football-field-size living room to greet me. He'd changed from whatever he'd worn to lunch to a pair of cotton shorts and a T-shirt. He led me onto a house-wide deck overlooking the sea, on which there was, on a rattan table, a jug of that potable unknown in California, freshly squeezed orange juice. With it a bowl of fruit and a beaker full of coffee. The reverend gentleman poured.

For starters, I said: "Dr. Coulter, Jesus was, by all accounts, stony-broke. You, by all the evidence, aren't. How come?"

"So that's the way it's going to be," he said.

"Or some other way, if need be."

"Pity," he said. "It is such a lovely afternoon."

e copy next

It developed that none of it—lot, house, furnishings—had taken a nickel from the ubiquitous collection plates passed in forty-five countries of the world by the Jimmy Coulter Evangelistic Association. The house and lot were, he said, a bequest. The furnishings were bought with royalties from his books. He couldn't live in a high-rise, could he? Or in some suburban rabbit warren. Privacy would be impossible, wouldn't it? Which it would: the man draws the curious as a magnet does iron filings.

"You'd like me to take what I have and give it to the poor, is that it?" he asked me.

"The poor you have with you always," I said. "If you're going to give it to anyone, let it be me."

He yielded the tribute of a small smile ("O faithless and perverse … how long shall I suffer you?") but as we went on, I got the feeling that a part of the reverend gentleman's mind was contemplating what punishment would be appropriate for the staffer who, on this lovely California day, had inflicted your obedient servant on him. ("Let him be cast into the lake of fire.")

Not wanting to wear out my welcome too soon, I changed the subject. Moreover, it was requisite to buy a little time. The Coulter office, in the person of a bumptious lackey by the name of TG Wheeler, had refused the request that a photographer be permitted to accompany me, and I hadn't yet spotted the fishing boat booked to park offshore with our man aboard equipped with telephoto lenses.

Question: Is he looking forward to returning to his old haunts—namely, Toronto? Yes, he likes the place and has fond memories of it, even though he lived there through the Depression. Moreover, he has family there. Question: Then why did he leave? "This is why," he said, taking off his T-shirt and moving to sit in the sun.

Let me report to Coulter worshipers who are accustomed to seeing their hero only on the platform and expensively accoutered: in his case, the suit does not make the man. Though past sixty he looks fit enough to kick sand in the face of any bully trespassing on his private beach.

f copy next

I put a number of stock questions and got a number of stock answers hardly worth the wear on a typewriter ribbon. Feeling like a serpent in Eden, I said to Himself, "Could we get back to money matters for just a moment?" He sighed. I looked properly penitent but nonetheless asked: "Dr. Coulter, according to my sources, this is only one of four homes you own. They tell me there's another on Georgian Bay in Canada, a condominium unit at Puerto Vallarta, Mexico, and a villa at Cap Ferrat on the French Riviera. Should I fire my sources or put them in for a raise in pay?"

It will surely show on the meteorological records; there came a sudden chill to the Malibu area. Dr. Coulter, his piercing blue eyes fixing me as a praying mantis might a slug, asked in an icy voice precisely what my assignment was. Had I been sent to discuss his ministry, and specifically the Toronto campaign, or had I been given a contract on him by the media Mafia. Was I, he asked, with the Los Angeles Journal or was it perchance the National Enquirer. He'd been led to believe, he said, that the purpose of the interview was to provide a background article for the Toronto campaign, and it had been for that reason only that he had allowed me to intrude upon his highly prized respite time.

I vowed that there would be no more questions on monetary matters if he would answer the one that had been left hanging. ("Let your Yea be Yea and your Nay be Nay.") He said, "I will say this and no more," and explained that (a) the place on Georgian Bay is a cottage he's owned for thirty years and which he'd given to his mother; (b) the condominium in Mexico was rented out; and (c) the place at Cap Ferrat was a retreat to which he repaired to write his books and to escape, among other things, "American journalists who have a fixation on money."

I didn't bother to explain that my fixation on money stems from not having much. Instead, I said that inasmuch as my sources hadn't been entirely in error, might I mention that they had further informed me that (a) the "cottage" on Georgian Bay has a dozen rooms, sits on a four-acre water lot, is assessed at a quarter of a million dollars, and is still registered on the Tay Township assessment rolls in the name of James Coulter; (b) the

g copy next

condominium in Mexico is indeed rented out, but the lessee is one Herbert D. Coulter, Jr.; and (c) the villa at Cap Ferrat is beyond question ideal as a writer's retreat, the British novelist, the late Somerset Maugham, having been a neighbor.

Whereupon, the Reverend Doctor gave me what is commonly described as "a look," told me I had come under false pretenses and was clearly bent on mischief. That being so, he had nothing further to say.

At which point things began to resemble nothing so much as a grade-B movie. In a strained silence he pushed a button. A guard arrived and I was ushered–with an Irish wolfhound big enough to have my head as an hors d'oeuvre, sniffing hungrily at my spoor–beyond the pale. ("Depart from me, ye accursed, into outer darkness.")

It's too bad, really. I was planning to ask him to compare the kitchens at Buckingham Palace and the White House.

TO: Clyde Rogers
FROM: HHH
SUBJECT: Coulter series

The Rodriguez article is acceptable, subject to the revisions listed below.

I will be candid to say that I would not have had him on staff as recently as ten years ago, but times change and we must change with them. It is unfortunately a law of life: adapt or perish. I have seen too many journals forced to cease publication because they would not change, continuing too long in what had once been a successful form, much as did the dinosaurs.

The Rodriguez piece is typical of what I gather is called the New Journalism, in which the reporter is as important as his subject. I can understand the vogue. This is an irreverent time, much given to debunking heroes, to sexual gossip and to the exploiting of former associations. It is of no importance whether I like it or you like it; it entertains and sells papers.

Now to the Rodriguez article:

Why, if the point of the piece is to list Coulter's real estate holdings, do we not list the assessed value of each property and how it was acquired? I made these points clear at our last meeting.

Delete the reference to our photographer on the boat offshore. It can only confirm in the reader's mind the common impression that the press has no respect for privacy. If he got acceptable pictures, use them, of course.

Omit the reference to the National Enquirer.

I am not too happy about the interpolation of scripture quotations in the text but will not object—they do form an oblique if snide commentary on the points being made.

I come now to a major deficiency in the two pieces I have seen. At no point is the reader told whether or not Coulter is a religious man. That he is a charismatic figure, that he has leadership qualities, that he heads a great church enterprise—all this is made clear; but does he believe in God? Coulter claims to be a Christian. The question then becomes: How did this apparently intelligent man "get religion," and how does he maintain a fundamentalist faith at a time when most educated men have rejected the simplistic premises on which it is based? The man is all paradox but you offer no insights. He is a grade ten dropout; from whence then come his gifts as an orator and his skills as a writer? He is a follower of "the meek and lowly Nazarene," and yet, as Rodriguez points out, he is wealthy and lives in comfort. He follows Jesus of Nazareth who said, "Woe unto you when all men speak well of you." Yet Coulter is on intimate terms with the eminent and the powerful, has millions of followers and annually tops the list of the "Ten Most Admired Americans." His Lord was a penniless revolutionary who challenged the religious establishment and drove the moneyed people from the temple, yet Coulter's campaigns get the backing of the churches and he is commonly feted and supported by some of the financial titans of our time. These contradictions stir curiosity.

Question: Is Jimmy Coulter a Christian in any sense that Jesus of Nazareth would have recognized, or is he simply a media-generated phenomenon, an attractive, gregarious, gifted preacher who finds wide acceptance because, in a time of uncertainty, he offers certitude, a sense of continuing order, and the conviction that (in the Rocky Graziano aphorism) "Somebody up there likes me"?

Clyde, do not misread my intention. I do *not* want the professional guesses of psychiatrists or sociologists on the Coulter phenomenon. It has been my observation that representatives of various disciplines can be found who will give scientific credence to any proposition in any field, in much the same way that clergymen can be recruited to bless in God's name any enterprise from total war to cock-fighting. Rather, give your readers the facts about modern mass evangelism and about the man, Jimmy Coulter.

PART TWO

9

As his first child, Herb Coulter had wanted a girl. He felt no need to perpetuate himself, and when Jimmy was born he was not overjoyed. He was himself the youngest of nine boys, whose mother, as a result of a profound exhaustion accumulated through years of unending housework and almost uninterrupted pregnancies, had expired with what sounded like a sigh of relief while giving birth to him. His father – The Pater, as he insisted on being called – was a Methodist parson, a man not given to sentiment. The closest he came to parental intimacy was to bestow a pat on the top of the head. In tribute to a good report card, he might shake hands. His remedy for any deviation from what he regarded as acceptable behavior was "a sound thrashing." Herb Coulter fled him and Ireland, and in his eighteenth year, made his way to Regina, Saskatchewan, where he met and married Lizzie Moore, a girl from his home town. Shortly thereafter, he joined the Robert Simpson Company, and within a dozen years had risen to become manager of the Ladies and Misses clothing department.

Whatever his skills in business, he lacked a father's gifts. He regarded boys as dirty, noisy and by nature undisciplined, and when there was no option, suffered them badly. So when on a Saturday morning he heard a sequence of unusual noises from the street – the catcalls of children and a man's voice raised in anger – he assumed that Jimmy was involved, and with a Job's sigh of resignation, put down his book and went to the front door.

A dilapidated pickup truck stood at the board sidewalk, steaming from exhaustion. Furniture, kitchen utensils and cardboard cartons were jammed into or hanging from it. The right rear tire, rubbed raw by a fender, had been jacked clear of the ground for changing. One of the cartons, bursting when the load shifted, had sent a torrent of books and a trickle of pamphlets onto the dirt road. A man, moving with the quick energy of a small bird, was picking them up and trying to stuff them back in the carton, pausing to shout at the children who were circling, laughing, taunting.

Herb called to them and they grew silent. He picked up some of the books, brushed them off and handed them to the man. He noticed two of the titles: *The Pedagogue as Student* and *The Circumscribed Mind*.

"Give you a hand?" he asked.

"Thank you, no," the man said crisply. "Are you Herbert Coulter?"

"I am."

"I'm told you own that shack at Indian Coulee."

"Such as it is."

"My name is Rimmington. I'd like to rent it."

Mr. Rimmington stood just over five feet, weighed perhaps 110 pounds and appeared to be in his late thirties. His oversize head was crowned with a brown derby hat, the brim worn through. A bulge of carrot-red hair of the texture of steel wool pushed from beneath it. His face was paper-white save for a rosiness of the nose, pinkish patches at the points of the cheekbones and lips so red they appeared tinted. The eyebrows, unexpectedly, were black and bristling and terminated in a Mephistophelean upturn, shading pale-blue eyes. His jacket and trousers hinted of Salvation Army castoffs. The shirt had no collar but was closed at the neck with a brass collar button which had left a permanent green spot at the base of his throat.

"That shack," said Herb. "I hadn't thought of renting it. I'm not sure you could live in it. There's no water."

"There's the creek. And snow in winter."

"I don't think the stove works ... Nobody's lived there for years."

He had bought the property from avarice – "One man's rain is another's sunshine." It comprised five or six acres of uncleared land edging on Indian Coulee. The soil was gravelly and useless for planting. At one time the government had deeded the land to a Métis in an attempt to appear concerned about the natives who had been left impoverished and starving with the disappearance of the buffalo. The Métis built a shack and tried trapping, but after a few years he gave up and went to the Peace River country. Herb bought the parcel from him for twenty dollars.

"Well," said Mr. Rimmington, "do you want to rent it?"

"I'm not sure you could manage a winter ..."

"Let me worry about that."

Herb looked at the man and wondered whether he'd have trouble getting him off the land once he was on. But, what the hell! The property was just sitting there.

"The rent will be six dollars a month."

"The land isn't any good for farming," said Rimmington. "There aren't enough mature trees to take off lumber. You said yourself the shack isn't habitable. I'll pay you three dollars and give you six months' rent in advance."

They settled for four dollars with a three-month advance. Mr. Rimmington, spurning help, repaired the tire, and after several tries at cranking the engine, got it going and went off down the street, the truck coughing and listing to the left.

In Regina the twenties were much as they were in other parts of North America. By 1924 the postwar recession had passed and there began five yeasting years in which the city changed and the people changed and the Canadian version of the American Dream seemed about to be realized.

The Coulters prospered with the times. Herb was now merchandise manager at Simpsons and had introduced a "groceteria," the first west of Winnipeg. He was seldom home, often working nights, and on Sundays sleeping late. In the dining room, with a packet of figs at an elbow, he would leaf through mounds of paper and pore over columns of figures.

The family was growing. Herb, Jr., two months old, was an animated doll in his bassinet, enchanting every visitor. Lizzie, after weeks abed – the baby had taken eighteen hours to have quit of her – was getting about more each day and was pale and lovely as a flower. Kathryn, chubby and boisterous at seven, was her father's favorite and the only one who dared break in on his Sunday-afternoon routine.

Jimmy Coulter was struggling with the growing awareness that all was not well between his mother and father. The knowledge had invaded his innocence long before he understood about such things. It had awakened him at night even when the angry exchanges between his parents were in whispers. It had fashioned a frown like a dropped stitch at the corner of an eyebrow and often caused him to withdraw to his room to lie listless on the bed until his mother missed him and came to fuss over him. Sometimes, at dinner, the tension made him ill.

"Lizzie, the roast is overdone. And the damned potatoes are cold." They were the first words his father had spoken since they'd come to the table.

Small pink blotches appeared on the skin of his mother's neck and chest. "I'm sorry, Herb," she said, her voice tense but quiet, "you told me six. It's past seven."

"I can't always control my time. You know that."

"Yes, I know that. But when I called your office at six, they said you'd been gone half an hour."

"I had a meeting with a supplier."

"I'm sure you did."

"And what's that supposed to mean?"

"Would you like me to reheat the potatoes?"

"They're all greasy," Kathryn said.

His mother went from the table and up the stairs to her bedroom. Nor did she return. The meal was finished in silence.

The Coulters lived in St. Margaret's parish, a small island of Roman Catholicism manned by French-Canadian priests in a predominantly Protestant neighborhood. The voters' list designated them as R.C. but their relationship to the church was tenuous. Under pressure, Herb had signed a document consenting that any children of the marriage "be educated in the religion of the spouse." At the time, he'd been indifferent to the matter, but when Jimmy completed grade six at St. Michael's, Herb (having developed a bias against "the Frogs" as a result of a dust-up with a Montreal supplier) enrolled him in Connaught public school.

Jimmy knew little of Protestants except that they were heretics and damned. In his first year he was called Mick, Dogan, Arsie or Catlicker, and as has been Christian practice over the centuries, was badgered and beaten up by zealous followers of his Lord. At the beginning of the fall term, he adopted the protective covering of the majority and passed for a Protestant.

58

But not on Sundays. On Sundays he and his sister Kathryn were the family's token Christians at St. Margaret's. Herb hadn't attended church since the wedding. Lizzie no longer went except on Ash Wednesday and Easter, but she insisted that the children go.

Seeing his parents' indifference to religion, Jimmy too became indifferent. But on entering adolescence, he began to feel intimations of spirituality. There came a longing for God. At times, alone on the open prairie or walking at night, he would be ambushed by tears and would pause, face upturned as though responding to a distant summons. He felt a hunger beyond sating, a need for completion, a longing for a cause. Sometimes he spoke the longing; sometimes he stood in silence, tears coursing down his cheeks.

St. Margaret's parish tempted him to atheism. The grubby building with its drab furnishings and banal priests seemed an affront to the ineffable stirrings within. The gaudy realism of the stained-glass windows, the vapid faces and mandatory halos on the plaster saints, the exhibitionistic parting of the Christ's meticulously folded garments to expose a bleeding heart: what institution could display for veneration such garish symbols? How could it have so much as a handhold on the infinite?

The mass angered him. It wasn't that he found incredible the changing of the wafer and the wine into the very body and blood of Christ. Didn't a seed become a flower, a caterpillar a butterfly? It was that, if such a miracle indeed happened, how could it be accompanied by disinterest and boredom in the officiating priests? If God was truly there (between the fingers of the priest, on the tongue of the supplicant, and finally within the blood and bone and brain and spirit of the worshiper), surely no sum of familiarity could breed such indifference.

He quit the church on an Armistice Day after Father Boissoneau urged the young people of the congregation to light three candles (representing the Holy Family) "for the souls of the brave boys of the parish who laid down their lives in the trenches." He was scandalized that the responsibility for the progress of these heroic young men from the pain of purgatory to the solace of heaven was being laid in part upon him – was dependent upon his prayers, upon his spending the requisite pennies for the candles. When his mother was informed of his action she nagged him for a few days, but she had known the time would come.

More disturbing were his failures at school. The truant officer had come by to report on his frequent absences from class and the principal warned that Jimmy would fail his year unless there was an immediate improvement in his grades. Herb sent him to his room to strip off his clothes and then thrashed him with a building lath, raising welts on his back and buttocks but inducing no tears. His mother threatened to hide his skates and hockey stick and to deprive him of desserts unless he applied himself. In his Easter report card, he stood thirty-second in a class of thirty-three.

10

The thought that Mr. Rimmington might be a teacher had stayed with Herb. On a Saturday morning he drove the few miles to Indian Coulee and followed the path through the woods to the shack. The lumber with which it had been built had been salvaged from a collapsed barn. The support timbers bore witness to the persistence of an early settler unskilled with an adze. The unfinished planking on the elevations varied in length, width and weathering, and the general impression was of imminent collapse. Within, the floor was compacted earth.

During his three years of occupancy, Mr. Rimmington had made changes. A barrier of felled young trees placed so that their branches intermingled provided a fence around the property. A gate made from an old packing crate opened onto a path of weeds which led to the door. The most extraordinary change was the growth of a forest of liquor bottles. When Mr. Rimmington emptied a bottle, he would cut a sapling, sharpen it, force one end into the soil and place the empty bottle upside down on the other. There were now perhaps a hundred, some leaning against each other, others bowed to the ground or surrounded at the base by shards where collisions had shattered the glass. In a breeze the bottles swayed and tinkled. In a storm they tossed and oscillated and often collided, measuring the velocity of the wind with the crescendo of their chiming.

Herb approached the gate, reached over, lifted the leather thong around the bent nail and swung the gate inward. A slight movement at one of the windows drew his eye. He paused before the door, then tapped on it. He rapped again. Silence except for the clinking of the bottles. He knocked again, insistently.

61

From within, a voice: "Yes?"

"I wonder, could I have a word with you?"

"What about? You have the rent."

"It's about ... my son."

A minute passed before the bolt was drawn. The door opened an inch. A blue eye peered out.

"My son, Jimmy. He needs a tutor ..."

"So?"

"I thought perhaps ..." Herb faltered.

"What makes you think I'm a teacher?" asked Rimmington.

"The books ..."

"Besides, what's wrong with the school? Foolish question."

"He's skipping classes. He's bored."

The solitary eye blinked. The brow drew down. A moment passed. The eye seemed to twinkle. "But what if I were to teach him anarchy and atheism and sexuality? Although I'm sure he's already well instructed in that by his grubby peers."

"I'll take the chance."

The door slammed shut. The bolt clunked. Herb stood for a moment, and when there was no sound from within, made his way back to the car.

The following Saturday, in the envelope with the rent money was a note written in a tight, exact hand. *I presume that even the dolts who run the Saskatchewan school system require some form of English composition. If such exist, leave it outside my door.*

Herb wrapped two of Jimmy's exercise books in butcher paper, drove to the shack and propped the package against the door. He knocked and left. When he was out of sight he returned; positioning himself behind a bush, he watched. When five minutes passed and the package remained where he'd placed it, he went on.

A week later there was a note in his mailbox. *I will see the lad. The conditions are these: He will present himself Saturday and Sunday mornings at eight. (If nothing else is accomplished, this may keep him out of church.) For my services, I will expect a reduction in my rent of a dollar and the provision of a 25-ounce bottle of Seagram's V.O. on the first and third Saturdays of each month.*

"Rattlebrain Rimmington! On weekends!"

Jimmy's voice, only settling in after having changed to a deep baritone, leaped an octave.

62

"Jimmy," his father said, "there'll be no more argument about it. I will not have a son of mine failing his year."

"It's only till summer," his mother said.

"But, Dad, he's a kook. And on weekends! What's the team going to do? The city finals start in two weeks. I'm captain."

"I warned you a dozen times, but you wouldn't listen."

"But Dad ..."

"Not another word. You'll be there at eight sharp Saturday, and that's all there is to it."

Now standing before the gate, studying the shack and its gleaming forest of bottles – their chiming the most macabre schoolbell ever sounded for a student – Jimmy grew apprehensive. He made his way through the weeds and raised a hand to knock. The door swung open and there was Mr. Rimmington.

"Enter, lad," he said with a deep bow, indicating the dark interior with a grand sweep of his hand. "The world awaits within."

Within was a shambles: a clutter of makeshift furniture, stacked canned goods, a stained sink heaped with dented pots and dirty dishes, and a mattress on the floor in a corner. Dominating the room was a wall covered almost entirely with books ranged on sagging planking. The other walls were papered with the *Leader Post*: Mackenzie King's 1926 campaign for Prime Minister butting against stories of crime and sport and business and a variety of 24-hour journalistic sensations.

Mr. Rimmington had prepared a desk for Jimmy's use by laying a plank across two stacks of concrete blocks. He lay down on a soiled settee from which wads of stuffing extruded like fungus. Placing his hands behind his head, he tilted his brown derby hat over his eyes and cleared his throat.

"Well now, lad, for your sins you've been put in my charge, the object being to jimmy a pinch of wisdom into your hard little head – and no play on words intended. My impression is that your father is something of a fool, but somehow he has glimpsed the importance of ideas. Recognizing the ineptitude of the public school system, he has turned to me. In a moment of weakness, I agreed to see if you're teachable."

He craned about to look at Jimmy. "You're listening?" Jimmy nodded slightly, piqued by the comment about his father. "Good," Mr. Rimmington said, his pale-blue eyes staring at the ceiling.

"I suppose the condemned have the right to know the shape of their fate," he continued, "so here's what's in store: There will be no assignments, no homework, no textbooks. You will listen and you'll read the books I shall lend you.

"What shall I teach you? Nothing. No man can teach another anything. But I shall inform you of the lies of historians, the vanity of kings, the naiveté of scientists, the presumptuousness of the clergy, the rapacity of bankers, the quackery of physicians, the wickedness of the military and the chicanery of politicians. We'll talk about life and death, love and hate, sex and lust, copulation and mitosis, the earth and the stars, the exquisite beauty and utter indifference of nature; about the engineering in a snail's shell, the aerodynamics of a gull's wing, the superlative design of a shark, the artistry of a wood duck's plumage ..."

Rimmington caught himself, sat up, pivoted on skinny buttocks and dropped his feet to the hard earth floor. "Words," he said with mild amusement, "they're my failing."

He studied Jimmy, a slight smile about his mouth. "Well, lad, what did you think of that?" Jimmy remained silent. "Did you understand anything of what I said? It *is* Jimmy, isn't it?"

"Yes, sir."

"Yes, sir, your name's Jimmy, or yes, sir, you understood?"

"Both, sir. Anyway, most of it."

"What didn't you understand?"

"Some of the words."

"For instance?"

"Well, copu ..."

"Copulation. It means fucking."

Jimmy flushed.

"Isn't that what you call it when you're with your chums?" Mr. Rimmington asked. "And that's what we'll call it here if we happen to discuss the subject. Fucking *or* copulation *or* sexual intercourse *or* making love *or* impregnating *or* being at stud – all good words as circumstances require."

When Jimmy remained silent, Rimmington asked, "Pose a problem?" His smile was a shade more evident.

Jimmy looked directly into his eyes. "No, sir."

"Good. Then let's continue. There's a marvelous new song writer – a man by the name of Noel Coward. What's the name?"

"Noel Coward."

"He's written a song about copulation. Goes like this: *The birds*

64

do it. The bees do it. Even educated fleas do it. Let's do it, let's fall in love .... What is it they do, lad?"

"Copulation?"

"Excellent. But the word in this instance would be copulate. They copulate. Copulation is a noun. It describes what's done. When it's being done, it's described with a verb. But don't worry about that. We'll be talking about what words mean and how to use them. Got it?"

Jimmy nodded and asked, "Could you also say they mitose?"

Mr. Rimmington threw back his head and let out a cackling laugh. "Jimmy, that's beautiful!" Then thinking he might have offended, he capped his amusement and said, "That's the best possible question you could have asked, lad. You're absolutely right. Mitosis and copulation are the same thing in that they achieve the same result: namely, the reproduction of the species doing *it*. There's one difference, though: when birds or bees or fleas or humans do it, it takes two. Mitosis is when a cell does it. You know what a cell is?" Jimmy nodded. "When a cell mitoses, does it, you might say, it doesn't need another cell. It divides in two. With most creatures, it's one plus one equals three or more. With cells, it's one divided equals two. Got it?"

From reproduction they moved to the differences between things that grow (the wooden plank on Jimmy's desk) and things that are made (the concrete blocks on which it sat). How wood could become as hard as concrete when petrified. The word petrified led to a discussion of fear; how the word *petrified* came to the language from the Greek *petra*; how Jesus named the apostle Peter *petra*, the rock.

Rimmington took the burl-handled cane with which he walked and they repaired outside to urinate against trees. Afterward, they sat on boulders in the warmth of the sun. Mr. Rimmington searched in the rubble, picking up rocks and tossing them to Jimmy, talking about how they'd been formed in the cooling of the earth's mantle, and how they came to be in the ground, the deposits of glaciers during the Pleistocene era, borne there millions of years earlier.

In the following weeks Rimmington lent Jimmy books or gave him titles to borrow at the public library. Jimmy was introduced to verse through a young poet, Ogden Nash. He learned that poetry is not merely the rhyming of words but often the best way to say something. And, sometimes, sheer delight. From there they went to Mother Goose. When Jimmy groaned at the introduction of the "baby" subject, Mr. Rimmington feigned umbrage that his favorite was so disdained and explained that some poems are "a kind of dancing with words," with the sound more important than the meaning. He had Jimmy chant *Hey-diddle-diddle* and did a mock Indian dance about the shack, jigging to the tempo and leaping into the air with wild cries on the rhyming words. At the end, he fell onto the pallet in the corner, gasping for breath, and they both laughed. Then came a "hard" poem by T. S. Eliot about a Mr. Prufrock, which only rhymed occasionally and wasn't funny and left Jimmy confused and Mr. Rimmington somber.

11

The weekends with his new teacher filled Jimmy with an excitement not unlike the sensation when the Pats won a play-off game at the arena. Thinking back to what he had learned was like remembering an intricate passing play or recalling the grace of "Duke" Keats as he split the defense and broke in alone on the opposition goal. Imagine poetry being interesting! With Mr. Rimmington as teacher, even the Plantagenets or keeping track of the Henrys and Edwards wouldn't be boring. Why couldn't school be like that?

Jimmy awoke trembling and rigid from the familiar nightmare. He was on the steep roof of a castle that reared high above a black, bottomless chasm. He was clutching at the tiles, but there was no crevice in which his fingers could get a grip. One foot was thrust against a rain gutter, but the metal was rotten and the trough was breaking away from the eaves. If he dared breathe it would rip loose, and fingernails screeching on the slate, he would slide over the edge to fall forever down ... down ... down ...

Voices! People below, calling up to him, trying to tell him something, but he couldn't make out the words.

He was awake now and realized that the voices were in the house. Downstairs. In the living room. His mother's and his father's voices. Shivering, he got out of bed and went softly to the door. The voices were louder now, his mother crying. He opened the door without a sound, and wormed his way on his stomach to where he could peer through the banisters into the living room.

His father, wearing his raincoat, was standing at the center of the room. His mother was on her knees at his feet, sobbing, clutching at his trousers. Her face was distorted, ugly. Her eyes were red. Saliva ran down from the corners of her mouth.

"Oh Herb, Herb," she moaned, "please don't. Don't go. I love you. I know where you're going. I know, I know ... Herb? Please ...."

His father, standing erect, leaned back with a military rigidity. Not looking down, he tried to disengage the fingers locked onto his clothing, speaking in a calm voice as though nothing extraordinary was happening, as though he was merely demonstrating patience before an unruly child while asking it to surrender a toy snatched from a sibling.

"Lizzie," he said, "will you stop this nonsense? Will you please let go of me?"

But she clutched even harder, sliding lower, her cheek against his calf, keening, pleading, "Please? Please? I know where you're going ...."

Looking down on them, Jimmy hated them – his father for what he was doing to his mother, and his mother for demeaning herself.

Mr. Rimmington was striding about in a grassy area, the forked branch of a willow clutched in his hands. He didn't look up as Jimmy approached. Jimmy watched in silence.

After a while he said, "What are you doing?"

"Dowsing. Some call it divining. Looking for water."

"Are you going to dig a well?"

"No," Mr. Rimmington said, "just want to know if I have the gift. Aha!" He doubled back, grimacing as the branch twisted downward. He crossed the spot twice more, the branch turning in his hands.

Jimmy was excited. "Does that mean there's water there?"

"Maybe. Maybe not. It's a curious phenomenon." He looked at his palms which were pink from friction. "Is there water there or is it auto-suggestion?" He hung the dowsing rod on the branch of a tree and picked up his cane. "We know almost nothing about the human mind."

As they headed for the shack, Jimmy said, "May I be excused next Saturday? It's the city championships in track and field."

"Of course you may. I don't mark attendance. I won't send 'round the truant officer." His voice was sharp. "I will, however, hold the hope that when you become a man you'll put away child-ish things."

They went on in silence. "In the ideal society," Rimmington suddenly said, "sport will be reserved for children. When adults play at it or watch other adults, they contribute to an evolutionary regression. They turn back the hands of time."

Jimmy realized that he had touched a nerve and that his teacher was about to zero in on a favorite target. He had learned to be silent at such times until the tirade was over.

"In no field of human activity, other than religion and politics, is so much nonsense uttered as in the advocacy of sport," Mr. Rimmington continued. "It's become an institution almost as sacred as the church. The athlete is hero. His exploits are the stuff of male conversation, and spectatoritis is the new social sickness.

"But, they say, doesn't sport make for fitness?" Rimmington trumpeted, flinging his arms wide. "Isn't that the modern gospel? It may for children, but all an adult needs is to eat properly and go for a walk each day. Spin the world with your stride! – that's the ticket. Time was when fitness was essential – a man had to wrest his supper from the wilderness. Today, supper's as near as the corner store, and journeys afoot were outmoded by the invention of the wheel.

"If we were even moderately good at things physical I could understand this prattle, but among the mammals we're clumsy, leaden-footed stumblers. There are only two ways in which we are superior: in the dexterity of our hands and the complexity of our brain. The trouble is, it's infinitely more difficult to labor with the mind than with the body. Unfortunately, manhood continues to be measured by the wrong criteria. At this stage in our evolutionary ascent a man isn't a man because he's brute-strong or animal-agile. He's more truly a man when he's reading, or meditating, or bird-watching, or trying to make music. We've outgrown our primitive past in housing, clothing, cooking and transportation. When will we revise our notions of man?"

Having reached the shack, they went in. Mr. Rimmington lay down on the settee and was silent. Jimmy went to his desk. He had wanted to argue but had restrained himself. Sport was not some-thing about which he felt indifferent. He studied the sports pages daily. He memorized batting averages and pitching records. He was stick-boy for the Regina Pats. He played in the Parks Hockey

League, and when his teammates went home, he remained, repeating stops-and-starts and dekes and wrist-shots. In summer he practised the pole-vault by the hour and ended each workout with a three-mile run. He exulted in the mastery of his body, in the effortlessness with which he jogged once he'd reached that plateau that distance runners achieve when they feel they can go on forever.

At home he put his feelings into an essay. On the Sunday he left it on Rimmington's desk. The following Saturday his tutor was waiting for him as he came up the path. He had the exercise book in his hand. They sat on the warm grass.

"Why did you write this?" he asked.

Jimmy shrugged. "I don't know ... just to put down how I feel about it, I guess."

"Did you have any help?"

"No."

Mr. Rimmington passed the exercise book to him. "I've made some changes."

Words and sentences had been struck out. Some had been replaced in Mr. Rimmington's crabbed hand. The result was half its original length. Jimmy felt a stirring of excitement.

"It says it now. What I was trying to say."

"Jimmy," Mr. Rimmington said, "you can write. We must work on it." He reached into a pocket. "I've made a list of the books you're to read. No textbooks for now – it can't be taught. We'll read for style, for form, for narrative line ..."

Jimmy felt the pleasant apprehension that formed within him before an important game.

12

Clyde:

I confess to feeling a hell of a lot better about doing the story on Jimmy Coulter than when you first assigned it to me. As I told you, religion is not my cup of tea and evangelists have always seemed to me either fanatics or ecclesiastical con-artists. Coulter appeals to me less than most, precisely because he is so success-ful. When I covered his press conference two weeks ago . toyed with the idea of using as my catchline the well-worn phrase, "As the Stomach Turns." The guy is too handsome by half, altogether too glib, and so self-consciously righteous as to make me wonder how he gets those Saville Row jackets over his wings. I'm predis-posed to dislike messiahs, political or religious, and it seems at this point in history we're overstocked with both.

HOW-ev-er, the Coulter piece has begun to grab me – perhaps because I've reread Sinclair Lewis' Elmer Gantry (now *there* was a scoundrel!). I'm beginning to believe that, contrary to my first reaction, there's a story here that hasn't been written. I've been through the files (nearly got a hernia carrying them) and have talked to some of his Toronto campaign organizers, all of whom are so obsequious and wary that, other than for the nuts and bolts, they'll be of little help. (God! what a strain it must be to be so everlastingly cheerful.)

I dug out a number of Coulter's Tribune columns and found to my surprise that the guy was good. Strong on factual stuff and human interest, with a spare, easy style that stands up well. Must have been quite a phenomenon in the business – not yet twenty

71

and his own by-lined column. Bobby Coombs, as you know, was assistant sports editor at the time. (Incidentally, he asked me to give you his best and to ask you why the hell don't you drop by and see him–Riverdale Hospital.) Anyway, Coombs tells me that sometimes Coulter even subbed (anonymously) for the legendary Pat Noonan, doing his column when Noonan was ill. All this didn't go down too well with some of the older hands on the paper or the ambitious younger types–among whom (according to Coombs) was our own Mr. Hoffman.

In looking into Coulter's years at the Trib, I have turned up something that I suspect will interest you. I thought I should pass it on in case you find Mr. Hoffman displaying more than usual interest in the series. It may be old stuff, but I hadn't realized that Coulter and Mr. Hoffman have known each other for many years. They were contemporaries on the old Tribune. Coulter was with the paper for nearly four years and Mr. Hoffman joined the staff some three years later. For seven months they worked out of the same newsroom, although in different departments. The editorial department was much more compartmentalized then than now and there wasn't much fraternizing. Nevertheless, Coombs tells me that the two whiz-kids (and they were that) clashed. They must have straightened things out, because in 1950 the Hoffman Press, under a direct order from the Chief, is credited with launching Coulter as an international figure.

The story Coombs tells is that (a) Hoffman very much wanted a by-line on some features he'd done and was turned down; (b) having met Coulter twice in the newsroom, Hoffman took a girl he was dating to the press box at Maple Leaf Gardens to introduce her, and Coulter didn't recognize him; and (c) when Coulter announced he was quitting to go into the ministry, Mr. Hoffman ridiculed the decision in a way that went far beyond the light-hearted fun being poked at the incipient preacher by other staffers.

I'm off to Regina tomorrow. Having been raised in the West, it's a prospect that doesn't enchant me this time of year. I'm not at all sure what I hope to find–perhaps no more than some feeling for the places where Coulter spent his childhood. (There has been surprisingly little written about it.) I'm anxious to track down at least one of his teachers at Connaught public school. Incidentally, how's this for pure Canadiana?–the three people I reached by phone at the school were surprised to learn that Coulter had been a student there. Migawd! if he had attended an American school they'd have a bronze plaque over the urinal he used.

There's some mystery about this man Rimmington mentioned in the Macdonald-Reimer kick-off article as having run a private school that Coulter attended. Macdonald says he got his information from a news story carried in the Trib when Coulter resigned to go into the ministry. In the story, Coulter is quoted as saying, "I did a few years at a private school in Regina run by Howard Rimmington. He more than anyone else kindled my interest in writing." Coulter goes on to say, "He was a great man and a great teacher. His ideas are still with me today."

But according to the records of the Saskatchewan Department of Education, no one by the name Howard Rimmington was ever licensed to teach in the province, nor have they any record of a private school operating under that name.

I trust the above is the kind of thing you want by way of a progress report ... unaccustomed as I am, etc.

Jenny

13

"Why do you live out here alone?" Jimmy asked.

Mr. Rimmington didn't answer. They'd been following a path through the woods while he talked about "the factory that is a tree: using the raw materials of earth and air and sunlight to manufacture wood and fruit." Now he went on slowly, eyes down, searching.

"Here we are. Walk in my tracks."

He went into the tangled bush, putting each foot down carefully. "I guess there isn't anything today," he said, and then leaned forward to add, "Here we are."

He reached into the long grass to pick up a metal animal trap at the end of a chain. Between the serrated jaws, so dark with dried blood that at first Jimmy took it to be a piece of a dead branch, was the foot of a small animal.

"Coyote," said Rimmington. "Pup. Chewed its foot off." He pried apart the jaws of the trap, and threw the paw into the woods. "At least the son of a bitch won't get the bounty."

He was silent until they were back on the path. "Why do I live out here? Why not in the city? That trap – it was set by Billy Miles, a city man. Not for food. Not for money. Not because he's an Indian doing what his ancestors have done for generations. He's a white man, making a good living."

"Owns Miles' Drugs. On Thirteenth Avenue," Jimmy offered.

"He's been trapping in these woods as long as I've been here. Doesn't give a damn what he catches. Doesn't give a damn whether it dies quickly or, like that coyote, just suffers. I've seen a raccoon caught by the jaw – just the tongue and the lower jaw. I've seen jackrabbits clamped by both forelegs. Right at the chest."

74

He stopped to pluck raspberries, giving a few to Jimmy. He wiped his stained fingers on his shirt. Not twenty feet ahead of them, a ruffed grouse burst from cover, threaded through the trees and disappeared. There was a gunshot and a whoop of elation. Mr. Rimmington walked on. Jimmy followed, remembering...

The bounty was a nickel a tail. He and a friend would go to a creek, a pail in one hand, a slingshot dangling from his hip pocket. Then to the nearest freshly dug gopher hole. One of them would pour in water while the other stood with the elastic cocked, a stone in the leather pocket of the sling. In the burrow, a rodent's face with matted hair and ruby eye, and the impact of the stone. Sometimes there was a trophy after the first pour. Sometimes it got bloody and sickening. In the end a limp body was fished from the hole, the head smashed with a rock and the tail sawed off with the dull blade of a jackknife. The reward for the carnage was a binge of chocolate and pop and ice cream. Sometimes the gore clung to the memory like burdock.

As though he'd read his thoughts, Mr. Rimmington said, "Gophers. They aren't the problem they used to be, but Billy Miles still hunts them. Likes to snare them, catch them alive. Then he holds them by the tail, gives a jerk and snaps it off like you'd flick a whip. Stands there laughing ...."

They'd come to the clearing near the shack. "Says he gets a kick out of doing in the government," Mr. Rimmington said grimly.

They sat on the grass in the sun.

"It's city types like Billy Miles," Rimmington said, "I can't stand to be around them ...." He paused and added, "Or to hear the sound of church bells."

"What's wrong with church bells?"

"They remind me of another Billy Miles." Mr. Rimmington jerked a thumb skyward. "The one who created all the suffering in the first place.

He was suddenly rigid with intensity. "To be the omniscient God! To be aware of *all* suffering – every horror, every brutality. To see the sparrow fall, yes, but also to see the antelope eaten alive by jackals, the caribou smothering in mosquitoes. To see the baby encephalitic, the ten-year-old being gang-raped, a thousand bodies putrefying in a plague, an entire town destroyed by an earthquake, twenty million dead from the flu!"

Mr. Rimmington strode off, hands jammed in his pockets.

14

"You'll do no such thing," Herb Coulter said. "I've just had a raise. We'll have our picnic basket prepared by the head chef at the Saskatchewan."

He was in an ebullient mood, had been for about ten days. Things were coming his way. He'd received another promotion, was now assistant general manager, and had an office and a secretary. The shares he'd bought on margin had doubled in value in three months.

Herb had become the soul of attentiveness to Lizzie. Each evening he brought home a long-stemmed rose until there were half a dozen in the crystal vase on the dining-room table, and had then continued, replacing a faded one each day. He'd begun again to kiss her on leaving for work and on returning. Jimmy and Kathryn were happy, each for their own reasons: Jimmy, because the world was like a Chinese box being opened before his eyes; Kathryn, because it was her birthday and she had no doubt the picnic had been planned in her honor.

Herb was up early to leave Herb, Jr., with Aunt Helen, after which he stopped by the hotel to pick up lunch. The chef, anxious to please, had packed it in an insulated hamper and had included with the soft drinks a bottle (illegal) of white French burgundy. The car packed, Jimmy took up his position awaiting the command to crank the engine. Herb gave his peak cap a tug, adjusted the magneto and gasoline levers and pulled the choke.

"Are we ready?" he sang out.

"Ready," came the chorus.

"Then switch on," he said, adapting the new jargon of aviation.

"Switch on," Jimmy echoed.

"Contact!"

Anxious to flaunt the new muscle that adolescence had brought, Jimmy set the crank and gave it a mighty tug. The engine started without even a second pull. Then off to Sandy Butte, the car running without a hitch beneath the magnificence of a cloudless Saskatchewan sky. *Yes Sir, That's My Baby*, they sang; and *Ain't She Sweet* and *Ninety-Nine in a Hundred Want To Be Kissed*. Herb even essayed an old Irish song:

As I went out one evening
From Tipperary Town,
I met a little Colleen
Among the heather brown.
"Ah!" says I. "Perhaps you're lonely."
She tossed her pretty curl,
"Well maybe I prefer it!"
Och! the dear little girl!

Says I, "Perhaps you're married?"
Says she, "Perhaps I'm not!"
Says I, "I'll be your gossoon!"
Says she, "I'll not be caught."
"Oh! your eyes are like the ocean,
And your heart is like a pearl!"
Says she, "Well then, I'll keep it!"
Och! the dear little girl!

Says I, "I've got a cabin,
And pigs that number seven,
And ah, with you, Mavourneen,
Sure the place would be like heav'n!"
Her eyes looked up in mine ... then
My heart was in a whirl;
The little pigs had done it!
Och, the dear little girl!

Sandy Butte was an isolated hill thrusting raggedly through the plain. On the south side was a rubbly slope surmounted by a ragged stand of poplars and cypress. A dusting of black-eyed susans and cone flowers formed scallops on the lower slopes. Herb maneuvered beneath the shade of a tree. Nearby, whiskered with long grass, was a shallow basin of fine sand. They spread the blanket and Lizzie sat on it, her face turned to the sun.

Now that they were no longer cooled by the movement of the open car they realized that the day was hot and close and without a wisp of wind.

While Herb and Lizzie set out the food, the children wandered nearby looking for something to do. There were no cliffs to scale and no trees to be climbed, but Jimmy was getting beyond that anyway. Kathryn, wondering what Herb had bought for her birthday, plucked a handful of wildflowers, and with Jimmy, made her way back.

"Well now, children," Herb said, "let's everybody sit down. Look at this food. Isn't it something?"

The display was not so entrancing to the children. The fried chicken breasts were covered with a gelatine embedded with what looked suspiciously like bits of green pepper and mushrooms. There were avocado pear halves filled with tiny shrimp (Ugh!). The potato salad had slivers of green pepper in it too, and worse, pieces of pimento. Kathryn wrinkled her nose at the green asparagus spears as Lizzie dropped a dollop of mayonnaise on them. There were carrot sticks and celery and sliced cucumbers, and heaped on a napkin, chunks of garlic bread. The peach tarts for dessert confirmed that there was no birthday cake.

"Can I have a bottle of Whistle?" Kathryn asked her father.

"Not before she eats," Lizzie protested.

Herb handed Kathryn a bottle, condensation beading on it. "Where's the opener?"

Consternation! They rummaged through the hamper. Was there one in the car? No.

"I can open it with my teeth," Jimmy volunteered.

"You'll do no such thing," Lizzie said, waving a napkin to drive off the flies which had scented the feast.

"I'll pry it off on the bumper," Herb said, going to the car.

"Couldn't it wait?" Lizzie asked. "Everything's getting warm."

"Are we supposed to eat this stuff?" Kathryn said grumpily, watching her mother prepare a brimming plate for Herb.

"This stuff!" her mother exclaimed. "It's special for your birthday." Kathryn wrinkled her nose and turned away.

Lizzie looked up at Jimmy. "What would you like, dear?"

"Is that mushrooms in that guck on the chicken?"

"Just a few. You can pick them off."

"No, thanks."

"What about some of this lovely avocado?"

"I was wondering what it was. It looks rotten."

"That's the way avocado goes. Look, I'll cut the brown part off. Some potato salad?"

Suddenly there came the sound of glass shattering and of Herb saying "Damn!" He was standing at the rear of the car, lips a thin line, eyes squinting, breath held against the onset of the pain. The broken bottle was at his feet. One hand was clasping the other. Blood was running through the fingers.

Lizzie went to Herb. "How bad is it?" she asked.

Herb only released his breath to take another. Lizzie was pale but composed.

"Let me see how badly it's cut," she said. "Jimmy, get me a napkin."

"Damn! I gashed all my fingertips," Herb said, grimacing with pain.

"Oh, Daddy!" Kathryn cried, eyes abrim.

"Take your other hand away so I can bandage it," Lizzie said. "It has to be done, Herb."

She daubed gently at the blood, peering closely. "All four fingertips," she said, shuddering.

Kathryn covered her face with her hands and began to cry. Jimmy felt sick.

"There are some brown flecks," Lizzie said.

"Rust. I had the neck of the bottle jammed in the bumper."

Lizzie wrapped the napkin loosely about the hand. "It's got to be washed out."

"Could you use the wine?" Jimmy asked. "It's alcohol."

"Yes," Lizzie said. "Get it."

"Why don't we drive to the nearest farmer's," Herb said uneasily.

"It must be washed out right away," Lizzie said in her unequivocal voice.

Kathryn jumped to her feet. "I don't want to see it!" She ran behind the car. "I don't want to see it!" she cried.

"Kathryn, will you stop that!" Lizzie poured the wine on his fingers. Herb turned his face away, baring his teeth, sucking air. "Steady. Just another second." Lizzie's grip was like iron on his wrist. "Good." She passed the bottle to Jimmy. "Pour some in a glass for your father."

Skillfully, she bandaged the hand. "All right, children, pack up."

Kathryn came from behind the car, her face full of misery. "Oh, Daddy," she moaned, "it was my fault."

"Don't worry, love," he said, drawing her near. "Give Jimmy a hand with the packing."

Herb couldn't turn the car about with one hand. Jimmy tried, but the car kept stalling. He stood on the running board and turned the steering wheel while Herb operated the clutch pedal. As Jimmy steered into the ruts, there was a sound like a gunshot. The right front tire had been punctured by a shard of glass.

Herb said, "Son of a bitch!" Jimmy said, "Jesus Christ!" Kathryn said, "Eek!" And Lizzie said, "Herb!"

Jimmy put the jack in position, but there was no flat stone nearby and the base of the jack sank into the sod.

The red stain on the bandage was spreading. Herb was pale and perspiring.

"We've got to get help," said Lizzie.

"There's some people over there," Kathryn said, pointing to a ridge. "I heard them drive up."

Herb went striding off, Jimmy at his side, the others following. As they topped the ridge they saw a man and a woman lying on a blanket spread on the grass. The woman's skirt was pulled above her thighs and the man's hand was beneath it.

The woman looked up. "Oh my God! Herb!"

She scrambled to her feet, face flushed, straightening her skirt. The man rose too, but seemed less embarrassed.

"Excuse me," Herb said, drawing back. "Sorry."

The woman saw his hand. "Oh my God! What have you done to your hand?" She grasped his forearm, holding the bandage up for inspection.

"I cut it," Herb said awkwardly. "On a bottle."

"Your poor dear hand," the woman said, her own hand hovering about the bandage as though to bless it. "My poor Herbie."

From behind them came Lizzie's voice. "What," she demanded, "is going on? Who is this woman?"

Herb pulled his arm away. "Uh ... Lizzie, this is Mae King. She ... works at Simpsons. And this is ..." The sentence collapsed.

"Hugh Oxley," the man supplied.

Mae remembered her unbuttoned blouse and tried to remedy it with surreptitious fingers. Lizzie looked at her, loading her gaze with disdain.

"Mr. Oxley," Lizzie said, taking command, "we must get Mr. Coulter to a doctor. He's gashed his hand."

Mr. Oxley said, "Well, I don't know, Mrs. Coulter. Mae and me come out here for a picnic ..."

"We blew a tire on the car," Lizzie said, "and he can't –"

She broke off as a sudden gust of wind threw dust in their faces. It was followed by a spatter of raindrops and a growl of thunder. Mr. Oxley went quickly to put up the top of his runabout. Before he could accomplish that, the rain was upon them. The Coulters made a dash for their car, and after the usual struggle, got the side-curtains in place.

They sat silent and sodden on the wet seats, the rain lashing and drumming on the roof, an almost palpable wall of estrangement between Lizzie and Herb. The rain eased for a moment and Mr. Oxley came over the ridge and replaced the burst tire with the spare. When he had gone, Herb said in an unnatural voice, "Well, we'd better be on our way."

They drove in silence toward the city. Twice they had to stop while Jimmy pried gumbo from the fenders.

15

Jimmy ran swiftly, moving in the shadows, crouching at times, his eyes on the figure ahead of him. The man passed beneath a street lamp, went on a few strides, glanced about, then turned onto the path leading to a bungalow from which no light showed. As he neared the front door, it opened and he went in quickly.

Jimmy waited a few moments. Then, staying close to the intervening houses, he approached the bungalow. Pressed against the wall, he went toward the back. The shades were drawn but there was a line of light beneath one of them. Pulling himself up until his eyes were on a level with the windowsill, he peered into the room and saw his father with his arms around Lettie Duggan.

His mother was at the ironing board when he came through the back door. He hung up his cap and was headed for the hallway when she said, "Well?"

He dropped to a knee at the bookcase, running a finger along the volumes. "The Henty books," he said. "Did you move them?"

"Never mind that," she said crossly, "tell me what happened. He went to Lettie Duggan's, didn't he?"

He turned to her, angry but taking care to soften it. "Mom, why do you do that? It isn't fair – to me or to Dad."

"Never mind, fair," she said. "He did, didn't he? Not that it's anything new. I've known since it started." She flipped over the shirt she was ironing. "That's where he went, wasn't it?"

He made his voice firm. "No, Mom, he didn't, if you want to know."

"Well then, where did he go?"

"I don't know. By the time I got to the corner he was nowhere in sight. Probably where he said – to Dan Fogarty's."

"He went to Lettie Duggan's," she said flatly.

He could tell she had been drinking; it was in her voice. Her eyes were on the shirt and he could study her. A great sadness enveloped him. Tendrils of hair had escaped the hairpins and hung about her face. Her skin was flushed and her eyes were red. Mascara marked the path of her tears and was smeared on one cheek and on the back of her wrist where she'd wiped them away. In the harsh light of the kitchen she seemed very old. For a moment he saw her as she had been only a few months ago . . . .

"Jimmy, do you think I'm beautiful?"

"Uh huh."

"You're not looking at me. Look at me. Do you think your mother is beautiful?"

He looked up from the floor where he'd been reading. Lizzie had come from her bedroom to stand in the sunroom, one hand on a hip, the other holding a broad-brimmed straw hat. In the crystal brilliance of the summer day her hair was dark and lustrous, gathered back with a wisp of green silk. Her skin was flushed pink. The dress, a filmy chiffon, picked up the green of her eyes and the coppery tint of her hair.

"Yes, you are," he said. "Don't you know that?"

"Sometimes. It's just nice to hear it, that's all."

"You're all dressed up. Where are you going?"

"To do a little shopping and see if I can talk your father into taking me to lunch."

"Does Daddy know you're coming?"

"It's going to be a surprise," she said and spun in a pirouette, the skirt following lazily. "Jimmy . . ."

"Yes."

"Am I as beautiful as Aunt Helen . . . ?"

"You know your father's leaving," Lizzie said, folding the shirt, setting it to one side and starting on another.

"He's just going for a few weeks," Jimmy said. "Vancouver's booming, he says. After a while we can all move there."

"I don't like to say this about your father, Jimmy, but that's a lie."

"Mom . . ."

"It's just another one of his lies."

She was silent, then said, "You think when I'm in the bedroom I have a drink, don't you?"

"Mom ..."

"Well, don't you?"

"I don't think anything. I just wish you wouldn't, that's all."

"So what if I do? Is that so wrong?"

"I got my oral comp mark today."

"... knowing what's been going on since the night you were born."

"Ninety-two."

"You're growing up. It's time you knew about your father."

"I don't want to talk about it."

"Well, you're going to talk about it whether you want to or not. You're going to be the man of the house around here so you might as well find out now. You know your Aunt Helen?"

"Mom!"

"My sister. My own sister. I take her into my home when she doesn't have anywhere to go and –"

"Will you stop! You're just getting yourself all worked up."

"The night you were born ... I'm in the hospital having my first baby, and your father and my sister ... my very own sister! Said she'd look after everything while I was in the hospital. Cook and clean. She cooked and cleaned all right. My first baby, and the doctor had to cut – no, it's time you knew. Six stitches. My insides have never been right since. There isn't a day goes by I'm not in pain. Nine pounds, ten ounces, you were. And while I'm there in the hospital, your father and my sister ... Right here in my home. In my bed. In my own bed!"

16

It was an oppressively hot day. The interior of Mr. Rimmington's shack was fetid, so they moved out-of-doors. A bird was darting about a clump of wildflowers, moving with crisp precision. They watched it, entranced.

"It's a ruby-throated hummingbird," Jimmy said.

"Has to be," Mr. Rimmington said sharply. "There's no other variety in Canada."

"It's the only bird that can remain stationary in the air and even fly backward," Jimmy said undeterred.

During the more than two years that Rimmington had been his tutor he had been encouraged to say without hesitation things he knew. "You can help diminish my vast store of ignorance," Mr. Rimmington had said.

"Where did you learn that?" Rimmington asked.

"A book I borrowed from the library."

"Well, it's not true, even though lots of people believe it and some books on ornithology – ornis, the Greek word for bird – assert it."

Rimmington had seemed preoccupied most of the morning, and sometimes testy. Jimmy had decided that it was the sticky heat of the day.

"Jimmy," he said, "don't believe something simply because it's in print. Accept most of what you read, simply because you can't possibly know everything first-hand, but keep your mind open. Be curious. Sure, curiosity killed the cat – and questing with the mind can sometimes get you into trouble – but ... What's the rest of the maxim?"

"Satisfaction brought it back."

86

"Exactly. You'll read that the hummingbird is the only bird able to hover and to fly backward, that the ruby-throat's feathers are green and red, and that it uses its long, curved bill to suck nectar from the base of flowers. None of these is true. Many birds can fly backward. The ruby-throat's feathers are all green. There are no reddish feathers on the throat except when light reflects their iridescence. And it doesn't suck up nectar; it uses a long tongue that emerges from the tip of the bill."

His mood suddenly changed. "Let's get away from here."

As they went, Jimmy asked, "Where were you born?"

"The Isle of Wight. Off the south coast of England."

"Do you have family there?"

"Why do you want to know?"

Jimmy grinned. "You said to be curious."

"They're all dead," Rimmington said shortly. "Just as well."

As they followed the path to the bottom of the coulee, Jimmy asked, "Will you ever go back?"

Rimmington smiled grimly. "Yes. When the time comes. In a box. The money for it is in an envelope under my mattress. Isn't that a cheery thought for a dreary day?" He ran ahead down the path.

Stripped to the waist, trouser legs rolled up, wading, they'd been looking for evidence of life in the creek at the bottom of the coulee. Heads down, only a segment of sky above them, they hadn't noticed the oncoming line squall until it blustered to the edge of the coulee and dumped grit and dust on them. Grabbing their shoes and shirts, they scrambled up the slope, clutching at tufts of grass and the sinewy shrubs rooted there. The storm buffeted them, spattering them with fat drops of rain. It had swept on before they reached the top. Winded, they collapsed in the long grass. Jimmy laughed at the dappled dome of Rimmington's derby, and he at the dust on Jimmy's hair.

They would freshen up with a swim. Jimmy was dispatched to the shack to get a towel. They met at a shallow pool where the creek backed up behind a ridge of rock. The water wasn't deep enough for swimming, but they stripped and cavorted and splashed about. Jimmy's shyness at his nakedness soon passed. Mr. Rimmington dried his back for him and passed him the towel. In turn, Jimmy dried Rimmington's shoulders. He was startled when the teacher turned and put his arms about him. He felt a hardness against his thigh. He stood motionless, trying to think of what to say; something light-hearted, chaffing, but couldn't think of anything, and so stood with his arms by his sides, the towel hanging from one hand. Mr. Rimmington was clutching him tightly, not breathing it seemed. Now he turned his head and Jimmy felt a bristle of beard against his cheek. And lips, warm and wet. Cold crawled on his skin and a sudden revulsion shuddered through him. He pushed away.

Mr. Rimmington's voice in his ear was almost a moan. "No, Jimmy. Don't."

He thrust with all his strength and broke free, turning away so he wouldn't see the man. He ran, tears blinding him, fleeing up the footpath to the plain above. He didn't stop until he realized he was naked. He went into the woods and crept to a spot from which he could look down unseen. Mr. Rimmington, dressed, was slowly coming up the path. Jimmy could see his own clothes by the creek where he'd left them. He hid, shivering, until Mr. Rimmington had passed, then made his way down.

17

The voices had continued through the night, rising and falling, and the pillow over his head hadn't blocked off the sound. He slept and awakened perhaps a dozen times and then started up, blinking and disoriented, when his mother swung open the bedroom door, banging it against the wall, and turned on the light.

"Time to get up," she said. Her voice was raw, clanging. "Your father's leaving. He should at least say good-bye. Come on, up you get." She was wearing the dress she'd worn at supper.

He heard her in Kathryn's room and again in the hall – a brief jousting of her voice with his father's. When he came out of the bedroom, Herb was passing by, lugging two suitcases.

"Hello, son," he said. His eyes looked tired and he was unshaven. A long, livid scratch ran across one cheek.

Jimmy went into the bathroom to put some cold water to his eyes. From the window he could see that it wasn't yet dawn. As he left the bathroom he passed Kathryn. Her eyes were down.

The front door off the living room was open. His mother was standing stiffly beside it. Her skin was the color of pie dough. Her eyes were puffed and red. She seemed unaware that Jimmy had come down the stairs. Not knowing what to do, he started for the kitchen.

"Where are you going?" she demanded.

"I don't know. I thought I'd set the table for breakfast or something."

"You'll stay right here. Your father's out packing the car." She called up the stairs, "Kathryn, get down here this minute."

He went to sit in a chair in the corner. His father came in and went upstairs. As he passed Kathryn, he put a hand gently on her

89

head and cupped the back of it. Kathryn, without a word, went to the sofa on the far side of the room.

When his father came down again, he was carrying two cardboard boxes, a pair of shoes and a peak cap. His pockets bulged, and binoculars bumped against his chest. "I guess that's everything," he said in a voice that sounded as though he was just getting over a cold.

As he went out the door, Lizzie said, "You *will* come back long enough to say good-bye?"

He turned on her, drawing a deep breath as if to speak, then compressed his lips. He looked across at Kathryn and said, "Back in a minute, children."

As he went out the door, Lizzie ran to the writing desk, searched frantically through an overflowing drawer, and returned with a small cylinder of paper.

She looked at Jimmy, who was sitting with his hands in his lap. "Are you just going to sit there? Your father's leaving. Do something! Say something!"

Herb came in slowly, wiping his face with a handkerchief. He looked at Jimmy. "Well, don't I get a handshake?" Jimmy went to him and awkwardly put out a hand. His father put his arms about him. "You're growing up, son, but not too big for a bear hug, eh?"

Jimmy felt his body stiffen. He wanted to put his arms about his father, but thought he shouldn't. Kathryn came across the room and stood waiting. Herb released Jimmy and put out a hand to the girl. As he did, she lost her composure and ran into his arms. Going to his knees, he brought her cheek to his own.

"There, there now." His voice was robust but phlegmy. "What's my little girl doing, for goodness' sake? I won't be gone for long. Just a few weeks –"

"That's a lie," Lizzie said. "Just one more lie."

"A few weeks and you can come out to Vancouver and everything'll be fine. Okay?" He pushed her to arm's length, smiling. "Tears all gone? That's my girl. A little smile? You wouldn't want your father to go without a smile, would you?"

Kathryn contrived a wan smile. Herb patted her cheek and got to his feet. "Well, better get going. I'd like to get as far as Calgary by dark." He put on his cap, pulling down the peak. "Take care, Liz," he said. "Kiss the little one for me. I didn't want to get him up." He turned to the door.

"Haven't you forgotten something?"

He paused, wary. "I have?"

"This," she said, and brought the cylinder of paper from behind her back.

Puzzled he took it, slipped the silk cord from about it, and then realized what it was.

"Our marriage certificate," she said. "Or had you forgotten about that?"

He held it out to her but she wouldn't take it. It fell to the floor between them and rolled against the doorsill. Jimmy reached down quickly and picked it up. Herb turned and was gone.

Lizzie stayed in bed until noon that day. Jimmy, who had slept fitfully, was awakened by little Herb, who was crying. He got out of bed, quieted him, and led him downstairs. He kept expecting that his mother would come to take the task off his hands, and at one point tapped on her door and looked into the bedroom. She was lying with her head in the crook of an arm, breathing heavily. On the night table was a tumbler with an empty sherry bottle.

He woke Kathryn to attend to Herb while he made some porridge. Kathryn was in a surly mood and refused to help. She sat at the table, head down, tracing the pattern on the oilcloth with a finger.

Jimmy was in the midst of fixing a lunch of milk and peanut butter and banana sandwiches when his mother appeared at the kitchen door. She was in her chenille dressing gown. Her eyes were puffed to where they were no more than slits.

"Why aren't you at Mr. Rimmington's?" she asked.

He didn't look up but continued to slice the banana, careful to position the segments equally on the peanut butter.

"I thought maybe I should stay with –"

"Well, I'm up now," she said, "so you can go. He hasn't paid this month's rent yet – he always pays on Thursdays, and today's already Saturday. And tell him you won't be taking lessons anymore. We won't have money for that."

Often, when his father hadn't been able to drive him, he'd jogged the five miles to Indian Coulee, enjoying it. On this morning, his limbs were heavy, and he walked all the way to the shack.

He approached the clearing through the woods. The area was flooded with sunlight. The sky was an electric blue, broken only by a single cloud. In the breeze, the bottles were chiming with a festive sound. The door to the shack was closed and there was no sign of Mr. Rimmington. There was a strong smell – a carcass in the woods, he thought. More of Billy Miles' work, probably.

For a while he lingered in the woods, then returned to the shack and knocked on the door.

"Hello!" he called out.

Silence, except for the chiming of the bottles.

"Anybody home?" he shouted.

The wind must have shifted; the stink from the woods was strong. He knocked on the door again and tried it. The bolt was on the inside. He called out again. Still no response. Obviously, Mr. Rimmington was avoiding him. Relieved, he was about to head home but something held him back.

He circled the shack and went to the window, putting his face to the pane. It was dark within, but he could see Mr. Rimmington stretched out on the settee.

He ran to the front door, banging on it with a fist and shouting. He kicked the door, driving it inward. A sickening stench issued from the shack. When his eyes adjusted to the darkness, he saw the body on the settee. An arm hung down to the floor, and beside the hand was a gun. The face was caked with dark blood, the features unrecognizable. Flies buzzed angrily about.

He ran from the shack and stood for a moment, breathing heavily. Then he began to be convulsed with sobs and fell to his knees. His arms about his head, his brow pressed to the soil, he wept. After a while he got up, took Mr. Rimmington's cane from its place beside the door and strode into the forest of bottles. In a silent fury he began to strike at them, smashing them. Soon there was blood on his face and hands and forearms. He continued wildly, blindly, swinging the cane in sweeping circles until it slipped from his hands and arced end over end into the woods.

18

It was a one-column newspaper clipping reproduced by photocopy and bearing the heading:

H. L. RIMMINGTON

Howard Llewellyn Rimmington, 43, who lived on the property bordering Indian Coulee owned by Herbert William Coulter of 2119 Angus Street in Regina, died of a self-inflicted gunshot wound to the head earlier this week. The body was discovered by James Coulter, 15, when he visited the property yesterday. County Coroner J. H. Smathers said Mr. Rimmington had been dead for at least three days.

Little is known of the deceased. He emigrated to Canada from England ten years ago and is believed to have lived for a time in Quebec City, teaching at Bishops' College. He moved onto the Coulter property five years ago.

Mr. Smathers said that the body was discovered when James Coulter went to attend the weekly classes of instruction he has been receiving from the deceased for the past few years. Coulter sustained cuts to his face and hands which were treated at Gray Nuns Hospital. No explanation has been given for the wounds, which were superficial, and police say no charges will be laid.

Mr. Rimmington has no known next of kin. The remains are resting at the city morgue preparatory to returning them to Mr. Rimmington's birthplace at Caithness on the Isle of Wight, England.

Hugh Hoffman put down the photocopy. He sat in silence, pondering, drumming his fingers on the desktop.

"Well, Clyde, what do you make of it?"

Rogers gave his deprecatory shrug. "Not much. That business about the cuts on Coulter's face and hands is a bit strange, but apparently it was of no importance. Jenny checked with the police. Had a hell of a time. It's so long ago now, and there was nothing in the official report."

Hoffman continued to look at him, the drumrolls accelerating. Behind the lenses of his glasses the magnified eyes blinked owl-like. "So there wasn't any fancy school, just this queer teacher and his student. How long was Rimmington his tutor – a few years?"

Rogers glanced at a sheet of paper in his hand. "According to his father, about two years. He was doing poorly in school, and when his old man learned that Rimmington was a teacher, he asked him to give the boy private lessons on weekends."

"Did Coulter Senior know why Rimmington shot himself?"

"He had no idea. He was an anti-social, reclusive kind of guy. Almost impossible to talk to. All the old man had to say was that it didn't surprise him."

"There's no question that he was a homosexual and that he was fired by Bishops' College for being involved with a youngster there?"

"None."

"Was it reported to the Quebec City police?"

"No, no. The boy was from a well-known Montreal family. It was all handled hush-hush, Jenny says. Rimmington was fired. I gather that Bishops' asked for his credentials and then notified Edinburgh, where he'd done his graduate work. It finished him as a teacher."

"Except for Jimmy Coulter."

Rogers said, "Jenny wants some guidance on it."

"What did you tell her?"

"That I'd get back to her."

Hoffman got out of his chair to stand looking out of the window. "We won't use it, of course."

"I didn't think so."

"However," Hoffman said, turning to face him, "I've been thinking back to Coulter's days at the *Tribune*. As I remember him, he was ... how shall I put it? – a little standoffish. Didn't fit in." He paused. "Bobby Coombs is still alive, isn't he?"

"Yes. Jenny talked to him a week or so ago."

"You might have her check him on this homosexual angle. He was assistant sports editor, I think, when Coulter was here."

Rogers scratched his head then carefully replaced and patted the thinning strands. "I'm not quite sure what we're after . . . ."

Hoffman came back to his chair and sat down. "I'm not suggesting that there's anything out of line, but let's be realistic. It's not impossible that there was something between Rimmington and young Coulter – he was only fifteen – and that maybe Rimmington killed himself after a bust-up. Apparently Coulter was the only boy this Rimmington was teaching. Then there's that business about the cuts."

"Yes, but as the clipping says, the police were satisfied."

"The clipping says," Hoffman said, picking it up, "that the wounds – wounds, not cuts – were superficial and that no charges would be laid. Would the police specify that no charges would be laid unless the question had been raised?"

"You'll excuse me, Mr. Hoffman, but there's nothing in the clipping or the police report to suggest that the question had been raised."

Hoffman leaned forward, putting his arms on the desk. "Clyde, you know and I know that this is the kind of thing that is not reported. As in the case at Bishops' College, it may have been hushed up. What's the point? Rimmington is dead and Coulter's a minor." He put his thumbs in his vest pockets. "I'm not suggesting there's anything to it or that we use it, but certainly it's background information that Wedger should be aware of while she's working on the story."

PART
THREE

19

After the flat plains country, Toronto was a daily marvel. The trees! Great horse-chestnuts and maples and elms, even apple trees laden with fruit for the picking. The lake! A veritable ocean stretching beyond the horizon. The city! Half a million people; more than lived in the entire province of Saskatchewan.

Lizzie's brother, Arthur, who emigrated from Ireland shortly after she did, had found them a house in the lush, aging Parkdale section of the city, an enormous, gingerbread-laden three-story structure with a basement. To the children it seemed a mansion. Lizzie's enthusiasm was tempered by the fact that the exterior needed painting, some of the floors creaked and were off-level and the ten-foot-high ceilings would make it expensive to heat; but the rent was only thirty dollars a month, and the extra bedrooms would permit Lizzie to take in boarders. She very much needed the money; a month after Herb had gone to Vancouver, he had stopped writing.

Finding roomers – or paying guests, as Lizzie preferred they be called – was not too difficult. The Great Depression had begun and thousands of men and women had come to the city from smaller communities looking for work and in need of lodging. Most guests stayed only briefly. Some went off, the rent unpaid. There was a Mr. Thompson who was found dead on the bed, an empty vial of medicine on the dresser.

Each year, on the first of July, all guests were given a month's notice, and during the first two weeks of August Lizzie prepared for the Canadian National Exhibition. Even the bedrooms on the third floor were pressed into service. She and the children slept on mattresses on the kitchen floor, using winter coats and even scatter rugs for covers when the nights were cool.

The Ex, as it was called, was the event of the year and the one financial bonanza the Coulters knew. The largest annual agricultural fair in the world, it ran from mid-August through Labor Day, attracting visitors from across Canada and the United States.

Each summer, on a slab of wood perhaps six inches by eighteen, Jimmy would letter the word ACCOMMODATIONS and make his way to Lakeshore Boulevard, the extension of highway 2 into the city. There, face scrubbed, hair brushed, dressed in a white shirt, he would stand at the curb, competing against perhaps two dozen rivals for the attention of the oncoming tourists. At seventeen, he had grown beyond six feet, with broad shoulders and his father's lean body. His face was callow and undistinguished except for the astonishing blue of the eyes. He gave an impression of openness and had discovered that adults tended to like and trust him.

When a car drew to the curb, Jimmy would move into action. "May I be of service to you, sir?"

"You've got rooms? How much?"

"We have accommodations in a number of approved private homes close by, yes sir."

"How much a night?"

"For a single bed, sir, two dollars. Three dollars for a double."

"How much for the kids?"

Here a judgment-call had to be made. It would be predicated on a number of factors: whether the license plate was American; the model and make of the car; and indications of affluence or lack of it. Jimmy might say, "For individual beds, the rate is the same as for adults." Or, "One dollar each." If it was early in the week and the traffic was light, perhaps, "Children fifty cents if they can sleep on the floor – blankets provided." If there was a baby or a toddler in the group, he might throw in, "No charge for the little one."

"How far from the exhibition grounds?"

He'd shrug. "A short drive." It was in fact more than a mile.

Once a tourist was sufficiently intrigued by Jimmy's bright, forthright manner, he would allow himself to be guided to the accommodations. Jimmy rode the running board, so that if there were objections to the distance being traveled, he could feign an inability to hear.

At the Coulter home, little was left to chance. As the car pulled into the driveway, Jimmy would reach in, touch the horn, leap from his perch and run ahead to alert his mother. He would then return to follow the visitors in, carrying their luggage, thus making it more difficult for them to refuse. Nor were they likely to do so, for Lizzie had been busy Creating the Atmosphere. She was a great believer in Appearances and in The Right First Impression. In order to make the rooms "comfy," she had spent the previous two weeks touching up painted areas, repasting curled edges of wallpaper, laundering curtains, linens and towels.

The house, especially in summer, had a pervasive smell: a combination of mildew, old dust and dry rot. Lizzie covered this by placing in the entrance hallway and in each bedroom a bouquet of crepe-paper flowers touched with Forest Glade cologne.

Jimmy's signal gave Lizzie time to close the bedroom windows (the rooms were aired until the last minute) and to draw down the shades so that direct sunlight wouldn't reveal bubbles in the wallpaper, peeling paint and worn spots on the carpets. She would then light two strategically placed lamps, each with a rose-colored silk shade, to give the room a friendly ambience.

Since the previous night's guests had departed, she had cleaned and dusted and done the laundry, with reluctant help from Kathy and with little Herb tagging behind. If there were no obvious signs of soiling, she didn't bother to change the sheets but ironed them right on the mattress. The down comforter was plumped and arranged at the foot of the bed, and carefully folded bath towels were placed on the bedspread, each with a matching face cloth. The clincher was a bone-china dish atop the dresser on which there were four freshly baked tea biscuits, a dab of butter and a tiny pot of raspberry jam.

Dressed in her best frock, a flowered chiffon, her hair freshly marcelled and the roots hennaed, Lizzie would greet the potential guests at the front door. The impression given was one of a private home being opened to the weary traveler.

In her best season, Lizzie took in more than four hundred dollars. The money carried the family through to Christmas. Taking in tourists also enabled the children to meet people from other provinces and from the United States, among them marathon swimmers, midway freaks, carnies and spielers. The freaks, the children agreed, were the nicest.

In contrast, winter was the bad time. Usually the rooms emptied in December. Guests gave up on the city and went home for Christmas, not to return. The house was so chill that it was hard to get new roomers. The drop in income caused Lizzie to conserve heat and this worsened matters. Hot-water radiators were drained in each room that wasn't rented. There were times when the coal bin was almost empty, and the children were sent to forage for wood in the neighborhood. Sweaters were worn indoors and sometimes to bed. The kitchen became the heart of the house, a Quebec heater and a wood-fired stove making it a warm and fragrant place.

The important date each month was the first, when the rent was due. Usually, within a day or so, the welfare check would arrive in the mail. It amounted to thirty-five dollars and was the only dependable income the family had. Jimmy had quit school, bored by unimaginative teachers, but had been unable to find work; married men with families were being hired first. He made an occasional dollar by shoveling snow from sidewalks. Lizzie earned a little extra by selling the paper flowers and silk lamp shades she made with such skill.

But the end of the month was the lean time and the children would sometimes come upon their mother seated in the kitchen, such cash as she had spread on the table, wiping her eyes with the handkerchief she carried in her woolen bathrobe. She often remained in her bathrobe all day, worn slippers on her feet, her uncombed hair more or less pinned on top of her head, yesterday's makeup unrepaired.

Toward the end of the month meals became predictable. Porridge and day-old bread for breakfast. Lunch was a glass of milk and bread and butter with brown sugar spread on it. For dinner there was usually soup or a stew. Kathryn would be dispatched to Melnyk the butcher to buy sausages or some chicken parts. That paid for, she would say to Mr. Melnyk, "You wouldn't have a bone for the dog?"

She was a pretty girl whose body had filled out early and who looked older than her fourteen years. She knew how to get around Mr. Melnyk. The butcher knew the Coulters didn't have a dog and that Mrs. Coulter didn't have a husband, and he would go into the refrigerator and return with a leg bone heavy with marrow. On the massive chopping block he would saw off a piece that would fit into a cooking pot, wrap it in butcher paper, tie it and snap the string with a flourish. Handing it to Kathryn, he would smile and say, "Tell your mother good luck from Melnyk the butcher. She should come and see me."

The bone, with some potatoes, turnips, onions and barley, would simmer for the rest of the day on top of the Quebec heater. With bread and a glass of milk, it was dinner. For dessert there might be "fish-eye pudding" – tapioca, of the consistency of lumpy mucilage – or rice pudding without raisins or milk.

One Monday during the Easter break at school, the relief check was a week overdue and there was not a morsel of food in the house. The furnace, having been hand-fed the last fragments of coal from the corners of the bin, had gone out. The previous day there had been soup and the heel of a loaf of bread, sliced and fried in bacon fat for lunch, but nothing for dinner. They all went to bed early to try to forget their hunger in sleep. That Monday Lizzie urged the children to drink water – "You'll feel full and not notice." She gathered them about the kitchen table, bundled in sweaters and overcoats, found a pack of cards and organized a game of Snap. At one-thirty, as a diversion, Lizzie made a ritual search of the cupboards and drawers; and to cries of delight, found a packet of Life Savers containing four mints.

Finally she dispatched Jimmy to find the postman, who normally made his delivery around three o'clock. He came upon him three streets away, and after following him for a while, asked politely, "Anything for the Coulters at 69 Beatty?" Mr. Montrose, the postman, was a dour man whose pelvis had been fused to the lower backbone as a result of a wartime injury. It gave him pain and caused him to rock as he walked. He didn't give Jimmy so much as a glance but growled, "If there's somethin', you'll get it when I get there."

Back in the kitchen, Jimmy broke up the foot stool with the wobbly leg and burned it in the Quebec heater. As they huddled about the heat, he proposed that each tell what they wanted for dinner after the check had been cashed. Lizzie said, "And you can all have a nickel for candy," thereby stimulating fervent imaginings: candy buttons on strips of brown paper, assorted flavors of icing sugar in paper packets, to be sucked through a licorice straw, maple buds, chocolate marshmallow brooms, miniature wax bottles filled with strawberry sugar-water, caramels, packets of raisins, jujubes, jawbreakers, peppermints, licorice whips, pipes, plugs or cigars.

At two-thirty they donned toques and overshoes and went to the living room to peer through the lace curtains into the street. The talk of food and candy had passed and they waited in silence, shivering in the cold, their breath hanging in the still air. After a while Jimmy pointed. They could see Mr. Montrose rocking up each path as he worked his way up the street. Finally before their house, it seemed he would go on.

"Please, God," Lizzie whispered.

But he turned in and he had the check. Lizzie caught it as it fell through the mail slot, tore open the envelope, and bearing it above her like a pennant taken in battle, led a snake dance through the house. There came the sudden, sobering realization that if they didn't get to the bank before three it would be too late to cash the check. Slowed to the pace of little Herb, until Jimmy picked him up and rode him on his back, they ran in a strung-out line to Queen Street to slip through the door of the Canadian Bank of Commerce even as a clerk was setting the lock.

20

Jenny Wedger came into Clyde Rogers' office, placed a fat manilla envelope on his desk and said, "I want off the Coulter story."

Rogers looked at her. "Have you had lunch?"

"No."

He reached into a drawer, took out a brown paper sack and held it up between thumb and forefinger. "Lunch," he said. Opening the bag, he peered inside, a look of distaste on his face. "My wife's on a health food kick. She's been packing me a lunch to keep me out of the cafeteria here." He rummaged around. "You wouldn't believe what's in here! The things they make out of soybeans!" He flipped it into the wastebasket, tightened his tie and went to get his jacket. "I see from the window there's a guy with a hot-dog stand parked over by Harbourfront. My treat."

They walked along Queen's Quay in the sunshine, bemoaning the theft of the view by the hotel and condominiums and remarking on the onset of spring. She was a tall girl, chunky of body but with a delicate Peter Pan face, the impression heightened by short-cropped black hair. With hot dogs and cokes, they went to sit at one of the picnic tables overlooking the lake. A dozen mendicant gulls deserted a passing sailboat and began to circle them.

After a while, he said, "You want off the Coulter story. Why?"

"Do we really need to go into it? Somebody else will do a better job. As I told you when you assigned it to me, it really isn't my cup of tea."

"Yes," he said, "you told me that. Then a few days later you write me a note and you're all gung ho."

"Okay, I'll tell you why," she said, looking off at the water. "You remember the series I did on Senator Brownlee?"

105

"Very well."

"It was a good story and it needed to be written – he's a crook. And part of the story was that the guy's a masochist. Fine, we all get our kicks some way. But in the Brownlee story, that was the key. It was the reason for the kickbacks. Now, what I don't want to do is to begin to specialize in that kind of story, and the way the Coulter piece is going ..."

He took a great bite of the hot dog. "I'm listening."

"The homosexual angle," she said. "Say Jimmy Coulter is gay – which I don't believe – so what? I can name you three members of the House of Commons who are gay. One in the cabinet. Do we do stories on them? Then why Coulter?"

"Jenny," he said, "you're not reading me rightly on this –"

She raised a hand. "No, let me get it off my chest." She took the remainder of her hot dog, broke it into chunks and began tossing them to the gulls. "I went to see Bobby Coombs yesterday. Great guy. Eighty-three last week. Lying there in that damn hospital bed but still full of piss and vinegar. I started asking him what Coulter was like when he worked for him, and after a while – he's no dummy – he said, 'What are you getting at, little lady? Are you trying to make him out a queer or something?' I said, no, of course not, and he said, 'I believe you, but take my word for it, you're wrong.' According to Coombs – and they worked together for nearly four years – he was a shy kid, self-conscious, ingenuous. If he didn't go out whoring or drinking or up to the Casino for the girlie shows, it was because it wasn't his style. Coombs says he made good money – very good for those days – but he never seemed to have any. Different from the guys in the department, yes, but queer, no."

She wiped the table top idly with a paper napkin. "So anyway, I go out of there feeling like a horse's ass. And on the way back to the paper I ask myself: 'Is this what you went into the newspaper business for – to become a purveyor of secondhand gossip?' So," she said, flinging the last of the bun into the air, "I want off the story."

Rogers tilted his head back, drained his drink, shied the can at a refuse basket, and missing, got up to put it in the container. "No problem," he said. "As I say, you've been misreading me. It was only for background information. But stay on the story. As you said, there's a hell of a story here that hasn't been written." When

106

she didn't respond, he asked, "Coulter's not getting to you?" She shook her head.

"Very persuasive guy," he said.

She smiled with him. "Christ, no! The guy's a bleedin' evangelist." She was silent, watching a ship heading through the Western Gap. "I have a question for you."

"Ask."

"It isn't you who's pushing the Coulter series, is it?"

"What makes you think that?"

"Clyde, it's my business to notice things. First, there was to be a series on Coulter to tie into his coming here. Fine. Then, all of a sudden, the complexion of the thing changes. You want written progress reports. Even after I've filled you in ... 'Put that on paper for me, will you, Jen?' Progress reports. Why? I saw the first draft of the story Macdonald and Reimer wrote – and then I saw the final. Like, wow! I stumble onto that Rimmington thing in Regina. When I tell you about it on the phone, you ask the usual. Then, overnight, you're after me to dig back to the thirties in the police files. Christ Almighty, what's that got to do with Jimmy Coulter today? Are we trying to nail the guy to the cross?"

"You're still misreading me, Jenny."

"Forgive me, Clyde, but I don't think I am. It's not you, it's Mr. Hoffman. Coombs was telling me that even when he was a young guy starting out, Hoffman had this thing about religion. Against it, I mean. And it's my private theory – kick my tail around the block if you like – that the Coulter series is a Hoffman series."

"Now I have a question for you," Rogers said. "If, as you say, Mr. Hoffman has this thing about religion – or about Coulter, if you will – answer me why he, more than anybody else, was responsible for putting Coulter into the big time."

She pursed her lips and looked out over the water, frowning. "You've got me there," she conceded. "I've tried to figure it out and it doesn't make sense."

He gathered the rest of their refuse and took it to the trash basket. "Stay with it a while," he said. "Maybe you'll find out. Maybe we'll all find out."

21

In the 1930s the sports department was on the second floor of the old Toronto *Tribune* building on Yonge Street, at the end of a row of telegraphers' stalls. Employees took the stairs, for the elevator was an ancient contraption, given to creeping and wailing and the gnashing of metal, and sufficiently unpredictable to give pause to even the most intrepid. The office was no more than a small room. Four mismatched desks, jammed side by side, lined the south wall. The sports editor's office, a narrow, rectangular cubicle, made private by the use of dimpled glass panels, occupied most of the opposite wall. The floor was covered with a heavy green linoleum which was usually littered with the debris once common to newsrooms.

One Wednesday evening Jimmy Coulter stood before the closed door to the sports editor's office, a sheaf of paper trembling in his hand. The next day the Australian oarsman, Bobby Pearce, was scheduled to compete against the world's best on the waterfront at the Canadian National Exhibition. Canada had a proud tradition in sculling – fostered mostly by that nonpareil in the sport, Ned Hanlan – and the race had created wide interest. Jimmy had written an article on Pearce, penciling in the letters his typewriter no longer struck, and without an appointment had taken it to the *Tribune*. He'd stood about awkwardly, watching the reporters and deskmen at work, and when after five minutes no one had so much as looked at him, he said to the man nearest, "Would you please give this to Mr. Noonan?"

"Give it to him yourself," the reporter said, jerking his head. "He's in there."

Jimmy knocked tentatively on the door. A voice bellowed

"Come!" He opened the door and was enveloped in a miasma of cigar smoke, rye whiskey, witch hazel and body heat. In a hinged-back wooden armchair was the great Pat Noonan, sports editor of the *Tribune*. He swiveled around and glared. "Who the hell are you?"

"My name's Coulter, sir. I've written an article on sculling–"

"On what?"

"On Bobby Pearce. I was wondering if you'd read it?"

Noonan, eyes squinted, appraised him for a moment. He reached into a hip pocket, extracted a two-dollar bill from his wallet, passed it to Jimmy and asked, "Do you know where the liquor store is on Adelaide?"

"No, sir."

"Northwest side, at York. Up the stairs. Get me a mickey of rye, Hiram Walkers 16-C. There'll be 80 cents change." The squint tightened. "You *are* eighteen?"

"Yes, sir."

"Well, don't stand there with your jaw down."

Pat Noonan had a round pink face topped by a nimbus of short-cropped white hair and spoke an obscenity-studded English in a voice normally stentorian. He had grown up street-smart and tough as saddle leather in the Cabbagetown section of Toronto, the son of Irish immigrants. On graduation from the University of Toronto, he'd gone to work for the *Mail and Empire* where his gift for vivid imagery attracted attention. He was stolen by the *Tribune* and after some years became sports editor.

When Jimmy returned, Noonan took the bottle from him and downed three great swallows without a grimace. He wiped his mouth on the back of a hairy forearm, punched a forefinger on Jimmy's manuscript, and said, "Where'd you get your facts?"

"You mean, in my article, sir?"

"Forget the sir."

"Mostly from my head."

"What do you mean, mostly from your head?"

"I've followed sport all my life. I clip stories and file them. I've got a good memory."

"For rowing?"

"No, sir. Mostly, major league baseball, hockey–"

"Who was the leading scorer in the NHL last year?"

"Bill Cook of the New York Rangers – 28 goals, 22 assists. Busher Jackson of the Toronto Maple Leafs was second – 28 goals, 21 assists."

"How many home runs has Lou Gehrig hit this season?"

"Forty-one so far. He's tied in the standings with Jimmy Foxx. Gehrig has a lifetime total of –"

"Never mind. Do you know what a color story is?"

"No, sir."

"It's a feature. It gives some human interest, some background to the news story. Understand?"

Jimmy nodded.

"Do you think you could do a color story on Pearce?"

"Yes, sir."

"Well, we'll see. Three hundred words."

He turned to his desk and had another pull at the bottle. Jimmy wanted to ask questions but didn't dare address himself to those humped shoulders. He backed out, pulling the door closed.

The following evening he went to the *Tribune* to turn in the story. Noonan was standing at the center of the department, convulsing the staff and himself with an account of how he'd escaped a police raid on a whorehouse in Sudbury by climbing onto a roof without his pants, and clinging to a chimney for half an hour in a blizzard. Jimmy hung just within the door. Finally, Noonan turned to him.

"Let's see what you've got."

Jimmy handed him the typed sheets and Noonan read them swiftly. He emitted a phlegmy chuckle and said to the others, "Listen to this."

The first words spoken by Australia's peerless oarsman, Bobby Pearce, after he won yesterday's challenge race at the Canadian National Exhibition waterfront were, "Will you get the hell out of my way, Sonny!"

Accosted by a Toronto youth in a fourteen-foot punt powered by a five-horsepower outboard motor immediately after crossing the finish line, Pearce seemed amused rather than angry. The Down-under oarsman, undoubtedly the greatest since Canada's immortal Ned Hanlan, was barely breathing hard, although sweat gleamed on his heavily muscled shoulders and arms.

He turned to Jimmy. "That was you in the boat?"

"Yes."

110

"Where'd you get it?"

"I rented it. A quarter for the gas."

"Why?"

"I wanted to race him outside the breakwall to see if he could beat an outboard. Which he did. I mention that lower down."

"I read it."

"And I wanted to see up close how tired he was before he had time to catch his breath."

Noonan looked at him for several seconds and tossed the pages onto Bobby Coombs' desk. "Cut it and run it as a sidebar to the Pearce story," he said, and went into his office and closed the door. When nothing further was said to him, Jimmy went home.

It was a hot, close night and he'd decided to sleep in the shed at the back of the house. He hadn't told anyone what had happened, and as he lay in the darkness, he cautioned himself not to get excited. The story wouldn't get into the paper. Something would happen to spoil it. Somebody famous – Ty Cobb maybe – would die; Hank Greenberg would hit four homers in a game; Sir Henry Seagrave would pile up his car at Daytona Beach ....

At four-thirty he pulled on his trousers. Barefooted and naked to the waist, he ran along the empty street, past the unlit store windows to the corner of Dufferin. No papers. When he returned an hour later, the bundle was there. He tried to undo the knot in the twine, but couldn't. He found a shard of glass in the gutter and sawed with it until the cord frayed and snapped. He dug two pennies from a pocket, placed them beneath the bundle of papers and streaked for home.

There it was! Under a two-column heading, his story! It had been reduced to eight brief paragraphs and the text had been altered, but it was most assuredly, incontestably *his* story:

PEARCE NOT EVEN WINDED
AS HE SETS NEW RECORD

Beneath the heading, in tiny 8-point italic type, were the words: *Jimmy Coulter, 18, a Toronto youth, was first to interview the great Aussie sculler after his record-breaking feat. Here is his story.*

After a while, he turned off the light and lay down on the mattress. Through the open doorway the sky was pearling but there was no sleep in him. He thought of Mr. Rimmington and of the day they talked about the essay he'd written. If he were alive he could share with him the excitement he was feeling. There was no one else to whom he could talk about it. His mother would be pleased, of course, but she'd want to know if he'd be paid and would press him to insist on it. He had few close friends, certainly none with whom he could talk about writing.

He suddenly felt very lonely and got out of bed and went into the backyard where he walked about on the wet grass in the darkness, fighting the tears.

Noonan let him sit a week before having Bobby Coombs telephone. Coombs offered him a job, to which he nodded yes before hearing the details.

"You'll cover things we usually assign to stringers: junior hockey and football, soccer, badminton ... Know anything about badminton?"

"Yes," Jimmy lied. He didn't but soon would, he told himself.

"Things like women's basketball and so on. Maybe the occasional color story. We'll see. The salary is twelve dollars."

There were a number of arguments with his mother, who seemed always to be complaining these days. "Do you realize that when the relief people hear about it, we'll probably be cut off? Then what?" Word did leak out, and the monthly stipend was reduced by half. There were harangues about that. "Nearly the same money's coming in, but more's going out. And you can't earn anything on the side anymore. There's your carfare every day and sometimes your dinner. And in the meantime, you're not here to help."

He closed his ears to it. Life was bliss. He had a press card that admitted him to the Gardens, to Maple Leaf Stadium and to the Mutual Street Arena. He soon came to know athletes on a first-name basis. Occasionally he was assigned a color story, and given a by-line. He would read his words in print again and again, often critical of his writing.

After two years at the *Tribune*, his nightly potpourri began to be carried under the heading "Coulter's Sportscape," and he was given more freedom in the choice of material. He'd begun to develop a style and discovered that he was a minor celebrity, sought out by athletes or promoters hoping for a mention in his column. On a few occasions he was invited to join others in the department for a few beers after the paper had been put to bed, but he declined, saying he didn't drink. In fact, each week he delivered his pay envelope unopened to his mother and he didn't have the money.

22

On a Sunday, while shoveling snow from the front porch, he heard his mother and sister shouting.

"I'll write him if I like! He's my father."

"He's not your father. He sired you, that's all. That's not being a father!"

"He's my father and nothing you can say will change that. He loves me and I love him."

"If he loves you so much, what's he doing out in Vancouver? And how come he doesn't send any money?"

"There's something more than money. At least *he* understands me!"

"And I don't? I understand you very well, Miss High-and-Mighty. I understand what you're up to with those letters of yours. Didn't think I knew, did you? Don't get many back, though, do you? Not from him. He's a taker."

They were in the dining room, standing at each end of the table, faces livid. Jimmy shouted above the clamor, "Stop it! Stop it right now!"

Giving way to tears, Kathryn ran to her room. Lizzie straightened up, tugging the belt of her bathrobe, her mouth a grim line. "I want to talk to you," she said, and went to the kitchen. He followed, pulling the door closed. There was an odor of rank garbage. The sink was a clutter of crockery. The top of the stove was crowded with unscoured pans. Lizzie's eyes had a glint to them and there were reddish blotches on her neck. He looked through the window into the backyard where a wind was toying with the weeds and his brother was swinging on a tire hung from the tree.

"They've been writing ever since we left Regina," Lizzie said in a ragged voice.

"How do you know?"

"Because letters have been coming with a Vancouver postmark. She's been lying. Told me she had a girl friend there ... But one came this morning and I opened it."

"You shouldn't have done that."

"Why shouldn't I? If she's getting mail from her father, it's my business." Her anger had brought her to tears. "When I think of everything I've done for him," she said into a handkerchief. "Treated him like a king. Whatever he wanted, he got. A lovely home, children, a wife who worshiped the ground he walked on ..."

Jimmy had to escape. "Is there anything for dinner?" he asked.

She shook her head, but only slightly, as though it was cruel of him to change the subject.

"I'll go to Maitland's and get some fish and chips," he said.

She called after him, "You'd better ask your sister. She's probably not going to want to eat. No sense wasting the money."

He tapped on Kathryn's bedroom door. A muffled voice said, "Go away."

He opened the door. The shade was drawn, and for a moment he didn't see that she was in bed, covered with blankets. "I'm going for some fish and chips," he said. "Okay?"

"Don't get any for me."

"You have to eat something," he said.

"I don't have to do anything. Leave me alone."

He went to sit at the foot of the bed. "Kathy?"

"I don't want to talk!" She threw back the covers. "Is that clear? Don't. Do not." She retreated under the covers again.

"Just one thing ... You have to understand Mom's side ...."

Out she popped. "Mom's side, huh? How would you like it if your mail was opened? And probably blabbed to everybody? She *lives* on that phone! I bet she's already blabbed to you ..."

"Kathy, try to put yourself in her place. Letters coming to you and none to her–"

"Coming to me! Do you know how many there've been? Two in the last six months." Her anger sagged and she finished in tears. "And I've written him I don't know how many times!"

He put a hand on the blankets at her feet. He was unmanned by tears, had never known how to handle them. His sister put her hands to her cheeks and swept the tears away.

"It's easy for you," she said, "you're Mom's pet. But she knows that I know Daddy didn't want to leave. She nagged him until she nearly drove him crazy. Okay – maybe he did something he shouldn't of, but how many times is he supposed to say he's sorry? She wouldn't forgive and she wouldn't forget. She's a bitch!"

"Kathy!"

"Well, it's true. I told her that, and now she's doing the same thing to me. And I'm leaving too. Soon as I can ...."

23

The Reverend Leo Francis McGeer was an American in his late thirties, film-star handsome, with a mound of dark, wavy hair, a lock of which often fell onto his brow when preaching. He cultivated a tan even in winter, and when in the pulpit wore tailored white suits with floral silk ties. A platform athlete, his preaching style was derivative of the famed American evangelist of the twenties, Billy Sunday. Having begun a sermon, he would seldom return to the pulpit. He paced and postured. He pranced and posed. He might drop to his knees in mid-sentence or turn his back on the congregation to address the choir. He'd been known to prowl the aisles and stand on the front pew through much of a sermon; even to leap onto the pulpit to position himself on tiptoe with upraised arms, straining "to bring heaven down."

He'd been an itinerant boy-preacher from the age of six, drawing turn-away crowds to an enormous tent. Most of his adult years had been spent trying to regain that early celebrity, for his fame had faded with the onset of puberty – the memorized sermons (written by his mother, herself an evangelist) which had charmed in his childhood seemed coy in his youth.

When, some twenty-five years later, he was called as pastor to Toronto's First Church of the Galilean, he'd become an accomplished pulpiteer, a gifted actor whose skill at theatrics was augmented by an extensive vocabulary and an innate understanding of crowd psychology.

A neighbor of Lizzie Coulter, an Irish woman by the name of Gillie Whittier, began urging her to go to church. "We've got a new preacher. He's not like anything you've ever heard. Come just once and you'll see what I mean."

With Jimmy seldom home, Kathryn in school, and withdrawn and sullen when at home, and little Herb away much of the day, Lizzie Coulter had grown increasingly lonely. A friend of Herb's from the Regina days, Harley Arnold, had come by to inquire about him and afterward had started to telephone and occasionally drop in. Sometimes Lizzie would let him take a kiss, but when he became passionate and pressed her to go with him to the bedroom, she became angry. She let him make love to her once, and thereafter wouldn't see him again.

On her first visit to the church, the emotions she'd been husbanding burst the dam. On the first invitation hymn she stumbled to the altar rail at the front of the sanctuary. When her weeping subsided, she rose, her upturned face radiant, filled with an elation she'd never known.

Lizzie Coulter had fallen in love with Jesus. The Christ presented in the Church of the Galilean was a romantic figure. In Sallman's Head of Christ, which hung on the wall of the sanctuary, he was depicted as handsome and virile. In Leo McGeer's sermons he was dynamic but gentle and understanding. And as she began to read the New Testament, she discovered that Jesus seemed to have a special bond with women: He comforted the widow of Nain when her son died, and Martha when her brother Lazarus lay in the tomb. He silenced those who sought to judge the woman taken in adultery and rebuked Mary Magdalene's critics. And at the end, when all the apostles had fled and were cowering behind locked doors, there, hard by the cross and at the tomb, were the women who loved him.

She found that many of the evangelical hymns were intensely personal; in effect, love songs. Her favorite became:

I come to the garden alone,
While the dew is still on the roses,
And the voice I hear, falling on my ear,
The Son of God discloses.
    For he walks with me, and he talks with me,
    And he tells me I am his own.
    And the joys we share as we tarry there,
    None other have ever known.
He speaks, and the sound of his voice
Is so sweet the birds hush their singing.

And the melody that he gave to me,
Within my heart is ringing.
For he walks with me, and he talks with me,
And he tells me I am his own.
And the joys we share as we tarry there,
None other have ever known.

Lizzie wanted very much to be near him. She went to church when the doors opened, and fell asleep whispering his name. She would share with him all that had happened as she went about her daily tasks. She gave him gifts; she took flowers to his sanctuary. She read his words over and over. ("The gospels are God's love letters to us," McGeer had said.) Her favorite verse of scripture was the promise given the night before he was crucified: *And if I go to prepare a place for you, I will come again and receive you unto myself; that where I am, there ye may be also.*

She let her hair return to its natural color and kept it clean and shining. She put away the mascara and rouge, using only a hint of lipstick. She sang as she went about the house: *Safe in the arms of Jesus. Safe on his gentle breast . . .*

She badgered the children to go with her to the Sunday-evening evangelistic service. Herb, Jr., went as on an adventure. Kathryn refused, then went sullenly to sit unyielding in the back pew. One night Leo McGeer, sensing her vulnerability as a jungle cat might a wounded animal, came from the platform to her pew during the altar call. *Tell Mother I'll be there* . . . sang the congregation as he put his handsome, perspiring face next to hers and whispered, "Do this for your mother's sake, dear one. And for your father's . . . your Father in heaven."

Running down the aisle on the verge of hysteria, Kathryn knelt at the altar. She never returned to the church.

Jimmy had a convenient excuse; the *Tribune* was a morning paper; he worked Sundays. He was impressed by the change in his mother – gone were the dark, despondent times, the blurred consonants, the reek of sherry – but sometimes she irritated him. She spoke of nothing but God and the church and Brother McGeer, and insisted on saying grace before each meal, using the opportunity to do a little preaching. He would watch her as, eyes squeezed shut, brow drawn down in concentration, she would go on and on.

"And, dear Jesus, speak to Kathryn. Soften her heart. Let her see the error of her ways. And, Lord, speak to Jimmy. You know, dear Jesus, how hard he works. Help him to make room in his heart for thee ..."

Jimmy Coulter was working hard. In addition to his duties at the *Tribune*, he was writing a daily feature called 'Sportraits,'' 300-word biographies of great athletes, which was being syndicated by Central Press Canadian. It yielded six dollars a week. At twenty-one, his face was immature and his manner diffident. Women found him attractive but he was ill at ease with them. He hadn't the money to take them out and felt self-conscious about his shabby clothes. He was younger than the other members of the sports department and had made no close friends among them. Sometimes he'd go to a movie – especially a Jean Parker film – and afterward buy something to take home to cook for a late snack.

In his room, he read Faulkner and Hemingway and Lewis and O'Hara and Fitzgerald and Steinbeck and Dos Passos. He also read Bernard Shaw and Arthur Miller and Thornton Wilder and Tennessee Williams. He wrote short stories and submitted them to *The Saturday Evening Post* and *Collier's*, and occasionally to *Argosy*, but after a first rejection, didn't send them off again. He read some under-the-counter books from the Olympia Press, rented at ten cents a day from a used-books store on York Street. There, he also bought erotic photographs which he hid under his mattress. Often, he would look at them, then in the darkness beneath the bedcovers, he'd masturbate and fall asleep.

He was a child of six, forlorn and wearing a man's suit. The jacket tented about him. The sleeves fell to the floor. The trousers were heaped in folds about his feet ...

He awoke from the dream with a start. A brilliant sun shafted through the open door of the shed at the back of the house where he slept in summer. Centered in the frame in a white suit was Leo McGeer. Light dazzled on his shoulders and made a halo of his hair.

"Good morning, slugabed," the god of light said. "I came by on the chance I might tempt you into going to church."

Blinking, Jimmy propped himself on an elbow. "What time is it?"

McGeer, flaunting the vivacity of an early riser, said, "Time to be up and doing. There's a world to be won and many a long mile e'er sets the sun ..." He smiled. "To tell you the truth, your mother put me up to it. Don't worry," he went on, "I'm not going to pester you."

Lizzie's voice broke in. "Is he coming?"

"In God's good time," McGeer said. He smiled wisdom's smile. "In God's good time."

Jimmy stayed on in bed, his arms behind his head. Despite the fact that it was obvious there was a conspiracy between the two of them to get him converted, he liked McGeer. He was bright but not sanctimonious. Dressed beautifully. Excellent English. He had dropped by the house a couple of times and once they'd talked sport. Knew what he was talking about. He seemed abreast of what was going on in the world. Obviously, he could have made it in some secular field – no flies on him. And there was none of that "Brother this" and "God that."

24

A ruddy-cheeked young policeman stood on the verandah. "Good morning," he said solemnly. "Constable Rowan of the Cowan Avenue station. Is this the residence of Mrs. Elizabeth Anne Coulter?"

"Yes," Jimmy said. He was alone in the house, his mother having gone off to the church with little Herb.

"May I have a word with her, please?"

"She's not in. I'm her son."

"May I come in?" the constable said. "We're in receipt of a communication from Vancouver concerning one Kathryn Louise Coulter."

Kathy had disappeared three months earlier. She'd quit school to take a job at Wilson's Drug Store where she worked at the soda fountain, and one Saturday night hadn't returned. There had been no word since.

The young policeman sat on the edge of a chair in the living room, removing the bicycle pants' clip. Then he produced a small black notebook and flipped the pages. "Here we are," he said briskly. "Your mother filed a missing-persons report on ... let me see now –"

"I'm sorry to interrupt," Jimmy said, "but is my sister all right?"

The officer would have preferred to persevere in his fashion. "If you mean is she dead or injured, no she's not. I have a full report here." He held up the notebook. Jimmy was almost rocking in his chair with impatience.

"As I was saying, a communication has come forward from the Vancouver police stating that Kathryn Louise Coulter, eighteen

122

years of age, female, Caucasian, presently resides at 27-C Burrard Lane, Vancouver. The report further states that the said Kathryn Louise Coulter was arrested on June twenty-third last on a charge of soliciting for purposes of prostitution ...' "

When the constable left, Jimmy paced the house. Kathy! His own sister! It was impossible. After a while, he got Kathryn's number from the long-distance operator. The ring sounded a dozen times before he heard her voice, thick with sleep.

"Kathy," he said, "it's Jimmy. How are you?"

"Do you know what time it is?" she asked. "It's the middle of the night."

"Sorry. I forgot the time difference. I just found out where you are. Why didn't you let us know? We've been so –"

"Well, I've been meaning to. How'd you find out?"

"Kathy ... what are you trying to prove? I mean ..."

"So I'm on my own. What's so terrible about that? If I'd let you know, Mom would have wormed it out of you and bugged me to death."

"The police say you've been in some kind of trouble."

"The police are a bunch of fucking liars!"

He heard a man's voice in the background.

"Look," she said, "I've gotta go."

"Kathy ..."

"No, I really do. Look out for yourself." The line went dead. He replaced the receiver and sat looking at it for a long time.

Jimmy arrived at the *Tribune* an hour late. A copy-boy passing on the stairs said, "Mr. Coombs has been looking for you. Mr. Noonan's in the hospital."

Coombs spun about in his chair. "Where the hell have you been?" He pointed at Noonan's office. "Get in there and write Pat's column."

"All of it?" Jimmy gasped.

"Jesus!" Coombs said, appealing to the ceiling. "This one doesn't understand English and I'm supposed to get a column out of him." He glared at Jimmy over the top of his glasses. "We," he said with a steely irony, "are up to our nuts in fuck-ups. Pat fell down some stairs and bust a hip. Gordo's off with the flu or the clap, for all I know. You drift in late like the bloody Prince of Wales, and I've got an edition to get out. So kindly get your ass into his office and let me see some ideas." When Jimmy hesitated, he roared, "Like *now*, goddam it!"

Jimmy had just finished the column, casting it in Noonan's style, when he was dispatched to the composing room to help in a major remake of the pages – Max Schmeling, in a stunning upset, had knocked out the undefeated heavyweight champion, Joe Louis.

The paper to bed, he slumped in Gordo's chair. Coombs and the others grunted their good nights and left. Only Ken Turner remained.

"That was a nice piece of work," he told Jimmy. "The column, I mean."

"Thanks." It was the first praise Jimmy had received in his years on the *Tribune*. "Some night, eh?"

"That's when this business is fun," Turner said.

He was a skinny man of about thirty-five, with a lugubrious face and a thicket of coppery-brown hair. He was the only unmarried reporter on the staff, and each Sunday night insisted on reporting to the others what he called his "box score" – the number and variety of "broads" he'd laid over the weekend.

"Any reason you gotta head right home?" Turner asked.

"Nothing urgent." Jimmy had been stalling in the hope that Lizzie would be asleep.

"Ever been to Mrs. Smith's?"

Jimmy shook his head. "No."

"Okay, Jimmy, my boy. Tonight you complete your education."

"What's Mrs. Smith's?" Jimmy asked. "A whorehouse?"

Turner laughed. "Don't worry, for Christ sake, you're not gonna lose your cherry."

They took the King Street car to Carlaw and walked north. "There it is," Turner said, pointing. As they approached the steps he asked, "You got ten bucks?" Jimmy nodded. "Good," Turner said, "because it's a fin each and I'm broke."

No lights were visible. Turner pressed the doorbell and a man appeared, leading them inside. When the hall light was on, Jimmy saw that he was enormous, very black, with a stubble of white hair on his head and jaw. Turner winked at Jimmy. "Give Mrs. Smith the ten."

"You want a shot?" Mrs. Smith asked in a high voice.

"Christ, I forgot." Turner turned to Jimmy. "You haven't got a two-spot, have you? I'll pay you Friday."

Mrs. Smith put the money in a wallet and opened the door into what had been a living room. It was fetid with sweat and stale air, and hazy with tobacco smoke. In the semi-darkness Jimmy could make out perhaps a dozen men. Mrs. Smith pointed toward two chairs in the back row.

The room was bare of furniture except for a small platform at one end. A spotlight was attached precariously to the wall above a bricked-over fireplace. The windows back of the platform were covered with gray, army-issue blankets. The men slumped in folding chairs, eyes unfocused, drinking and smoking. Jimmy noticed an old man with white wavy hair sitting low in his chair, his hands shielding the sides of his face as if in a prayer for anonymity.

Mrs. Smith entered with drinks for Turner and Jimmy, turned on a gooseneck lamp and directed it toward the platform. On tasting his drink, Jimmy felt revulsion. A man seated nearby coughed and was caught in a paroxysm which intensified until he was bent double. When the seizures eased, he hawked phlegm into his handkerchief. Someone in the front row began a slow, measured clapping, which was picked up by the others.

"And now ... Princess Nadia!" Mrs. Smith announced from the doorway. A woman with a dark, gypsy look entered. She was wearing a costume fashioned of green cheesecloth, imitating harem attire. She walked to the mantel over the fireplace, turned on a radio and searched for music. Then she began to stalk back and forth on the platform, bumping and wiggling her hips and shaking her slack breasts. Midway through her performance, the music ended and a news broadcast began. She continued her act while a voice spoke of accidents, fires and death, and of Adolf Hitler. In sudden exasperation, she turned off the radio. To the accompaniment of sporadic applause, she began to remove her pants, exhibiting a tangle of black pubic hair. Then, naked, she walked sullenly from the room.

Mrs. Smith put his head in the doorway. "Anybody?"

Three men raised their hands. While they waited for the drinks, the man in the front row tried without success to get the cadenced clapping going again. The door opened and Mrs. Smith called out, "Joy Sublime!"

Joy had stretch marks on enormous breasts and a belly that made Jimmy wonder if she was pregnant. Turner greeted her with applause and whispered to Jimmy, "Look at the knockers on that one!" Joy didn't turn on the radio but went straight to the platform and began a series of exercises, wheezing as she worked. At one point she interrupted her routine to snatch a cigarette from the lips of one of the spectators, smoking it as she went on. After shedding her skirt and G-string, she displayed her pubic area, doing knee bends, legs akimbo. Then she bent far forward, her head between her legs, to stick her tongue out at the audience. The applause mounted when she lay on her back, spread her legs, and raised and lowered her pelvis, while finishing her cigarette.

Then came the star attraction, with Mrs. Smith reading from a card. "And now, ladies and gentlemen, direct from the world-famous Minsky's in New York City, the sensation of three continents, the very lovely, the very provocative, Ima Lover and her partner, Happy, the luckiest piece of ass in town!"

A great clattering came from the hallway and a naked woman appeared, pulling a donkey by its halter. She had difficulty getting him to mount the platform. Then she began moving about him, writhing and twisting. She stroked him, rubbed a hip against his flank, brushed her breasts against his side, then with a look of abandonment, mounted him to post on his bare back. She dismounted to do bumps and grinds against his rump and moved to his head to lower it to her crotch. As she tugged his ears, the donkey bunted its muzzle against her and the men applauded . . . .

It was past two when Jimmy got home. In the bathroom, having washed his hands he washed them again. He was filled with the vague discontent he had been feeling for weeks. After three years on the *Tribune* he had become disenchanted. There was an estrangement between himself and the reporters in the sports department. He had made attempts to close the gap but they had failed. It wasn't simply that he was younger, that he didn't go to the beverage room on breaks, or hang around to shoot the breeze after the paper had been put to bed. There was jealousy. He had his own column, and despite their seniority earned what they did. Some of the younger men were put off by his facility with words, his encyclopedic memory. He didn't belong. It was one of the reasons he had gone off to Mrs. Smith's with Ken Turner. What a mistake *that* had been!

And he was seeing the sports community differently. It seemed a world of forced camaraderie; elitist, separate even from other

126

journalists. Sport was all. Jimmy's initial excitement at being admitted to their world had ebbed. He was no longer thrilled that during a break in a practice at Maple Leaf Gardens, Chuck Conacher or King Clancy might lean on the boards to chat with him. It all seemed trivial. Mr. Rimmington's words echoed: "Sport should be reserved for children. When adults play at it, they contribute to an evolutionary regression . . ."

Nor was he at ease at home. His mother had two themes: Jesus and Herb Coulter; all praise and all blame. When occasionally he thought of Kathryn he grew heavy with guilt. Little Herb often pressed him to play games with him, but he seemed never to have the time. The unfinished manuscript of a play lay on his dresser top, untouched for weeks. He was restive, tense. He often thought of inviting out a girl but avoided it, telling himself he didn't have the money.

There was a tap on the bathroom door. His mother whispered, "Jimmy, is that you?"

"I'll be out in a minute."

"I haven't been able to sleep. I wanted to apologize for the things I said . . . about Kathryn and your father. Will you come see me before you go to bed?"

"Yes."

"I've been praying about it," she breathed through the crack in the door. "During the service tonight, God showed me how selfish I've been . . ." Her voice broke. "You won't forget? You'll come see me?"

Leaning on the sink, he studied his face in the mirror. What a loathsome person he was. Others might not see it, but he knew. The clear blue eyes, the handsome face, the deferential manner, the ingratiating shyness – all part of the disguise that hid the real Jimmy Coulter from the world. Tonight, with his sister far away and in trouble, with his mother struggling to hold the family together, where was he? Wallowing in filth. Throwing away half the rent money to watch whores.

Why had he gone to Mrs. Smith's? He hadn't wanted to, but was too gutless to say so. Also, he had wanted to avoid his mother with her bitter words about Kathryn and his father. Couldn't wait to get out of the house to leave her to face her problems alone. Off he'd gone, all wrapped up in himself. And in his conceit, stopping off on the way home to pick up half a dozen copies of the paper so he could clip Pat Noonan's column, thinking that some day he could use it to make himself look good.

What would his mother think of him if she had seen him in that sleazy place? What would Leo McGeer think? From the time he had arrived at the *Tribune*, had he given a thought to Kathryn? How often had he thought about her in the months since she'd gone? How self-centered could you be? On the morning his father had left for Vancouver, what had he felt? Nothing. And now his sister ...

He was suddenly overtaken by a sense of unworthiness. He went to his knees on the tile floor, his brain numb. Guilt! Overwhelming guilt! A great, swelling groan shuddered through his body and burst from his throat. In a moment he was drenched with perspiration and began to be shaken by panting sobs. They bore him to the floor where he lay on his side, knees drawn up, quaking.

Tears streaming, he whispered over and over, "Oh God, forgive me. Forgive me ..."

After a while, a calm settled. A burden that weighed what he did lifted off. He felt buoyant. Clean! An excitement began to tremble in his limbs. He pulled himself slowly to his feet and stood in the center of the bathroom, face upturned, not daring to move or speak lest the moment be broken.

The words came of themselves, softly to his lips. "Thank you, Jesus ..."

He went to his mother's bedroom to tell her what had happened. She saw it in his face and burst into tears. They talked and laughed until close to dawn. In his room, he took the photographs from beneath the mattress, tore them into bits and flushed them down the toilet. Back in his room he drew the shade, undressed and climbed into bed. In the darkness he lay motionless, his eyes brimming with tears, washed over by waves of warm, exultant joy.

25

TO: HHH
FROM: Clyde Rogers
SUBJECT: Coulter series

I enclose a report from Jenny Wedger on a new development in the Coulter series. It speaks for itself. Granted that the "proof" offered is genuine, I am prepared to pay the asking price. We will, of course, offer a lower figure and do some negotiating.

Progress report – coulter   wedger

Clyde:
We may be onto something substantive on Coulter. It has to do with (a) his alienation from his son, Jonathan, and (b) the distinct possibility that Coulter no longer believes what he preaches and may be an agnostic.

The more you talk to people who know them, the more obvious it becomes that Coulter and his son are seriously alienated. Normally, that kind of personal problem is not the sort of thing you want to dig into too deeply, but in Coulter's case there appears to be a great deal more to it than a father-son rift.

Jonathan Coulter at twenty-four seems very much like his father was in his early twenties. You'll remember Coombs told me that Coulter was pretty much of a loner. So is Jonathan. Doesn't have many friends. Works as a corporate design consultant – packaging, company logos, letterheads, that kind of thing – but wants to be a painter. And, I'm told, works hard at it. I've seen some of his work – gifts to friends. And while I'm not an

129

expert, neither am I a philistine. He's good, yet he's never had a show. Had one scheduled at the Cummings Gallery. Posters and a mailing were printed, the whole thing was set, then suddenly he canceled it. Cummings is still pretty hot about it–at one point he was going to sue. He says Jonathan just called it off and gave no reason.

A week ago the city desk passed on a call to me–a man named Barry Beale who claimed to have "the lowdown on Jimmy Coulter." We all get crank calls and usually they're a waste of time, but I called him. He was cautious at first, then he asked if the Tribune would be prepared to pay for a "sensational exposé" (his words) on Jimmy Coulter. Like what? I said. He wasn't pre-pared to give details on the phone. I was almost certain it would be a blind alley (Jimmy Coulter cheated on an exam back in high school!) but I agreed to see him. To my surprise, it was pro-ductive.

Who is Barry Beale? I've been asking around. Seems to be a professional shit-disturber. Active in any number of citizens' pro-test groups. He's currently chairman of a committee set up to object to the Coulter campaign on the grounds that they're get-ting a break (at the taxpayer's expense) on the rental at the CNE. The committee is a cover: he's planning to go into politics and the Coulter campaign is a hook on which he can hang the hat he's going to throw into the ring come the next civic election. The thing that's important to us is that he's a friend of Jonathan Coulter. They're both graduates of York University (fine arts) and have mutual friends. They both paint, although I gather Beale is little more than an accomplished dauber. I doubt that they're inti-mates but they seem to move in overlapping circles.

I found Beale repulsive. He's about thirty, balding, with a puffy face and blotched skin. Chain-smoker. Various signs of inner ten-sion. Some paranoia. He was afraid any conversation with me would be bugged. Wouldn't come to the Trib for a meeting; wouldn't meet for a drink. Insisted on getting together at his office (he's an insurance broker in Willowdale). And when he hung up my coat I saw him run his hands over the pockets.

Here's his story: He says he's been with Jonathan a number of times when he teed off on his father. According to Beale, Jona-than says his father no longer believes what he preaches and hasn't for years. I told Beale that the allegation was a serious one, and interesting, but that it would be of no use to us without specific proof. He said he had proof – a letter from Coulter *père* to Coulter *fils* in which he admits that he no longer accepts the principal doctrines of Christianity. I asked him how he happened to have the letter but he wasn't telling. I said I would have to see it to satisfy myself it was authentic. He said he didn't have the letter with him, and would let me see it only if we made a deal. He was reluctant to commit but finally said $5,000. I told him that before I could recommend the payment of so large an amount, I would need to be assured of the authenticity of the letter.

He then admitted he had the letter and was prepared to let me see a paragraph from it, including Coulter's signature.

The paragraph I scanned in the ten seconds allowed was to the effect that in light of the indifference of the universe to the suffering of mankind and other forms of life (as evidenced in natural disasters, disease, etc.), it was impossible to conceive of God either as a Father or as a God of love.

I didn't allow myself to show much enthusiasm and expressed doubts that I could get an okay for the amount he was asking, but I said I'd give it a try and get back to him.

Jenny

TO: Clyde Rogers
FROM: HHH
SUBJECT: Coulter series

Now you're making progress. Give Wedger whatever help she needs. In my view, it would be worthwhile to dangle before Mr. Beale an even larger carrot in order to obtain the rights to reproduce for publication the Coulter letter to his son. I have no doubt that he stole the letter (how else would he come by it?), and Wedger's assessment of the man leads me to believe there's a strong Judas strain in him. Tempt him with as many pieces of silver as seem appropriate. Clear the legal aspects first, of course. We would not want to be implicated in a theft of documents.

26

Jimmy pushed through the double doors into the sanctuary, smiling as though he'd come to the edge of Eden. An electric organ was playing, the organist often doubling back to retrieve a fumbled chord. The sun was shining through the amber panes of a great window, gilding and making glad the shabbiness of the surroundings.

Jimmy slipped into a pew. In front of him was a girl of about eighteen, her shoulder-length red hair radiant with sunlight. She glanced at him from the corner of an eye. How beautiful, he thought, and how pure. And how pure the women in the choir: their eyes clear, their faces free of makeup, their hair long and shining.

The sound of the organ swelled and the congregation came to its feet, rustling the pages of their hymnbooks. The tunes were unfamiliar but sung with open-throated zest. McGeer's prayer stormed heaven. The choir ricocheted hallelujahs off the walls. He took his text and launched into his sermon:

"I'm talking about lies, brother! Not little white lies. Not falsehoods. Not prevarications. Not a shading of the truth nor a bending of the facts ... but lies! Deliberate, willful, black lies! And you know what God's Word has to say about liars? Hear me now! *All liars shall have their part in the lake that burneth with fire!*"

Outside, on the steps of the church, waiting for Lizzie, Jimmy's hand was shaken a dozen times. The congregation stood about in small groups – none apparently wanting to go home – all whispering and glancing shyly at him. Two boys on bicycles went by, shouting "Hallelujah, brother!" but no one paid attention.

All the world was new to Jimmy. It was a world of certainties in which the church was center and circumference. The King James version of the Bible became the rock on which all of life was built. It was God's Word, without error, accepted without question. It taught that God created the world in five days (in approximately 4,000 B.C.), whereupon he created Adam and Eve and placed them in the Garden of Eden. Their sin (which was taken to be fornication) cursed all men and made them sinful. The Devil was real and was present everywhere, "seeking whom he may devour." Noah built an actual ark. Jonah was swallowed by a whale. Gideon caused the sun "to stand still in the heavens." Jesus Christ was himself "very God of very God" and was born of a virgin. All his miracles were fact. He was crucified by the Romans at the instigation of the Jews. Having risen from the dead and ascended into heaven, he would return (any day now) "in clouds of glory" to rule the world for one thousand years. The wicked (those who had not been born again, including all the unsaved and most members of other churches) would be banished to "outer darkness," a place of endless agony where there would be "weeping and wailing and gnashing of teeth." Born-again Christians, on the other hand, would enter into an eternal life of unbroken bliss, ruling on earth with Christ for the first thousand years, and forever in a heaven where the streets were paved with gold.

One was to love God and one's neighbor, of course, but the Church of the Galilean took literally Jesus' declaration that "strait is the gate and narrow the way that leads to life everlasting." Prospective members were required "to give evidence in their daily lives that they were in a State of Grace." They were not permitted "to smoke or drink or to traffic therein." Nor were they allowed to attend movies or circuses or go dancing or play cards or indulge in "other forms of worldly entertainment." Makeup, while not expressly forbidden, was disapproved of and often preached against – "You see these modern women, looking for all the world like the painted whore of Babylon!" – as was the cutting of a woman's hair. The reading of secular books and magazines was frowned upon. Conversation tended to be about God, the Bible, the church and each other. No church suppers, bazaars or bingos were held, nor was there any canvassing for funds. Money was raised through the contributions of the membership, many of whom earned small incomes but tithed one-tenth of their wages.

On the Wednesday, Jimmy filed his column, and there being nothing pressing, talked Bobby Coombs into letting him leave work early. He made no mention of going to Prayer Meeting. As

133

he entered the basement auditorium of the church, he was surprised to see that the attendance approached Sunday morning's.
He slipped into a row beside Lizzie and she handed him a hymn-
book. McGeer was leading the singing, the volume of the confined
sound enough to set ears ringing. He then read a portion from the
New Testament, commenting on each verse as he went. Everyone
had a Bible and followed his words. Then came the collection ("I'd
like a silent offering tonight. I don't want to hear the clink of a
coin."), after which he announced "a season of prayer." "I'll ask
Brother Jameson to lead off, followed by Sister McCready."

The entire congregation went to its knees by the kitchen-type
chairs. Within a dozen words, Brother Jameson was in full bellow
but was unheard. Everyone raised his own prayer; all were lost in
their own pleading, and the sound rose and fell like the surf, casting up a phrase of praise here, a sentence of petition there as the
intensity ebbed and flowed.

As though at a signal the tumult fell off and ceased. The people
were seated and the meeting "thrown open for testimonies." With
the randomness of jets leaping in a geyser pool, men and women
got to their feet to give halting or set-piece witness to what God
was doing in their lives. Victories over the Devil were reported.
Triumphs over temptation were recorded. Requests for prayer
were made: for a husband who drank, for a friend scornful of the
gospel, for a son or daughter, wayward and rebellious. Some
sought to outdo the others, striving to coax "Amens" of approval
from the others. A Brother Pike arose. In the voice of a dray-
man he launched into his testimony. He was a converted drunk.
With the freshness of the great actor in a long-run play, he told his
story, ending with a leap into the air and the words, "Once I was
pickled but now, thank God, I'm preserved!"

Jimmy became aware that the congregation was waiting for him.
He began to tremble. Twice he marshaled his courage, but each
time, before he could rise, someone else got to his feet. Finally a
silence fell. He felt McGeer's eyes on him. A nudge from his
mother sent him to his feet.

"I'm not sure I know how to say this," he began, his voice
reedy with fear, "but I want to thank all of you for praying for
me." He broke off, feeling terror, but was able to go on when he
heard voices calling out encouragement. "All I can say is, it's as if
the whole world is different, as if I'd been born all over again ...."

An explosion of joy. A man leaped to his feet, turned his face to the ceiling, and with tears streaming down his cheeks, began to shout, "Thank you, Jesus! Thank you, Jesus!" Others joined him. Minutes passed before the silence settled again. Almost in a whisper, McGeer began a slow, rhythmic singing:

I'm so glad that Jesus took me in,
Jesus took me in, Jesus took me in.
I'm so glad that Jesus took me in,
Glory to his name.

The congregation picked up on the old spiritual, accenting the rhythm by clapping their hands and swaying their bodies, the music growing until it was at full flood.

I'm so glad that Jesus took me in,
Saved my soul from sin, saved my soul from sin.
I'm so glad that Jesus took me in,
Glory to his name ...

God was calling him to preach.

Jimmy Coulter had become the focus of an almost worshipful attention from the small, tightly knit community of fundamentalist Christians in the city. They formed a clearly delineated sub-culture. Most were poor, and few had completed secondary school. University graduates were rare, even among their clergy. They were the hewers of wood and drawers of water in the society: the clerks, salesmen, truck drivers, day laborers, housewives and pensioners; and they thought of themselves proudly as "The Lord's despised few." Among them, a tall, handsome, well-mannered man of twenty-one who, despite his notoriety, affected no airs but rather was deferential, was an exotic figure. As such, he was welcomed, encouraged and plied with requests to speak at young people's functions. In the circumscribed world of "Bible-believing Christians," he was a celebrity.

Each Sunday, from the vantage point of the choir at the First Church of the Galilean, he was able to study Leo McGeer in the pulpit. He could see the volume of his notes, could watch his footwork and his gestures. And he could study the congregation, noting the relationship between the preacher's words and their responses.

At home in the basement he fashioned a crude lectern and practised, whispering the words, not wanting to be overheard even by his mother. As he walked the streets, he would speak under his breath, learning to articulate his thoughts. Often he would force himself to speak without interruption for a full two minutes about such mundane things as a crack in the sidewalk, a broken pop bottle, a bare patch on a lawn. He was training his unconscious mind to bring forward the desired word or phrase, to fashion the syntax of his sentences. He studied the sermons of the master pulpit orators. In bed each night he read a page of a dictionary, checking the meanings of each word he didn't know, speaking it aloud in a sentence.

When he was ready, he went to Lem Washington, the caretaker at the church.

"Who you gonna preach *to*?" Lem asked.

"Nobody," Jimmy said with an awkward smile. "It's to get used to being behind a pulpit."

"You gonna preach to empty pews?"

Washington looked at him out of the corners of red-rimmed eyes. After a moment he tilted his head and shrugged a shoulder. "Go right ahead, Mista Jimmy. Don' make no neva mind to me. Some a them pews could use a little patchin' up of the Sperrit." Pleased with his witticism, he went off, chuckling loudly.

It took Jimmy a few days to get used to the echoing sound of his voice. He read the scriptures aloud, speaking them in different ways, experimenting. He prepared sermons and preached them. He practised gestures, movements. He learned to whisper in a way that would carry to the back of the auditorium, to shout so that his voice wouldn't break or be shrill.

Some weeks after he'd begun, he was declaiming what Leo McGeer called "The Gospel in a nutshell," John 3:16, seeking to improve his interpretation with each restatement of the words: "For God so loved the world, that he gave his only begotten son, that whosoever believeth in him should not perish, but have everlasting life."

Suddenly, from the shadows beyond the topmost row of the balcony came the sound of a voice: "Amen ... and Amen!" It was the Reverend Leo McGeer.

"Hello," Jimmy said, blushing. "Sorry. Am I disturbing something?"

"Not at all. I'll be right down."

Jimmy was in an agony of embarrassment as McGeer descended from the balcony, mounted the platform and went to the pulpit. "Sit there," he said to Jimmy, pointing to the front pew.

McGeer placed his hands on the pulpit and for a moment stood motionless except for the blinking of his eyes. Then his voice rang out, strong, passionate, controlled, the sound of it resonating:

"For God so loved the world, that he gave his only begotten son – *his only begotten son* – that whosoever believeth in him should not perish, but . . ." His voice fell away to a whisper filled with awe, "*but have everlasting life!*"

He waited until the sound had died.

"So you want to preach?" he asked, leaning over, peering down.

Jimmy looked up at him. "Yes."

"Has God called you?" The voice was stern, the tone that of a watchman guarding sacred ground.

"I'm waiting for a sign."

In his dream he was in his bedroom in the old house on Beatty Avenue. Above it, a sundeck could be reached through a trapdoor. The trapdoor was stuck. His mother climbed a stepladder and tried to raise it but couldn't. His father pushed. Others also tried and failed. Mr. Rimmington climbed the ladder but descended without raising a hand. Then came Leo McGeer. He thrust, he shoved, he pushed. He put his shoulder to the trapdoor and heaved. It would not dislodge. Every eye turned to Jimmy. He put a foot on the ladder, mounted it, placed his fingertips to the trapdoor, and without effort lifted it off. A sudden thrust and it flew spinning into infinity.

Sunlight poured into the room.

In McGeer's car enroute to a youth rally in Lowville, New York, Jimmy was questioning McGeer on the difference between churches. He'd been doing the prescribed reading for a candidate wanting to become a Licensed Evangelist.

137

"Does every church believe in being baptized?"

"Baptists sure do. You don't make it unless you've been immersed. Not sprinkled. Not poured. *Dunked!*"

"Would they say we won't make it? We believe it doesn't matter which way it's done."

"Depends. There are as many kinds of Baptists as Heinz has pickles."

"Apart from baptism, do all Protestants pretty well believe the same things?"

"Such as?"

"In being born again, for instance."

"The standard-brand churches – the Presbyterians, the United, the Anglicans – sure don't."

"But they all believe the Bible."

"And pigs have wings. The only churches that believe the Bible are the gospel churches. The liberals believe that while parts of it are true, you can't take it literally. The modernists believe that it's just a history of how God dealt with the Jews."

"So we don't even agree on the Bible?"

"Never mind the Bible – take the virgin birth. Some say Jesus was born of a virgin, others say he wasn't – which in my book would make him a bastard. Some believe Jesus is God, others say he's a man. Some believe he rose from the grave, others say it was only a spiritual resurrection. Some believe there's going to be a Second Coming, others don't. Some believe in the Trinity, others say there's only one God. Some believe in heaven and hell, others say it's all allegory." He laughed. "But we're all Christians, of course."

"It's confusing."

"You think *that's* confusing? Seventh Day Adventists believe that Saturday, not Sunday, is the Lord's Day. Mormons believe in two Bibles, not one. Christian Scientists believe this world is an illusion, and so is sickness and death. Spiritualists believe that not only do people die, but you can contact them after they do. Quakers – Friends, they call themselves nowadays – believe there's no need for preachers. Plymouth Brethren don't believe in preachers either, but they think Quakers are going to hell. Jehovah's Witnesses don't believe in preachers *or* churches, and they say the Second Coming has already happened. The Salvation Army got rid of the clergy, and then replaced them with uniformed officers – and

138

while they were at it, they threw out baptism and the Lord's Supper. Some Mennonites believe inventions like the automobile and electricity – even buttons on your clothes – are of the devil. There's a sect that believes you prove your faith by handling rattlesnakes. Another that believes you should wash the other guy's feet to prove you're humble."

He turned to Jimmy. "I haven't even mentioned the *big* differences. Roman Catholics, for instance, have bishops and a pope. Episcopalians claim they're Catholics too. They have bishops, but they won't accept the pope. From there, you get into the differences between the Eastern and the Russian Orthodox churches, and the Coptics and –"

Seeing Jimmy's dismay, McGeer went on, amused.

"I haven't even touched on those religions that believe that Jesus was a manifestation of God, but only one of many – the Bahai, for instance, and the Muslims and Hindus. Then there's Judaism, various kinds of Buddhism, Taoism, Shintoism, Confucianism and on and on."

McGeer glanced at Jimmy and grinned. "Clear up your confusion?"

27

STONE MILLS METHODIST EPISCOPAL CHURCH
Stone Mills, New York
J.A. Garvin, Minister

February 27, 1939

Dear Reverend Coulter:

I am, in the words of the Psalmist, "drawing a bow at a venture." I wish to invite you to conduct our Annual Spring Revival. The dates are Thursday, March 18, to Sunday, March 30, incl. I realize that this isn't much advance notice, but the Board of Elders has agreed to go ahead, and since we haven't held our Annual Spring Revival during the ten years I've been here, I want to move on it immediately.

I have some friends who heard you speak at the Youth Rally at Lowville. They praise you highly. The fact that you are young and can lead the singing (as well as preach, of course) is why we are contacting you. God knows we need someone who can appeal to the youth.

We will pay your expenses and give you a love offering on the closing Sunday night. Mrs. Garvin and I will be happy to have you stay with us at the Parsonage.

Yours faithfully
(Rev.) J.A. Garvin
Minister

The headline read:

TRIBUNE COLUMNIST FORSAKES
TYPEWRITER FOR EVANGELISM.

140

The story, a five-column feature on the section page, also carried a photograph of Jimmy Coulter smiling self-consciously as he removed a sheet of paper from a typewriter.

McGeer reacted with a pitchman's alacrity. He hustled a display ad into the Saturday religious section, announcing in bold type:

GREAT FAREWELL SERVICE
Hear Canada's Top Sportswriter's
Triumphant Testimony For God!

The advertisement also trumpeted that the Reverend Leo Francis McGeer would preach on "God's Athletes." (At the time he drafted the ad, McGeer hadn't troubled to consider which biblical characters could be employed to illustrate his themes; but hadn't Joshua leaped over a wall? And surely Samson could be worked in.) A signwriter was hired to paint a 30-foot-wide paper banner bearing the message:

GOD BLESS YOU, JIMMY! OUR PRAYERS GO WITH YOU!

An orchid corsage went to Lizzie with the request that she "grace the platform with her presence."

Jimmy had hoped he might be asked to preach, but McGeer envisioned a packed church (with possibly a reporter present from the *Tribune*) and had decided that with such an opportunity for the harvesting of souls, God would want the gospel sickle in an experienced hand.

The church was filled. Early on, the service caught fire, the flames being fanned by an ebullient McGeer who interpreted the excitement induced by the crowded pews and the presence in front of a stranger taking notes as evidence of a moving of the Holy Spirit – only to learn afterward that the "reporter" was a preacher from Detroit on a busman's holiday.

McGeer was in fine form. He welcomed the visitors. He announced the hymns and led the singing. He introduced the choir, the male quartet and Lizzie (entreating all to "remember the missing Kathryn" in their prayers). Finally, he introduced Jimmy, his presentation of the fledgling evangelist falling short of being a sermon only through his failure to take a text.

Pale and trembling, Jimmy moved to the pulpit. As he began, his voice was almost inaudible, and it was minutes before he and the congregation were at ease with each other.

Then his words came pouring forth, passionate, intense. In a voice that rang like a bell in the lively acoustics of the tabernacle, he described the emptiness of his past and his lifelong yearning for purpose. To a hushed congregation, he told of his obduracy in the face of his mother's entreaties, and of the moment when he sank to his knees and prayed for forgiveness:

"God was as surely in that room that night as he is in this sanctuary now. I saw his face through my tears. I heard his voice through my pleading. In my agony, all I could say was his name: 'Lord ... Lord Jesus ...' But in those words was the memory of a lifetime of sin and selfishness. Oh, the profound sense of unworthiness! I can't begin to describe to you the overpowering, numbing sense of guilt. In that moment I knew I was deserving of the darkest hell and that my only hope was in 'the love that wilt not let us go.'

"And then ..." He paused. "And then ..." His voice was a whisper and the silence was almost palpable. "And then ... I felt the burden go. It passed through my body and lifted off. A weight that weighed what I weigh simply went. I could have leaped over the house. It seemed in that moment that every impurity had been cleansed, that every wrong had been expunged. I was clean! I was forgiven! Oh, my friends, the joy ... the radiant, inexpressible happiness! There by my bedside, as a new day dawned, I found 'the peace that passeth understanding'..."

Overcome, he broke off, struggling to contain his emotion. In the audience there was audible weeping. McGeer went to Jimmy and put an arm about his shoulders, repeating, "Praise God. Praise God." The rat-tat-tat of Amens and Hallelujahs crescendoed to a tympany-roll of sound. McGeer signaled to the Elders and they came to the platform to encircle Jimmy and place their hands on his head as he went to his knees. Each wave of emotion induced another. McGeer took Lizzie by the hand and led her to stand with the Elders. Softly, the choir began to sing:

Just as I am, without one plea,
But that Thy blood was shed for me ...

McGeer raised his organ voice. The prayer of dedication became an invitation. "Who is here tonight to whom God is especially speaking? Who is here tired of sin and wants to know the same loving Savior our brother Jimmy has found? Who is there here to whom God is giving one last chance? Which of you will join this fine young man, this choice servant of the most high God, and go with him to labor in the vineyard?''

They came down the aisles: some weeping, some with teeth clenched in determination, some pale and shaken. When the last seeker had clasped the prize and given a testimony, there was unanimous concurrence with McGeer's pronouncement: ''Surely we see here the proof that God has set his seal on our brother Jimmy Coulter's call to be an evangelist. These new converts are the first fruits of a mighty harvest of souls yet to come. '

28

TO: HHH
FROM: Clyde Rogers
SUBJECT: Coulter series

I enclose a manuscript by a local free-lancer, Alec Vickery. He heard scuttlebutt about the Coulter series, and having had three years in a theological seminary, decided to submit the attached on spec. I find it interesting, but don't have a spot for it in the series as planned. Perhaps consideration should be given to it as a separate feature.

a copy – evangelists   vickery

The old-fashioned hellfire-and-damnation mass evangelist is dead – done in by television. And Dr. Jimmy Coulter, soon to arrive in Toronto for a 15-day campaign at the CNE stadium, is the last of the great evangelists.

This from a man who ought to know, the Reverend Billy Joe Harewood, himself formerly an itinerant preacher and now advanceman for the Coulter organization – Jimmy Coulter's John the Baptist.

Billy Joe, as he insists on being called at first meeting, could pass for the stereotype southern United States senator (he is, in fact, from Fargo, North Dakota). The image is complete: the leonine mane of white hair, the string tie, the double-breasted vest

b copy next

144

with heavy watch chain, the modified Prince Albert jacket. Back
in the thirties he took his best shot at stardom on the international gospel circuit but lacked the one mandatory skill – the
ability to "pull the net." A dramatic preacher whose loud-hailer
voice needed no microphone, he could bring sinners to the brink,
but then let them get away – fatal flaw in an evangelist.

A good advanceman is preeminently a salesman. The product
Billy Joe sells is Jimmy Coulter. His territory is the western world,
with occasional forays outside. His clients are the preachers, lay-
men and assorted media types in a city scheduled for a visit by
the Coulter team. His responsibility is to fashion the base for the
enormously complex organization required to conduct a city-wide
evangelistic campaign.

Early last week Billy Joe sat with a reporter in Toronto's Inn on
the Park. A room-service meal of a dozen raw oysters, sixteen
ounces of rare steak, a baked potato, two pieces of apple pie
with ice cream and numerous cups of coffee in his rotund belly,
he loosened his collar, put his high-top boots on the coffee table,
shoved a finger into his mouth to dislodge a morsel of meat, and
sat back as the reporter began to fish the pool of his memories.

"There have only been five great evangelists," Billy Joe ponti-
ficated, covering a belch with a large liver-spotted hand. "Charles
G. Finney, Dwight L. Moody, Billy Sunday, Billy Graham and
Jimmy Coulter. When Graham and Coulter go, it's the end of an
age. They're the last of the great evangelists."

"What about the television evangelists?" the reporter asked.

A snort of disdain. "They're not evangelists. They're purveyors
of pious pablum. Electronic eunuchs. Let me tell you what an
evangelist is: The word means Herald of the Good News. That
good news is that God was in Christ, reconcilin' the world unto
himself – II Corinthians 5-19. Christianity's a call to take up your
cross, not an invite to sit around jawin' about how sweet Jesus
is. Real evangelism goes back to the disciples, even to the Old
Testament prophets. You wasn't in for no patty-cake sermonettes
from *them*!"

Billy Joe pushed together the crumbled bits of pie remaining

c copy next

on his plate and slid them into his mouth. "When I first started preachin'," he said, "there was dozens of evangelists in the field. In many cities the annual revival meetin' was the event of the year. Sure, with some the dollar sign was more important than the sign of the cross, but there was a lot of the genuine article too – men who loved souls. And that's the way it went till some-time around the fifties. Then television come along. Nowadays, even born-again believers ain't willin' to turn out weeknights, 'specially when they can sit home eatin' potato chips and lis-tenin' to what passes today for God's word."

It happens that the reporter had spent three years in a theo-logical college before deciding that his bent was for the news rather than for the Good News. He had done research on mod-ern evangelism. It is a fact, as Billy Joe argues, that television has killed revivalism and produced a new breed, the electronic evangelist. He bears little resemblance to his predecessors. He is a smooth-talking, perpetually smiling, expensively dressed master of the simulated intimacy demanded of any television performer. His church is a channel on your set. His pulpit is a TV screen. His pew is an easy chair in your living room. His techniques are the commercial pitchman's. His "live-on-tape" services are "bicycled" from station to station or bounced around the world by satellite. Contact is effected by placing the hands on the tele-vision set while the frequency modulated voice of the two-dimen-sional man of God offers forgiveness of sins, answers to prayer, happiness with no need for its pursuit, and miracles of healing that would astound the Mayo Clinic – authenticated on the ground of a 30-second telephone call from a stranger.

Unlike his predecessors, the electronic evangelist never raises his voice (they never lowered theirs), delivers brief homilies in lieu of sermons and wouldn't dream of preaching on hell – bad for ratings. Some don't preach at all, but from behind a Johnny Carson desk, chat about the Deity in a manner that makes the *mysterium tremendum* seem a mere Mr. Fixit in the sky. Prayer takes the form of a conversation conducted in terms of buddy-buddy intimacy, and the "sacred music" tends to be trendy – God's Country-and-Western.

d copy next

It's an easy undemanding faith, a mediapostacy bearing no resemblance to its rigorous New Testament beginnings. Standards of membership are so low that some "television ministries" are prepared to enroll as a believer anyone willing to say no more than, "Thank God it quit raining."

In one area, however, the traditional evangelist has been surpassed by his electronic counterpart—in the taking of an offering. The former made a plea and passed a plate. The latter offers a "free gift" and flashes a mailing address on the screen. Any respondent is automatically enrolled as a full-fledged member of a computerized mailing list and becomes the recipient of a volume of mail as personal as a post-office box and rivaling in its volume and frequency the more energetic book clubs. These mailings are the television church's equivalent of a collection plate which, having been passed is passed forever and ever, Amen. The "offerings" amount to millions of dollars annually. Relatively few of these dollars are used to give succor to the needy, to put food in empty bellies or to help the helpless. Most are spent to buy more broadcast time, to put up satellites and build studios, or to perpetuate the founder's name in a variety of institutions.

"Getting back to mass evangelists," the reporter said, "who of the men you named—Dr. Coulter excepted—was the greatest?"

Billy Joe reached into a vest pocket for a stainless-steel toothpick and probed as he talked. "They *all* were, in their own way. Graham is the most successful. Finney was the greatest revivalist. Moody did the most with the least talent. And Sunday was the best organizer."

"Billy Sunday!" the reporter marveled. "What a name for an evangelist."

"It was his real name. Played major league baseball from 1883 to 1890. Saved when he was drunk in one of them missions for down-and-outs in the skid-row section of Chicago."

"He was a great organizer?"

"He was an organizational genius," Billy Joe said, chomping on some celery and pitching a half-dozen olives into his mouth with rifle-shot precision. "You see, it isn't enough to hope people

e copy next

will come to your meetin's, you *see to* it that they do. Sunday left nothin' to chance. The day before he opened, there'd be a parade and a reception at City Hall—the mayor, probably the governor. I mean he put on a *parade*! Flags and banners and balloons. Bands playin'. Floats. Whole congregations marchin'. Billy'd bring up the rear in one of them open cars, a Packard or a Pierce Arrow, and there beside him would be Ma Sunday, dressed fit to kill, wearin' one of them big hats. Maybe a couple of dead birds stuck on. Mark me, son, it was somethin' to see."

"Didn't he build his own meeting places?"

"There wasn't many sports arenas in them days, so they built these tabernacles. What they was was a big, sprawlin', one-story buildin'. They'd build 'em in an open field. To save puttin' in a floor, they'd cover the weeds with sawdust—that's where your sawdust trail comes from."

Three olives in swift succession—pop, pop, pop. "You'll be interested in this," he continued. "The boards on the walls was attached with only one nail. If there was a fire, you could push out the walls. More important," Billy Joe said, smiling his admiration, "when the campaign was over, they'd knock down the tabernacle and sell back the lumber. Not bad when you remember the money to build the thing was raised before the campaign began."

He'd been eyeing the reporter's tray. "Ain't you gonna eat your pie?" When the answer was no, he picked up the wedge and scoffed a great bite of it, working his words around the food.

"The way you was converted in a Billy Sunday meetin' was by shakin' Billy's hand. The critics say that Billy's converts got saved in job lots. What they don't understand is that a Billy Sunday campaign was an *event*. The whole city was in on it. The meetin's was based on delegations. A factory would attend on a given night; the president, the foremen, the workers—all there in a reserved section. When Billy'd get through and give the invitation, the president or one of the foremen would lead the way down the aisle and the others would fall in behind 'em. And the whole shebang'd be converted."

"But surely they wouldn't be making a real decision. How could they?"

f copy next

"You'd think that," Billy Joe conceded. "But I've met hundreds of men and women saved in his campaigns. Lots of 'em preachers. Or out on the mission field." He poured himself some coffee. "Here's one guy who made his decision for Christ in a Billy Sunday meetin'. April 17, 1930."

"Tell me about Finney."

"Charles G. Finney was a lawyer. All reason and logic. Didn't trust emotion. If he was preachin' and somebody broke into tears or started to sob from conviction of sin, he'd stop. If that person didn't get control of himself, he'd dismiss the meetin'. Funny thing is, though, he was the center of more emotion than any great evangelist in history. Sometimes the presence of the Holy Spirit in his meetin's would be so real that people would be slain of the Lord –"

"Slain of the Lord?"

"Just keel over and lie there. Or they'd start quakin' or rollin' on the floor – that's where you get the words 'quakers' and 'holy rollers' from. In some towns business'd be suspended. Farmers would even forget to milk their cows. It was a real Holy Ghost revival. No organization. No advertisin'. Just the power of God. Finney once walked through a factory, and as he passed the workbenches, the workers fell like ninepins. When they come to, they was saved."

Billy Joe put down his cup. "Billy Sunday had a secret – his organization. Finney had a secret too – a man by the name of Father Nash."

"A priest?"

"No, no, no. Everybody just called him Father Nash. He traveled with Finney for years, and in all that time never once heard him preach. While Finney was upstairs preachin', Father Nash was down in the basement prayin'. Wrestlin' with God for souls. *He* was Finney's secret."

"And Dwight L. Moody ... what was his secret?"

"God."

"But beyond that?"

"There's no other way to account for Moody. He had nothin' goin' for him. He was a layman, a shoe salesman in Boston

g copy next

149

earnin' fourteen dollars a week. Never got past the eighth grade. Weighed about 230 pounds. Had this big paunch, an ugly face and a bushy black beard. Talked like a gatlin' gun – 200 words a minute. And his English! Somethin' awful!"

"But what was it? In human terms?"

Billy Joe turned the coffee decanter upside down and was rewarded with a trickle. "In human terms? Well, he was as direct a man as ever lived, and he was blessed with incredible energy.

"Give me an example of his directness."

"Okay. When he went to England, he started with nothin'. No big build-up, but he swept the country. So, he got an invitation to hold a campaign at Cambridge. A bunch of undergraduates figured to run him out of the place – you know, this uncouth American evangelist comin' to the heart of British culture. On the first night, Moody got up and said, 'Good evenin'.' The students applauded. He welcomed them to the service. They applauded. He announced the first hymn. They applauded. He had a singer with him by the name of Ira Sankey. When he was introduced, they applauded. When Moody took his text, more applause. He stopped, looked at the students and said, 'Gentlemen, I'd been led to believe that comin' here I was comin' to the heart of English culture. I thought I would meet English gentlemen, and that even though you might disagree with my views, you would show me some courtesy – me bein' a guest and a foreigner. I've been misinformed. The meetin's dismissed.'

"Eight of the students ran to the platform. 'We're terribly sorry for the behavior of these men,' they said. 'Will you accept our apology?'

"Moody said, 'No, I will not.' They said, 'Why not?' Moody said, 'The insult was public, the apology will have to be public. Tomorrow night I'll save eight seats for you in the front row.'

"He opened the meetin' by sayin', 'Some of your fellow students have a word to say.'

"One of the undergraduates got up and said, 'I want to apologize for the boorish way we've treated our guest from America,' and sat down.

h copy next

150

"Moody stood up. 'We'll sing hymn number such and such.' He went right ahead as usual. Turned the campus upside down. Hundreds were saved."

Billy Joe eyed a hard roll remaining in a basket on the table. "Don't you want that roll there?" When the reporter said no, he split it, slathered butter on the two pieces and wolfed them down.

The reporter asked, "Which of these men you've been talking about is Jimmy Coulter most like?"

"That's a hard one," Billy Joe said. He pondered, his brow drawn down, his lips pursed. "None of them, actually. None of the great evangelists have been like those who came before them. I think maybe that's how God shows there's no trick to it. Nothin' you can copy or imitate. He just uses whatever channel he can get and pours the water of life through it.

"Amen. Praise the Lord," he said, and belched.

TO: Clyde Rogers
FROM: HHH
SUBJECT: Vickery article

I am returning herewith the article on evangelism. I suggest that you not use it for the following reasons:
(1) With the Coulter series plus the news coverage we will be giving to the campaign, the Tribune will be doing more than enough for the cause of evangelism.
(2) While Vickery's analysis of television evangelism seems insightful, I see no point in needlessly antagonizing the followers of these electronic evangelists who may also be our readers. Newspapers must sometimes alienate readers in pursuit of their obligation to report and comment on the news, but to do so unnecessarily is self-defeating.
(3) I suggest that we give ourselves to completing the Coulter series and not be diverted.

PART
FOUR

29

The instructions had been: "Cross the U.S. border at the Thousand Islands Bridge. Take the Watertown bus at Ogdensburg. Stone Mills is twenty miles north of Watertown, and the church is right on the highway. I'll meet the afternoon bus."

As the bare landscape moved past the window of the bus, Jimmy was filled with excitement. Stone Mills would be an old town, postcard-pretty, with clapboard and fieldstone houses set on the slopes of a river. There would be an historic mill, and a stream chuckling and cavorting in celebration of spring. In his mind the church was a structure with gothic arches, a pipe organ, a gowned choir and a congregation of men and women of consequence. How typical of God's grace that it be given "pressed down, shaken together, and running over."

The Church of the Galilean wasn't given to the building of impressive places of worship – few congregations could afford them. As McGeer said, "We don't believe in worshiping God with costly bricks and mortar, but with temples of the spirit." Most Galilean churches were stark, box-like. Many were mere concrete block basements. Not uncommonly there was at the front of the auditorium a simulated thermometer on which the progress of the Building Fund was recorded. Often it was dusty and warped, the red line stalled.

"Stone Mills."

The driver's voice broke his reverie. The bus slowed and veered to the shoulder of the highway. There were only open fields and distant hills and a solitary building.

"Move along, please," the driver said.

155

Puzzling, Jimmy hauled his bags from the overhead rack. "Stone Mills?" he asked.

"This is it, mister."

Jimmy stepped down to the gravel shoulder. The bus ground through its gears and went off, leaving its stink in the clear air.

Jimmy stood at the summit of a gentle rise of land, surrounded by faded yellows and browns and beiges: roadside weeds, wheat stubble, tattered corn stalks pale from the struggle with winter, and an old oak, last autumn's leaves still clinging. Nearby, a wire fence, felled by the years, lay expiring on its side. Overhead, telephone lines skipped to the distant hills, their humming the only sound in the enveloping silence.

He crossed the highway to the building he took to be the church. It resembled a large farmhouse surmounted by a steeply pitched roof. The color had been barn red. The trim was a faded white, and the sheet-metal roof was streaked with rust. The only evidence of its ecclesiastical function was an afterthought steeple topped with a lightning rod. A sign at the front door was set in concrete:

STONE MILLS CHURCH
(Methodist Episcopal)
"I WAS GLAD
WHEN
THEY SAID UNTO ME
LET US GO INTO
THE HOUSE
OF THE LORD"

SERVICES
Sunday 11:00 A.M.   8:00 P.M.
Prayer Meeting. Wed. 8 P.M.
J.A. Garvin   Minister

Jimmy tried the door, and finding it locked, circled the church. He came upon a row of open-faced sheds once used to shelter horses and buggies. A disemboweled piano lay behind the church, with two broken chairs and a cord of stacked firewood.

Returning to the highway, he pivoted on a heel, scanning the distance. There was no sign of habitation. Where would the people come from?

An ancient Chevrolet clattered up the slope and jerked to a stop beside him. A gangling man with a ruddy face, a shock of white hair and a white moustache, leaned across the front seat and flung the door open.

"Reverend Coulter?"

"Yes."

"J.A. Garvin. Throw your bags in back."

The Reverend James Alvin Garvin seemed perpetually pleased by some secret knowledge. He smiled constantly and laughed frequently, often inappropriately. During the five-mile drive to the parsonage, he delivered a cheerful diatribe against Franklin Roosevelt for his attempt to pack the Supreme Court – the President not being mentioned by name but being referred to as "That Man."

At the parsonage, Jimmy was introduced to Mrs. Garvin, who seemed to have been poured into her clothes by a heavy-handed Creator to whom no prudent angel had cried "When!" The taut bodice of her dress gave evidence that her cups runneth over. Her ankles overflowed her shoes, and her fingers, diminutive at the ends of cylindrical, baby-creased arms, were like teats on an udder. Her face was incongruously youthful, free of wrinkles. On meeting Jimmy, the gray, owlish eyes locked on his as though to restrain them from lowering.

During dinner she seldom spoke, while the Reverend Garvin rambled on, pausing only to swallow.

"I was wondering, Reverend Garvin –" Jimmy began as the Reverend JA was spooning his second helping of deep-dish apple pie into his mouth. "I didn't see any sign at the church and ..."

Garvin's guffaw spread pastry crumbs on the tablecloth. "You been wonderin' 'bout the advertisin'," he grinned. "Don't need nothin' like that. Been waitin' till everybody's home to dinner."

He shoveled the remainder of the pie past his moustache, wiped his mouth on a sleeve and went to the wooden telephone on the wall. He turned the crank several times, removed the receiver from the hook and winked at Jimmy. "Give 'em a chance to get on the line."

"Good evenin'," he said, his voice attuned to the presumed number of his audience, "this is Reverend J.A. Garvin speakin'. The annual spring revival at the Stone Mills Church begins tomorrow night at eight. We are privileged to have a very special guest evangelist with us, the Reverend James Coulter. Likes to be called Jimmy. Only twenty-one years old –"

"Twenty-two," Jimmy said.

"... but wise beyond his years. He's a former sports editor on one of the biggest papers in Canada and illustrates his sermons with stories about sport. Leads the singin' too. He appeals to the youth, so bring the children. Haven't heard him preach myself, but I'm told he can scrape the stars and bring heaven down. Straight enough to send the Devil scurryin' with his tail 'tween his legs, they tell me." The image pleased him and he laughed some pie into the telephone. "Tell your neighbors, tell your friends and tell-a-phone. God bless you and yours. See you in church."

Chuckling, he returned to the table, looked at Jimmy and winked again. "Great invention, the party-line telephone," he said. "By bedtime, everybody in the county'll know you're here."

There was no heat in the bedroom. Jimmy undressed and kneeled to pray but was soon shivering, and finished his prayer in bed. He continued to tremble as excitement rebuffed sleep. Whispering in the darkness, he asked God's forgiveness for the pride that had fashioned gothic arches and a distinguished congregation. Stone Mills would be his enrollment in the school of evangelism. God in his wisdom had chosen that he make his mistakes before the few.

There was much to be done. He had five sermons, all oriented to young people. If he included Sunday mornings, thirteen services lay before him. He'd begin tomorrow night with his sermon on King David's son, Absalom; best to engage the Enemy on familiar ground. For the older audience he could alter those segments dealing with the pleasures of the flesh.

There had been a heavy snowfall through the night. A strong wind was driving it into drifts. The road leading to the highway was impassable, and Jimmy felt sure that the opening service would have to be canceled.

J.A. Garvin chuckled at Jimmy's concern, showering corn flakes and laughter over half of the breakfast table. "Take more'n a bit a snow to keep Stone Mills folk from doin' what they've a mind to do," he said.

By noon a neighbor had plowed the access road, and when Jimmy and JA drove to the church to "lay a fire" the highway had been cleared. The interior of the church was unornamented and austere. Bare light bulbs on exposed roof joists glared at every flaw on the unpainted walls. Folding chairs were ranged in rows on each side of a center aisle that skirted a squat, rusting coal stove. At the far end was a small platform with three carved oak chairs and a matching pulpit on which lay a large open Bible.

Jimmy counted the chairs: 109. There was room for more if they were moved closer to each other and if the space at the back was utilized. In the basement, in the Sunday School cubicles, he discovered a few dozen mismatched chairs and benches.

He asked to be left alone. He wanted to get the feel of the acoustics and to dedicate himself to God. The Reverend JA had errands to do, so it was arranged that he would return in an hour. The sound of his car gone, the auditorium became a cold cavity of silence. Jimmy went to the platform, put his hands on the sides of the pulpit and stood looking out at the empty chairs.

"My text tonight," he began, "may be found in Second Samuel, the eighteenth chapter, verse thirty-three: *And the King was much moved, and went up to the chamber over the gate, and wept: and as he went, thus he said, O my son Absalom, my son, my son Absalom! would God I had died for thee, O Absalom, my son, my son!*"

He preached the entire sermon, moving about the platform with a feline grace, enhancing his words with the gestures of the born orator. He preached with his entire body and with the actor's feeling for the rhetorical pause, the quiet aside, the touch of lightness, the sound of thunder. At the end he was drenched with sweat.

At 7:45 that evening there was only one car parked by the church. A man in a navy pea jacket and peak cap with earlaps was clearing a passage to the door.

"Evenin', JA," the man said.

"Karl Todd, meet our evangelist, Reverend Jimmy Coulter," Garvin said heartily. Todd pulled a calloused hand from a leather mitt and offered it. "Pleased to meet you, Reverend. The wife's inside."

Jimmy went to the basement, where he paced the cold concrete floor, talking to God. Only one car parked outside the church! His despair deepened as the minutes passed and there were no footsteps on the floor above. The first service of his first campaign and there were only five people upstairs.

The voice of J.A. Garvin in the stairwell: "It's ten past. We should get started."

A verse from Matthew's gospel flashed into his mind: "*Thou hast been faithful over a few things, I will make thee ruler over many things.*" God was testing him! He went up the stairs and directly to the platform. Positioning himself behind the pulpit, he stood smiling until his congregation had turned their chairs toward him: five gray figures against a field of chairs.

"Good evening," he began. "Welcome to the opening service of what is going to be one of the great revival meetings in the history of northern New York State. Not long ago I heard the late great 'Uncle Bud' Robinson preach. He said that if four people came to a meeting, he talked. If five came, he preached. It is my intention to preach. Before that, will you open your hymnbooks to number one hundred and sixty-nine. 'Amazing grace, how sweet the sound that saved a wretch like me. I once was lost, but now am found, was blind but now I see ...'"

The following morning the word went out. From J.A. Garvin: "The lad's a born evangelist. Preached up a storm – a real gully-washer." From Mrs. Todd: "I've never heard nobody like him since Dwight L. Moody was in Albany when I was a girl." From Karl Todd, in town to pick up some seed grain: "Kept me awake right through. That hasn't happened in twenty years." From his daughter, Arla: "He's *interesting*. He really is. And cute."

Overnight the weather improved and there were twenty-four in attendance at the second service. Sunday, the church was filled. The closing Sunday night, chairs were brought up from the basement. People stood against the wall and crowded at the back. Many were turned away. The love offering totaled $39.45. Karl Todd threw in another 55 cents to make it an even forty dollars.

It was past eleven when the last worshiper had gone. While the Reverend Garvin was banking the fire, Jimmy started off down the highway. The night was crisp and clear. The moon was high and almost full, and the stars gleamed at tree height.

He stood at the center of the highway and raised his face to the sky. Tears blurred his eyes. "Thank you, Lord," he said aloud. Then he added, his voice husky, "I love you, Lord Jesus."

30

In the Church of the Galilean, the itineraries of Licensed Evangelists were carried in the denominational magazine, *The Beacon of Holiness*, under the heading "Evangelists' Slates." Jimmy Coulter listed his name and began to get inquiries. Most of the evangelists listed were only occasionally engaged. These tided themselves over by selling Bibles or Fuller brushes door-to-door, or by taking employment that would enable them to go absent when a call came to conduct a campaign.

Most were seedy-looking extroverts given to wearing flamboyant clothes, loud men with braying voices, permanently hoarse from exhorting. Many were failed pastors, men who couldn't endure the drudgery of ministerial duties. Each had a specialty, a gimmick of some kind to set him apart. Some specialized in faith-healing or Bible prophecy. Others traded on a criminal past, or on a life of dissolution which enabled them, at the climax of the campaign, to recount their "life story" under titles such as "From the Gutter to God." Some sang as well as preached, which was an economy for the church calling them.

The sermons of most of these men were little more than "illustrations" strung together on a thin theology; and because a meeting wasn't considered a success unless a good number of "seekers" came to the mourners' bench, they motivated listeners through fear or sentimentality or by telling horrendous tales of men and women who rejected God and went to hell for it. They received little for their efforts: their travel expenses and a love offering on the closing night.

From Stone Mills Jimmy Coulter went to Carbondale, a coal-mining town in southern Illinois. The church was an unpainted tarpaper shack, the studding revealed on the inside. Rows of hand-made benches provided seating for seventy-five. The pastor, the Reverend Ulysses A. Boyleston, was a brother-in-law of J.A. Garvin. He worked part-time at the mine, being incapacitated by the "black lung." He wheezed as he talked and split his sentences into short segments that he might breathe in the spaces.

As Coulter took his place on the platform on the opening night, he saw half a dozen young mothers on the front bench with their babies. As the infants became hungry and began to cry, each mother opened her dress and began to breast-feed the child. Jimmy, his eyes averted, stumbled through the sermon. Afterward he pulled Boyleston aside.

"You've got to do something!"

"Jimmy! A mother feeding her baby ..."

"But publicly! It's distracting."

"It's not ... distracting anybody. That's why we ... have them sit ... on the front pew. Their backs are ... to the congregation."

"Doesn't it distract you?"

"Most natural thing ... in the world," Boyleston said, a smile creeping onto his face.

"Maybe it's the way I was raised," Jimmy said, growing self-conscious.

"What do you ... do in Canada? Tell the young mothers ... they can't come to church?"

"Some churches have what they call a Bawl Room. A big window so they can see, and a sound system so they can hear."

Boyleston smiled tolerantly. "Jimmy, my boy ... we don't even have ... Sunday School rooms."

Amused, Boyleston told his wife. From that night on, some of the mothers covered their breasts with a handkerchief or a folded diaper; a few of them didn't bother to, smiling up at him archly.

The next crisis arose after he preached his new sermon on David and Goliath. He'd been preparing it for days, polishing the phrases, developing the ideas. Now, dramatically, his voice communicating excitement, he set the scene:

"There they are – the two antagonists. Goliath, a tremendous figure of a man, head and shoulders above his people. A fierce, mountainous, black-bearded, terrifying giant of a man, the lust for a fight in his eye, the earth shaking beneath his feet as he advances to the fray ... "

Jimmy crouched, gliding across the platform like a boxer. "And there is David. Lithe and lean and bronzed from a thousand days on the hills, but a mere stripling. They strap Saul's armor on him. It is sizes too big, and he clanks comically along, looking like an anemic turtle.

"Then off comes the armor. And clad in nothing but a tunic – no spear in hand, no shield, nothing but a shepherd's rawhide sling and five smooth stones – he moves toward Goliath."

In short swift sentences Jimmy pictured the confrontation and brought it to a climax: "The stone goes whizzing across the gap between them. It strikes the giant full between the eyes and drops him in a sprawling heap, twitching on the ground ... dead!"

He paused, looking out at his audience. "The impossible has happened. An unknown shepherd boy has single-handedly defeated Israel's most dreaded enemy. An hour before, you might well have asked, 'What possible difference can this inconsequential youth make in the face of this gigantic challenge?' The answer comes to us across the centuries ... *all the difference in the world!*"

He moved to the pulpit, and leaning on it, spoke in an almost conversational tone. "Why have I told you this story? Who am I talking to tonight? To you. You who think you don't count. You who think of yourself as a small cog in the machinery of our civilization, as someone who cannot have any influence for good or bad. At your work you're a mere extension of a machine. At home you do a daily round of boring tasks. Can you influence Washington? Can you fight City Hall? You're one of millions in a world that doesn't even know you exist." His voice dropped to a whisper. "A shepherd boy by the name of David comes here tonight to tell you that you are wrong, that you *can* make your life count."

He warmed to his theme, holding an imaginary dialogue with a member of the congregation. " 'But,' you say, 'what can I possibly do? I'm so insignificant.'

"So was David. So is an atom. Yet there is enough latent power in the atoms in a thimbleful of water to drive an ocean liner to Europe and back.

" 'But,' you say, 'I am so weak and unstable.'

"So was David. So is water. But let some water trickle into a crack in a rock and freeze, and it will split the largest boulder on a mountainside.

" 'But,' you say, 'I'm so inconsequential.'

"So was David. So is a snowflake – a fragile flower crystal, so light as hardly to move the most delicate scale. Yet it is one flake of snow joined with dozens and millions of others that blocks highways, halts the mightiest locomotives, cuts off the greatest cities and blankets a continent.

"Unimportant as you may seem, impossible as the challenge may appear, I say to you tonight that the promise of the Bible is: *With God, all things are possible!*"

He moved aside from the pulpit so that his entire body was visible, and leaned forward, the intense blue eyes blazing. "How do you begin? You begin by stopping dreaming impossible dreams and by doing the simple tasks that lie at hand.

"How do you go to a distant city? You begin by taking a first step. One step! All great achievements have simple beginnings:

"You begin to fly by lying on your back studying the gulls at Kitty Hawk.

"You begin to invent the automobile by running a bicycle shop in Dearborn, Michigan.

"You begin to discover the theory of relativity by memorizing your multiplication tables.

"You begin to write Hamlet by learning to write.

"You begin to compose the Fifth Symphony by practising your scales ..."

He carried them forward with Bible texts and illustrations, urging, entreating, badgering, and moved to the conclusion. "Do you still doubt that God can use you because your talent is ordinary and your opportunities are small?" His voice rang out. "Let me remind you of the people he called to be his disciples in Galilee. Who were they – scholars, kings, rulers? No, they were ordinary men. Working men. Fishermen, tax collectors – the common people who heard him gladly!"

He gave the invitation. No one responded. Drenched in sweat, he pronounced the benediction. Boyleston called him aside.

"Jimmy," he said kindly, "I and the Board ... have just had a meeting ... and we have a request. Please understand ... we all love you. We think you're ... going to be a ... good preacher some

164

day. But, you're young and ..." He paused, embarrassed. "They wanted me ... to ask if ... maybe you wouldn't use ... so many big words."

By bus from Carbondale to Rome, New York, to Utica to Oswego to Binghamton to Bradford, Pennsylvania, where he bought a car, or rather, put fifty dollars down on a second-hand Ford Victoria. No more stifling, spine-jolting bus rides. No more shabby waiting rooms. Now he could come and go as he wished; get out of the hotel, buy a sandwich and a coke and have lunch by a stream; drive to the meeting house alone, with the opportunity to focus his concentration without the need to make small talk. He could practise sermons as he drove through the city, and on the road between campaigns.

In Bradford, Pennsylvania, the church burned to the ground on the first Thursday night. The pastor wanted to cancel the campaign. Jimmy pleaded with the Board of Trustees and convinced them to rent the Masonic Temple – at least to complete the week. The fire had been a spectacular one, with pictures and stories appearing in the newspaper. Jimmy prepared an advertisement which was carried on the Saturday church page:

OUR BEAUTIFUL CHURCH IS BURNED
BUT!
"ALL THINGS WORK TOGETHER FOR GOOD
TO THEM THAT LOVE GOD."
Hear the story of the fire.
Sunday night, 7:30

The auditorium was jammed. During the second week attendance doubled, and then tripled. On the closing Sunday night Jimmy raised pledges for a new building. They totaled $9,792.

In his diary he wrote: "Bradford, Pennsylvania. Best attendance, 550. Worst, 53. Love offering, $76.33. Behold! The power of the press."

31

Each day found Jimmy Coulter in a state of euphoria, despite the poverty in which he lived. Sending money home at the end of each campaign left him with little to spare. During the Utica meeting, a woman whispered to the pastor's wife, "Does he only have one suit?" He had two, but one was shiny with wear, the lapels curling and the trousers too short; it could be used only away from the platform. After each service his suit was soaked with perspiration and he had to hang the jacket in the bathroom overnight to dry.

Mornings were spent in his room, in prayer, in the study of the Bible and reading the orations of great preachers. After lunch he would work on new sermons, scribbling phrases and thoughts, and then go to the empty church to try them out. To get away from his spartan quarters, he'd often drive to the country, where he roamed the fields or sat reading beneath a tree. At such times he sometimes thought of Mr. Rimmington.

And he would talk to God:

"Lord, you must teach me. You must help me to understand you better and to apply myself with more.discipline. Why did I fail so miserably last night? Not a soul responded. And yet I was conscious of your presence. I felt liberty as I was preaching. Was it a sowing time rather than a reaping? Or could it be that I was trusting my words and not putting my trust in you? Humble me, Lord, if that's what I need. Make a fool of me if it will make me more effective for you ..."

Each night he stayed at the altar until the last seeker had been prayed through. How much sadness there was in their lives! Sometimes he felt guilt at his own good fortune. He was healthy and strong and bursting with energy. He was doing work that he loved.

On the platform he exulted in his growing power. To take a crowd of strangers and fashion them into a unit, a unit so caught up in what he was saying that sometimes you could *hear* the silence. The satisfaction of knowing that God was using you to change lives! He could see the rewards of his labor in the glowing faces, hear it in fervent thanks after a service, read it in letters telling him how he'd enabled someone to deal with his problems, or to find God.

During his Pennsylvania campaign, a handsome woman of about thirty-five came forward. Afterward, on the front pew, eyes lowered, she told him her story. Her husband had deserted her and their three children. She'd found a job, but the money went for food and clothes and baby-sitters and, recently, for doctors' bills. The youngest had been taken with an illness that wouldn't yield to diagnosis. She had faith that God would touch the child if only he would pray for her. Would he? There were tears on her face.

The following afternoon he went to her home, a small house, neatly tended. He pressed the doorbell and heard her voice through the screen. "Reverend Coulter? Come in and sit down. I'll be there in a minute." He sat leafing through a magazine until he saw her at the top of the stairs in a white, transparent negligee. As she descended, he saw the shape of her breasts and the shadow of pubic hair. He fled from the house.

And so, on to Jamestown and Warren, Pennsylvania, to Lackawanna, New York, and into Canada to Windsor and Guelph and Newmarket. Then on to Cherry Valley, Michigan.

He'd accepted the invitation because he had a two-week gap in his schedule and had heard that in early April Cherry Valley was exquisitely beautiful.

His information had been wrong: it was a hamlet of perhaps 175 ("if you include dogs and chickens," he'd written his mother) incongruously set, not in a valley, but in a slight declivity in an austere and barely arable plain. There were three churches in the town and they existed in an implacable rivalry, each plowing its own furrow. ("The ecclesiastical Hatfields and McCoys.") To heap misery on disappointment, through most of his ten days in town the weather ranged from rain to sleet, raw winds sweeping in from Lake Superior.

The Reverend Cyrus K. Kleet, the minister, was a bachelor, a short, slat-thin man, bald and cavern-eyed, whose skin seemed drawn over the skull. It would be difficult, Jimmy thought, to find a man less suited to the ministry. He didn't visit his parishioners. He was shy and blushed when spoken to. His voice was nasal and grated on the ear, and his words were infelicitous. He was a secret smoker who reeked of tobacco. He seemed incapable of casual conversation, lapsing quickly into silences.

Jimmy was quartered with him in the parsonage, there being no hotel nearby. Kleet had an extraordinarily large library. Jimmy took Thomas Paine's *The Age of Reason* to his room, reading through the day and after the service, until dawn. Within a week he had read François Voltaire's *The Bible Explained at Last*, Bertrand Russell's *Why I Am Not a Christian*, and Robert Ingersoll's *The Mistakes of Moses*.

He was shattered. Nothing had prepared him for the thrust of their logic or the persuasiveness of their arguments. He'd had moments of doubt but not over matters of consequence. Jesus' cursing of the barren fig tree couldn't be fact – the vindictiveness was out of character. Gideon couldn't have caused the sun to stand still – even Jimmy's rudimentary knowledge of cosmology recognized that as patently impossible. The feeding of the 5,000 (or 4,000, if you read Mark or Luke instead of Matthew) undoubtedly had some less miraculous explanation. But such doubts hadn't shaken him. They were accretions to the text added by over-zealous followers. The record of Jesus' life and teaching had the ring of authenticity. No genius could have invented *him*! And if one's mind caviled with details, it was of no consequence; the central facts were so.

But the words of Thomas Paine! Jimmy was defenseless before that precise mind. Bertrand Russell's unornamented arguments left him disarmed. They struck to the heart of the matter. Often he flung out of the parsonage to walk for hours in the rain, shouldering aside the buffeting winds. Evenings he preached without passion, his sentences lifeless. He tried to pray, but his mind strayed into the brambles, hounded by the questions that pursued him.

A week passed before he emerged from his depression. On the closing night, he found himself caught up in his own words, words he'd spoken so often that they spilled out almost without thought:

"The resurrection is important because the Christian religion is based on the faith that Jesus was right about the nature of the universe. If he was wrong, we're fools to follow him. As the apostle Paul said, 'If Christ be not risen, then is our faith vain and we are of all men most miserable.' Why? Because Jesus had predicted that he would rise from the grave, and if he was wrong about that he might well be wrong about everything else.

"Jesus taught that at its heart the universe is friendly and God can best be described by the word 'Father.' He said that there is meaning to life; things don't just happen. God stands in control of history.

"Let's face it: Jesus was either right or wrong. And if he wasn't vindicated after his death, it means he was wrong about life, and that God either doesn't exist or doesn't care. It means that morality is a fool's dream. It means that Pilate was right in getting rid of this troublemaker. If Jesus was wrong, Hitler is right – take what you want. If Jesus was wrong, it means that life is indeed, 'a tale told by an idiot, full of sound and fury and signifying nothing.'

"But the other side of the coin is this: The resurrected Christ is the evidence that God *is* at the heart of life, that evil will *not* triumph and that life *does* have meaning."

As he heard his own words, his spirits began to rise. His voice took on some of its old assurance and rang out in the tiny enclosure. "But how can we be sure there is a God? What is the evidence? Can you *prove* that God exists?

"You can no more prove God than you can prove beauty. I may say that a certain painting is beautiful, but if it doesn't seem so to you, no argument will convince you.

"Then, can God be defined? No. You can no more define God than you can catch a fragrant spring breeze in a paper bag. Catch the breeze in the bag and what do you have when you open it – a fragrant spring breeze? No, you have a sackful of stale air. Catch God in a definition and what do you have – God? No, you have a string of finite words.

"What, then, is the proof of God? It is the changed lives of those who believe in him. The miracle of Easter is the miracle of human transformation.

"Look at his disciples. Before the resurrection they were a ragtag bunch of semi-literate nobodys: craven, dull-witted, self-seeking and unfaithful. They had fought each other over who would be first in the Kingdom. They had wanted to call down fire on their enemies. They had fled when the soldiers came, and even Peter, their leader, had denied him.

"But what were they *after* the resurrection? Overnight, they were changed. They became men aflame with zeal and bold with courage. Ineffable mystery! Jesus was alive, and the disciples were so sure of it that they were ready to lay their lives on the line. They ... *they* are the proof!"

There were seekers at the altar. In his room he thought back to the night God had changed his own life and was able to pray.

32

Hugh Hoffman was accustomed to getting his own way. He had observed early in life that some did and most did not, and that life was much more enjoyable for those who did. He had observed also that getting one's own way seemed contingent on the acquisition of money and power. Early on in his career as a journalist – at the end of a day filled with frustration – he had made the resolution that he would not long subject himself to lesser men. Upon being named editorial director of the Toronto *Tribune*, his first act was to fire fourteen members of the editorial department (it so happened, within a fortnight of Christmas), replacing them with reporters from other newspapers across Canada. Staff morale plummeted; efficiency soared.

Within eighteen months he changed the character of the paper. He slanted the news unashamedly, crusading with equal vigor against big government and big business while pandering to the burgeoning middle class. He disdained the traditions of the Fourth Estate, there being but one dictum, set in 72-point headline type and displayed in the City Room. It read: JOURNALISM IS LIKE POLITICS – THERE ARE NO PRIZES FOR SECOND. In his thirty years as owner, the *Trib* was seldom second.

On a Friday morning in May, padding in bedroom slippers about the dark expanses of his home high on the knolls above Malibu, he was in a foul mood. As was his custom, he had risen at six-thirty, and first thing after shaving had gone to the teletype in his study to do a swift scan of the overnight wire copy. Two items had soured his stomach as he went to breakfast: the annual poll of America's Ten Most Admired Men, which listed President Adam Scott in first place and Evangelist Jimmy Coulter in third; and a feature

171

datelined Washington dealing with the economics of the newspaper business and with the probable impact of a tax bill undergoing examination by congress.

Having checked his wife's bedroom to see if she was stirring (unlikely as that might be), he went to the kitchen, poured a glass of orange juice, broke three eggs into a pan, beat them and immediately forgot them. When the scent of burning alerted him, it was too late. He shoved them to the back of the stove, wrapped a wedge of cheese in a piece of bread, poured a cup of instant coffee and went to his study.

The burning of the eggs irritated him, following as it did the argument he'd had only the day before with his wife Tammy about the hiring of a maid.

"I will not have a stranger living here. You have a cook now, and a cleaning lady. That's enough."

"You're gone all day. How could it bother you?"

"How many times must I repeat it? No live-in help."

"Then you can make your own breakfasts. I'm damn well not getting up at seven."

He called Toronto on the WATTS line.

"Clyde. Hugh Hoffman."

"Good morning. How's the weather in California?"

"Are you at your desk?"

"Yes."

"Good. You'll want to make some notes. Clyde, I am at a loss to understand why we aren't making better progress on the Coulter series."

"I wouldn't worry about it, Mr. Hoffman. Things are in hand."

"That may be, but there is precious little evidence of it at this end. Let's review. I have before me a memorandum from you dated April 6 in which you list five stories to come. To date I have seen the Macdonald-Reimer and the Rodriguez pieces, and some odds and ends of progress reports, one purporting to show that Coulter has lost his faith. As yet, I have seen nothing by way of an analysis of the effect of Coulter's preaching on a community and very little on his financial affairs."

"Mr. Hoffman, believe me, they're all underway."

"Well, let's just see. Who's doing the analysis of Coulter's effectiveness?"

"Jim Findlayson in Washington. Coulter's going there to launch Salute America Week and Findlayson will tie his analysis to that."

"Findlayson is a columnist, not a reporter. And he's wordy."

"I've talked to him a number of times. I think you'll be pleased."

"The letter from Coulter to his son."

"We've negotiated a fee with Beale. Cost a bit more than I'd hoped but we have the letter for publication."

"Why have I not seen the letter?"

"Sorry. I'll put it on the printer this morning."

"Not on the printer – let me have a photostat of the letter itself."

"Yes, sir."

"Coulter's financial worth. I was talking to Bill Lennock of the *Register* earlier this week and he tells me he has heard nothing from your office."

"Yes ... I'm afraid there's been something of a foul-up there. I passed it to Grady –"

"Who?"

"Grady Solomon, our new executive editor. I'm afraid that, in taking over his new responsibilities, he –"

"I fail to understand your handing it off to an associate. I thought I made it crystal clear that it was a matter demanding the utmost discretion."

"Yes. Yes, you did. I might say, however –"

"Where does it stand? Have you been in touch with Lennock?"

"It's on my calendar as a priority for today."

"It's already ten-forty Toronto time."

"I'm aware of that, Mr. Hoffman. It's been a chaotic morning."

"I received a telex from Lennock yesterday with the following information. It's from his source at the IRS and can be trusted. I would emphasize again the need for discretion. Coulter's salary from the Jimmy Coulter Evangelistic Association is, as Macdonald-Reimer reported, $50,000. However, they did not report that he has additional income as follows: from his syndicated newspaper column, $118,545 –"

"One hundred and eighteen thousand, five hundred –"

"There's no need to take it down. I'll put it on the telex. Dividends from investments, $37,392. Miscellaneous fees, $12,995. Expenses – whatever that means – $13,000-odd dollars. Additionally, Lennock was able to learn that he owns $875,000 in annuities. Interesting. How does one purchase nearly a million dollars in annuities on a salary of $50,000?"

"Perhaps from his books."

"I seem to remember that all the revenue from his books is given to the Inasmuch Foundation."

"Oh yes. Right."

"I am interested to note also that Mrs. Coulter paid taxes on an income of $63,568, part of which was salary paid to her by the JCE Association."

"That's interesting."

"I would have thought your people would have gotten to that by now."

"I believe you said you would put all that on the telex?"

"There's one other thing. What's being done by way of examining Coulter's relationship with President Scott?"

"Findlayson is looking into it."

"I hope so. Frankly, Clyde, I would have thought you would have given the matter priority, especially in light of the Democrats' proposed increases in the tax on newsprint, color presses and binderies, which are, in my view, little short of punitive."

"Yes."

"You might point out to Findlayson that Coulter is, in effect, chaplain to the President, and inasmuch as some 150 million Americans are church members, this could be a significant factor in next year's election ..."

"Yes, of course."

"... when, needless to say, the Hoffman newspapers will oppose the reelection of the incumbent."

"I'll draw it to Findlayson's attention."

"I have only one more note. I was interested to see that our Jimmy Coulter was one of the speakers at a recent convention of The American Association of Community Churches ..."

"I'm afraid I don't know anything about them."

"Not a significant group. Headquarters here in Los Angeles. A membership of around twenty thousand."

"I'm afraid I don't follow."

"It's of no great importance other than the fact that it's a distinctively, although not exclusively, homosexual denomination. I mention it only because your Jenny Wedger was so sticky in the matter."

33

Twelve hundred people thronged to the closing meeting of the Jimmy Coulter Albany campaign in the spring of 1941. So great were the crowds at the church that it had been necessary to rent the Orpheum theater for the closing service.

After two years on the campaign trail, Jimmy preached with assurance and a new sense of power. His subject was Life's Decisions, and he ended by pressing his listeners to make the most important one:

"There was once a very wise man who lived in a humble shack on the outskirts of a little town. People came from all the region thereabout to ask him questions. There was a boy in the town. He decided to find a question that the wise man couldn't answer. Finally, he had it: He would snare a bird, and holding it alive in his hands, would ask the wise man whether it was dead or alive. If the wise man said it was dead, he would open his hands and let it fly away. If the wise man said it was alive, he would give a quick squeeze and open his hands to show the bird dead.

"So he went to the wise man and said, 'Mr. Wise Man, is the bird in my hands alive, or is it dead?' Oddly, the wise man didn't look at his hands. Instead, he looked full into the boy's eyes and said, 'That decision is yours, my son. It's whatever *you* want it to be.'"

When Jimmy gave the invitation, the response was immediate. He was backstage talking to one of the new converts when a man drew near. "There's a girl wants to see you," he whispered. "Says she knows you." He checked a card. "Arla Todd from Stone Mills."

Jimmy followed the man to a room that normally served as a

175

dressing room. It was lined with mirrors. "That's her," the man said, pointing to a young girl who seemed backed against the wall by a short, dumpy woman with straggly hair – Jimmy recognized her as one of the personal workers.

Arla Todd appeared to be about eighteen. Dark auburn hair fell in soft curls on her shoulders. Her lips were scarlet with lipstick, and blackened lashes made her green eyes larger. She was wearing a dirndl skirt with a white peasant blouse. The bodice was tight and the drawstrings were neatly tied.

"Reverend Coulter, this is Arla Todd," said the woman with the straggly hair. "She's a backslider."

Jimmy extended a hand, and as he began to withdraw it, the girl would not release it. "Reverend Coulter, could I ..."

"'Seek ye the Lord while he may be found; call ye upon him while he is near,'" said the personal worker, anxious to impress the young evangelist with her zeal.

The girl spoke over the woman's head. "Reverend Coulter, please. Can I talk to you a minute?"

The woman was rummaging in the quiver of her New Testament, looking for an appropriate arrow. Jimmy spoke to her. "Sister ..."

"Hawkins," said the woman.

"Thank you, Sister Hawkins. You can leave Miss Todd with me. I know her family in Stone Mills." When the woman hesitated, he repeated firmly, "Thank you, Sister Hawkins." She went off, piqued.

In the harsh light of the room Arla Todd was beautiful. In the mirrors, Jimmy could see their images reflected to infinity. "Are you here with your parents?" he asked. She shook her head, looking into his eyes. Her gaze was so open it unnerved him. "Is there a delegation from Stone Mills?" he asked. She shook her head again.

"You don't remember me, do you?"

"Well, to tell you the truth ..."

"I was saved at your meeting in Stone Mills two years ago. And when I read you were coming to Albany, there was no way I wasn't going to be here."

He vaguely remembered her – one of the five in the congregation that first night of his first campaign. But she'd been a child then, shy, withdrawn.

176

"It meant a lot to me," she continued, "being saved at your meeting, I mean. It made my parents happy, that's for sure. They were always bugging me about going to church." Her eyes were shining with admiration. "You were wonderful tonight. I could just listen to you forever."

His heart was beating rapidly and he was slightly bewildered. In his meetings, he'd dealt with dozens of girls. Some blushed when they were introduced to him. Some were attractive. Occasionally, when shaking hands, he felt a strangely poignant sensation, but he'd never been powerfully drawn to any of them.

Arla Todd was different from the rest. He was aware that the girl before him was a woman, aware of her red lips, her great green eyes, the swell of her breasts.

"Sister Hawkins says you've backslidden," he said awkwardly.

She looked at him with a small, sweet smile. "I just said that because I wanted to talk to you."

"Would you like me to pray with you?" he asked, and then felt foolish.

But she bobbed her head, and they went to their knees by the chair. As she bent over, the neckline of her blouse fell away and he saw her breasts within a flimsy brassiere. Afterward, he couldn't recall a word he'd uttered, so conscious had he been of the head bowed next to his, of her perfume, of the beating of his heart, and of a sudden, intense longing to remain near her.

Up came Sister Hawkins, leading a half dozen women and a man. "Here's Reverend Coulter," she said officiously. "I'm sure he'd like a word with each of you before you go." She herded them toward him as a sheep dog might a hesitant flock, and then took Arla's arm. "Now, Miss Todd, you come with me. You'll want to sign a decision card, and I'll give you some literature ..." Her voice trailed off as they disappeared beyond the door.

Jimmy Coulter talked to the new converts, saying the words that needed saying, shaking hands, but his mind was elsewhere.

He was already in bed when the phone rang. It was Arla Todd. Her voice was so low, he scarcely caught her words. She had wanted to talk to him at the theater, she said, but hadn't been able to. "I've run away from home, Reverend Coulter. A friend, Bud Harvey, gave me a ride ...."

"Do your parents know where you are?"

"No."

"They'll be worried." She made no response. "Where are you staying?"

She hesitated. "I don't know. Bud wants me to go to a hotel."

"And?"

"I don't want to, if that's what you mean. But we can't sleep in the car, the window's broken ...."

"How old are you, Miss Todd?"

"Eighteen. Anyway, going on eighteen."

"You realize you're underage, that your friend could be in trouble if you went to a hotel?"

"I said I didn't want to go."

"You should call your parents. They'll be very worried."

After a moment, she said, "Tonight was the last night of your campaign here – right?"

"Yes."

"And, like you said in the service, you're going on to Ottawa?"

"Yes."

"I was thinking ... since it's on the way, maybe you could drive me home tomorrow ...."

It wouldn't be out of the way to go through Stone Mills. The thought of Arla with him on the drive started his heart to beating quickly again. But it was out of the question. Perhaps he should loan her the bus fare, he thought. But it was past eleven and she'd have missed the last bus.

"Do you have any money?"

"About a dollar."

"I'll tell you what," he said decisively. "I'll call a bellboy and leave an envelope with five dollars for you at the desk – to pay for your room. In the morning, I'll meet you in the parking lot at eight and drive you home."

He gave the bellboy the envelope and went back to bed. His hands behind his head, he lay thinking of her and of the journey tomorrow. He saw her again in the Inquiry-room, kneeling at the chair, and felt a stirring in his groin. He reached into a drawer and found the Gideon Bible. After finishing the first three chapters of Paul's epistle to the Romans, his eyelids were heavy and he turned out the light. When the telephone rang, he started and glanced at his watch – 1:45.

It was Arla Todd.

"Where are you calling from?" he asked.

"The lobby. . . . Bud just wouldn't take no for an answer and I thought . . ."

"Why don't you check in and call me from your room?"

"Well, you see, I can't do that. When we finished eating, Bud said if I was ditching him he wasn't going to pay. So I had to come to the hotel and get the money. The bill was nearly five dollars."

"I see."

"I'm sorry."

"What you'd best do is check in anyway. I'll take care of the bill in the morning."

"Well, if you don't have any luggage, they want the money in advance."

He was at a loss to know what to do. He couldn't call the desk and tell them he'd pay her bill – at 1:45 in the morning, it would seem strange. And the clerk knew who he was. "Come up to my room," he said, "and I'll give you the five dollars. We'll straighten it out in the morning."

He turned on the lights, put on his bathrobe, and went to wash his face. As he combed his hair, he saw that his hand was trembling. Ten minutes passed before he heard an urgent knocking. He took out five dollars and opened the door.

The girl brushed past him. "The lights!" She put a finger to her lips, touched the switch by the door and went to turn off the lamp on the night table. In the dimness he saw her slipping off her shoes. Coming to him on tiptoe, she put her head close and whispered, "The house dick!"

There was the sound of a board creaking in the hallway. A shadow broke the slot of light under the door. Arla clutched his arm tightly. "Shhh!" Her hair was fragrant against his cheek. There was a scent of liquor on her breath. The door handle was tried and the footfalls moved off.

Arla led him to the bathroom, where she closed the door and switched on the light. She lowered the toilet seat and sat. He felt awkward standing above her in his old, short robe with no pajamas underneath, so sat on the edge of the bathtub. She smiled in a pleased conspiratorial manner. "Now we can talk."

"What in the world is going on?" he asked sternly. "Why did the house detective try my door? And why are we hiding in here?"

She laughed merrily. "Isn't it crazy?"

She told him how she had evaded the desk clerk and the house detective. "Don't worry," she said, "nobody saw me come into your room."

She smiled cheerfully, her teeth white against the vivid red of her lipstick. Her eyes were shining and wide with the excitement of the game. He noticed that the drawstrings of her blouse were now tied differently.

She looked at him in her direct way. "Can I stay here tonight?"

"You know you can't do that ... Arla."

"I don't mean in the room. I'll just curl up in the tub. Snug as a bug in a rug."

"Arla, that's not –"

"I've slept in worse places," she said, and laughed. "Don't worry."

His face was flushed. "I'll see if there's a blanket."

There was. He took it with a pillow to the bathroom. Arla was washing her face. "I look just awful," she said to the mirror. "I don't know how you can let me stay." She turned toward him. Her skin shone and was pink from the toweling. Her eyelashes were thick and clotted, and damp wisps of hair curled on her cheeks and forehead.

"You wouldn't have a shirt I could borrow?"

"A shirt?"

"I can't sleep in my dress. It would look awful in the morning."

"Yes, of course."

He unpacked a shirt and passed it to her. "Good night," he said, and got into bed.

The bathroom door was partly open and he saw her reflection in the mirror as she brushed her hair. Then she pulled the drawstrings of her blouse and lifted it over her head. As she did, she stepped away from the mirror. He heard a faucet squeak and water running in the tub and was suddenly cold. Wasn't she going to close the door?

Now she was before the mirror again. She reached behind her back, undid her brassiere and slipped it off. Barely breathing, he watched as she pinned her hair high on her head.

She was gone from sight again and there were the sounds of bathing. He shivered. It broke upon him that he was feeling the same chill fear that seized him when in his teens he'd begun to masturbate.

There came a rush of water down the drain. In the mirror there were fleeting glimpses of Arla's face, of a shoulder, an arm, of breasts.

Finally the bathroom light went out, and Arla entered the room, buttoning the shirt. "Are you asleep?" she whispered.

"Just falling off."

"We forgot something," she said. "How can I sleep in the tub? I took a bath."

When he did not reply, she came to stand by the bed. "Reverend Coulter, can I talk right out to you? Look, here I am in your room, but nobody knows and nobody's going to know. Right? So why don't we be sensible? I won't be able to sleep in the tub, and you'll just worry about me. So, nobody gets any sleep. We're not children. Why don't I just lie down on the bed? We both know nothing's going to happen."

His brain felt numb. He couldn't bring himself either to refuse or to acquiesce, and so lay silent. Half laughing, she said, "I could even sleep on top of the bedspread if you're afraid of me."

She slipped in beside him. He moved to make room. Their bodies weren't touching but he could feel her warmth and smell the scent of soap and freshly bathed skin and the faint muskiness of a perfume. He was trembling, and tried to control it.

"Did you know I've kept your picture ever since you were in Stone Mills?"

Her breath was warm and sweet with the scent of his toothpaste. Her thigh pressed lightly against his. She put a hand on his shoulder. "You're trembling. You're like a steel spring. Are you afraid of me?"

"No," he said. "Good night."

"Good night," she whispered.

She lay on her back, her hip pressed against his, their shoulders touching. After a few minutes she turned toward him. "You're not sleepy, are you?" she asked, her lips at his ear.

"I'm afraid not."

"Can I ask you something?"

"Yes."

"Do you trust me?"

"I'm not sure what you mean."

"You're like a steel spring. You really are. You've been kind to me and I want you to relax. Let me massage your shoulders."

She slipped a hand into his bathrobe, kneading his muscles with strong fingers.

"Now, isn't that good?"

"Yes it is."

She shifted the better to reach him, stroking his chest in small circles. Her mouth was close to his ear. She was breathing quickly with the exertion. "Now your tummy," she whispered, and moved her hand to the flat of his belly. The belt of his bathrobe obstructed. She untied it and pushed the robe aside. After a moment she let her hand rest, fingers spread, at the center of his stomach. "Was that good?" she whispered, her voice thick, her lips brushing his ear with each word.

"Yes it was."

"Can I ask you one more question? Have you ever been like this with anybody – I mean in bed? Have you ever made love? I think it's beautiful if you haven't. You haven't, have you?"

"No."

She lay still for a moment, then whispered, "I'm in love with you, you know, Reverend Coulter. I have been ever since you came to Stone Mills ...."

34

A newspaper photograph of the interior of a church. At the far end of a long center aisle, like tiny figures on a wedding cake, a bride and groom, facing a clergyman. In the foreground, in the aisle, a white satin slipper, the heel jammed in the wrought-iron grill covering the cold air return of the heating system. The caption read:

MODERN CINDERELLA. Helga Nostrand, former Miss America, lost a slipper on the way to the altar to marry Canadian evangelist, Rev. James (Jimmy) Calder. The beauty queen was a convert in Mr. Calder's recent Sandusky, Ohio, campaign.

Progress report–coulter   wedger

Clyde:
Thought you might be interested in the enclosed photo and news story on the Coulters. It's something of a rarity and might be useful to the photo desk when they do their layouts. I was able to dig it out through Ed Ashby, city editor at the Sandusky Beacon. He tells me the neg is available. I was amused that the caption writer identified him as Jimmy Calder. Understandable: an obscure, young preacher marrying Sandusky's very own Miss America.
I'm planning to go to Los Angeles next week. Hoping for an interview with Coulter, but not confirmed. I have Mrs. C definite. Talked to her on the phone yesterday. Capsule description: cool customer. When I mentioned the photograph and broached their courtship and wedding, she dismissed it with, "That was *so* long

ago." She is very sensitive about her age and made it a condition of the interview (off the record) that I make no specific reference to it in my story. I pointed out that it's almost impossible to avoid, she having won the Miss America contest in a specific year. She said snappishly, "What's wrong with simply, 'a former Miss America'?" It's entirely an intuitive thing, but I have a strong impression that the Coulters aren't close. You would never get that impression from their public appearances, where sometimes their references to each other and their mutual deference skates very close to the maudlin.

Planning also to spend some time at the JCE Association. Will see what I can turn up to supplement your information on Coulter's income. I understand now how he can afford those $500 suits.

Jenny

35

Had God ever created anything so beautiful as Helga Nostrand? Jimmy Coulter thought not. It was a view held also by her parents, Anna and Pieter Nostrand. Since childhood she possessed a fragile loveliness that stopped passersby on the street. Strangers would look at the child and at the parents and wonder how such a lovely flower could come from such roots. Her mother was a plump, pleasant hausfrau with taffy-colored hair; the father was short, balding and appeared crestfallen. Their daughter's beauty was the heart of their existence. They fussed over her and showed her off as others might primp and preen and wrap their lives around a Best-of-Show cat.

Sometimes the lineaments of Helga's face would take Jimmy's breath away. She would look off as though engrossed, so that he might gaze freely at her. He was filled with wonder at honey-blond hair, skin that seemed transparent beneath the sheen of a flawless tan, eyes so deep a blue as to verge on violet (a marvel amid all that fairness), a delicately formed nose, and lips the color of roses behind which perfect teeth bore witness to genetic luck and orthodontic skill.

There were other joys to be contemplated – described in the press as Miss Nostrand's vital statistics: 5' 5", 112 pounds, 36-23-36. Her voice was modulated and perfected through elocution lessons during The Year of Her Reign. And she sang, "Ciri Biri Bin." It was her talent, without which, needless to say, the Miss America judges would not have chosen her as a finalist.

Despite her beauty and fame, her parents, a pious couple who belonged to the Evangelical Free Church, were worried about Helga. The moment she placed the crown upon her successor's

185

head, the spotlight swung away from her. Her retinue of reporters, photographers, public relations people and various civic officials abandoned her.

"The Queen is dead, long live the Queen," Helga said. Then she became irritable. Her parents could do nothing to please her, and she denigrated anything relating to Sandusky. She had acquired a new vocabulary of obscenities, which she used at home with the inventiveness of a stevedore.

During the Jimmy Coulter campaign in Sandusky, Helga agreed to attend, and her parents were tremulous with hope. Little did they know that she had assented only because she was afraid that a refusal might tempt God – three weeks earlier, she had gone to bed with a Los Angeles talent agent who had flown east to try to sign her to a contract, and she was now three days overdue.

At the service she was escorted to a seat in the front row. Two thousand people jammed the Shrine Auditorium. The lighting was theatrical; there was a press table, and photographers prowled about. Helga was overwhelmed by the young evangelist's charisma and responded to the altar call. Afterward, as she posed with Jimmy, she overheard someone in the crowd say, "Don't they make a handsome couple!"

At a special youth night the following Wednesday, Jimmy invited her to give her testimony. When she finished, there was applause. Each night thereafter she attended the services. She began to see herself on the platform as the young evangelist's wife, heard the applause, imagined herself traveling all over the country, singing ...

Jimmy, too, began to fantasize. The loneliness of life on the campaign trail had begun to be burdensome, and he sometimes wondered whether he shouldn't marry.

On the Monday following the campaign, he spent a day with the Nostrands at their cottage, and went for a walk through the woods with Helga. Coming on a clearing warm with sunlight, they sat and talked. "I'll miss the meetings," Helga said, and then added, "I'll miss you too, Jimmy."

Awed by Helga's beauty, Jimmy had not dreamed of winning her affection. Sitting on the grass, she leaned back, her face tipped to the sun, her lips parted. She closed her eyes.

Helga had had little experience with men. Beneath the gloss of sophistication, she was an emotional child. She hadn't dated as much as her peers and had often been lonely. Men didn't phone

186

her as they might a plainer woman. She found Jimmy handsome and gifted, and although he was a preacher, she felt at ease with him.

"Maybe you'll come back soon," she said.

Jimmy moved to sit beside her. He leaned close to put a long, gentle kiss on her mouth.

She lowered herself to the grass, putting one hand behind his head to draw him down with her, and the other behind her own so that she wouldn't get her hair dirty.

Never in its history had the Sandusky Evangelical Free Church seen such a crowd. Some had stood in line since dawn. At least six hundred packed the pews, with others standing along the walls and sardined-in at the rear. Many waited out in the street. A police officer was dispatched to keep traffic moving. Five press photographers were on hand: from the Cleveland *Plain Dealer*, the Sandusky *Beacon*, the Columbus *Post* and the *Associated Press*, with a free-lancer covering for the Toronto *Tribune*.

Lizzie Coulter was the only family member who came to the church for the wedding. Jimmy's father sent a night letter, carefully composed to stay within the 50-word limit: *Congratulations, you lucky stiff. Picture of you and Miss Nostrand in Vancouver paper recently created quite a stir. Please extend my warmest and most cordial wishes to the beautiful bride. Regret cannot be present for the ceremony. Annual meeting CanBiz Ltd conflicts. Wish you both much happiness. Dad.*

His mother had been driven to Sandusky by her brother Arthur, but she took ill within an hour of checking into the hotel. His sister Kathryn couldn't be contacted. Nor was Herb, Jr., able to attend: he was at a Christian summer camp which had a rule against making refunds without sixty days' notice and Lizzie decided it was sinful to waste the money.

Dressed in a pink satin bed jacket, Lizzie received the Nostrands in her hotel room. When Mrs. Nostrand asked if she was in pain, she gave a small, brave smile and admitted to being "a wee bit fatigued." She insisted that the group kneel about the bed while she led in prayer.

"Dear Lord Jesus," she whispered, "Helga and Jimmy are our children, but they are also your children. You understand how much we love them and have loved them from the moment they were born. We understand too, Lord Jesus, how much you love them – for didn't you lay down your life for them at Calvary? We cannot know what plan you have for their lives, nor do we seek to know – thy will be done. All we ask is that you go with them as they now begin to walk as one. You brought them together, Lord. Be by their side as they go out into the world to proclaim your word . . . ."

To Jimmy Coulter worship was as normal as breathing. He took literally the biblical injunction to "pray without ceasing," and talked to God as readily as he might to a friend. Upon awakening, he would lie quietly and put the day in God's hands. The words "Thank you, Lord" formed almost reflexively on his lips when something went well. He prayed as he did his work, as he walked the streets, as he drove his car. Rarely did he ask for things, but often for guidance. He prayed before each service, usually in some out-of-the-way place – a boiler room, a storage space, a stairwell. So accustomed did he become to God's presence that walking in an open field one night, face turned to the sky, he looked down only in time to see a skunk in his path, tail at the ready. He stepped back with a grin. "One of your creatures, Lord."

He fell as easily into an adoration of Helga Nostrand. Even when her actions puzzled him, he was untroubled. He was accustomed to waiting upon a deity who didn't always respond as he might hope, having worshiped for years at the heart of an enigma.

36

When Jimmy and Helga returned, tanned and clear-eyed from a two-week honeymoon in Jamaica, heads turned as they passed through the airport. In Sandusky, there was a box filled with letters awaiting them: congratulations from friends, "God bless you" notes from converts, and invitations to conduct campaigns from churches in a dozen states—most of them addressed to "The Reverend James Calder." Within weeks they were booked for a year ahead.

Jimmy was developing an approach to preaching that was unique. There was no cadence to his sentences, nor did his voice rise at the end of a thought. And he avoided the style of the exhorter with its familiar evangelistic buzz words—which in the hands of a skilled practitioner can create a counterpoint between pulpit and pew as intricate as the interplay between soloists and backup men in Dixieland jazz.

His style confused the "old saints," and as he began, the nostrils of some of the veterans of revivalism would twitch, scenting heresy. Not hearing the usual evangelistic jargon, but wanting to encourage, they would interject their "Amens" and "Hallelujahs" with the awkwardness of a long-ball hitter chopping at a change-up pitch. But once he was in stride their doubts dissipated. The congregation fell into silence, borne away by the images his words conjured up. His gift was akin to the painter's, who sees his subject in the mind's eye. Coulter *saw* the three-dimensional body of the dying Christ ... "*muddy and bloody and brutalized. Is this the serene teacher who has been ministering to the sick and needy? Would you recognize him if you didn't know it was he? — 'his visage marred as no other man's,' his face a red smear of sweat and blood and spittle, his*

189

body dirty, naked and bleeding, his hands and feet pierced, his poor, tired body sagging ... "

Often he would begin a sentence without knowing its end and would be surprised at the turn it took. He believed it to be the Holy Spirit working through him. So it was that he often felt closest to God when he was preaching.

In the early months, there was little for Helga to do but sit decoratively at Jimmy's side, occasionally speaking a few words of testimony. Later she learned some gospel songs, but her singing was a problem. "Ciri Biri Bin" had been acceptable from a Miss America contestant – the song moved quickly, a nimble larynx could skip through it without being betrayed – but in churches and local auditoriums, where the sound systems were poor and there were only local accompanists, her inadequacies were sometimes embarrassing. Her voice had the quality of a tin whistle, and her ear was untrustworthy. Depending on her mood and level of energy, she might go sharp or flat when the song ventured beyond the middle register. It troubled Jimmy but seemed of no importance to their audiences.

"Darling ... "

"What?"

"I've got an idea. The crowds are getting bigger and I thought it would be great if, when we're planning future campaigns, we find out in advance who's the best vocal teacher in the city and –"

"What are you trying to say?"

"Nothing. Except that –"

"You don't like my singing."

"No, no. Just that –"

"I've sung to bigger crowds than we ever see. I sang on the whole network, coast to coast, at my pageant. Dozens of guest shots. In fourteen foreign countries ... "

"It couldn't do any harm to –"

"The accompanists you get me – Deanna Durbin couldn't sing with them."

"Everybody has to study. I practise every day."

"Why don't you just keep on doing that?"

He dropped the subject but hired a pianist to travel with them, and his fortissimo accompaniment covered most of the musical misadventures.

Having rejected Jimmy's suggestion, Helga then adopted it. In

190

each city she sought out a teacher and practised long hours. But she was no longer content merely to sing, and the audiences were disappointed if she did no more than bring greetings. Jimmy prepared a dozen five-minute talks, carefully tailoring them to her style.

She had an innate sense of drama and a good speaking voice, and though the stilted quality of the elocutionist remained, she made the words her own, each time delivering them with greater effectiveness.

"Ladies and gentlemen," she would begin, then break off with a laugh of feigned embarrassment. "Forgive me, I should have said, Brothers and Sisters in Christ. I can't tell you what a joy it is for me to stand here tonight to tell you something of what God has done in my life. I have traveled this great nation of ours from coast to coast and to foreign lands as a representative of America, of the Miss America Beauty Pageant which I was honored to win. Tonight, I stand on this platform as a representative of the Kingdom of Heaven. Not as a beauty queen but as a sinner saved by grace. Not as a spokeswoman for a commercial enterprise but as a servant of the Most High God ..."

Strikingly beautiful, standing to one side of the pulpit so that there was nothing to obstruct anyone's view of her, a bank of spotlights trained on her and the lights of the auditorium dimmed, she seemed to radiate an inner flame.

"Three years ago," she would conclude, "it was possible to say that the greatest thrill of my life was that night at the Miss America Beauty Pageant when the judges said, 'We have chosen you,' and a crown was placed on my head. It was a moment I will never forget. But, my friends, exciting as it was, can it begin to compare with the moment that is coming soon when the judge of all the earth will say, 'You have not chosen me, I have chosen you. Enter into the joys of thy Lord,' and a crown – not a temporal crown but an eternal one – will be placed on my head. And not only on my head, but on the head of the humblest Christian."

In the silence that followed, she would put her lips to the microphone, and the amplified whisper would reach to the back rows: "Oh, my Brothers and Sisters in Christ ... *will that not be a DAY!*"

Taking a step back, she would give a slight nod of her head, and there would be applause of an intensity usually heard only in opera houses.

37

On the wall in Lizzie Coulter's kitchen was an Imperial Oil road map of North America on which she traced in blue crayon Jimmy's and Helga's travels. It showed forays as far west as California, as far east as Bangor, Maine, and as far north as Edmonton, Alberta, with one deep V reaching to Miami, Florida. There was a circle around the town of Wheaton, just north of Chicago, where the couple had bought a tiny, two-bedroom house, partly because it was central but also because Helga didn't want to live too close to the parents of either of them.

After Helga joined the campaigns, the attendance doubled. In most cities the churches were too small to handle the crowds that thronged to the doors each night. And there was a professionalism to their presentation that caught the attention of the press.

But there were also disheartening times, times of doubt and questioning. Jimmy recorded some of them in his journal.

CLARKSVILLE, TENNESSEE. (April 3-18, 1944)
Our first outdoor campaign. Tabernacle on outskirts of the city. Open on all sides. Heckling and wolf whistles from young people driving by. Pulpit was focus of lighting, so dozens of moths, June bugs, etc. orbited our heads. Helga refused to go on unless problem solved. Mounted two bare 300-watt bulbs at each end of platform and bugs went there. Campaign a great success. At closing service, 2,300 present. Many converts. Cultural note: invited to parsonage for "great treat" – chicken stew, mountain style. Cooking pot brought right to table. Fragrance exquisite. To our horror, entire chicken afloat in broth, including feet and head, complete with opaque eyes. Host nibbled on feet as "a delicacy." The prophet Job had it easy!

SYRACUSE, NEW YORK. (Mar. 3-17, 1945)
Pastor Abernathy after me every night to "Get down where the people live. Preach on adultery, on gossip, about smoking and drinking ..." Yet, he had to admit that we had the largest attendance in the history of the church and that he will take in a dozen new members as a result. God helping me, I will *not* descend to that mindless browbeating that passes for evangelism in the Church of the Galilean.

LANSING, MICHIGAN. (Oct. 12-27, 1945) Crestwood Evangelical Free Church. Rev. Douglas "Doug" Kip, pastor.
Arrived here to find pastor in jail. A converted alcoholic and former boxer, "fell off the wagon" and beat up a police officer trying to arrest him for drunken driving. Front-page story with pictures. Pastor released on bail put up by church. Reporters at the service when he returned. Insisted on making detailed and sordid confession. Publicly asked forgiveness. Congregation split on whether to fire him. Much bitterness in membership; one fist fight in the sanctuary before Sunday-morning service. (The press are like jackals around carrion.) I have sympathy for Kip's problem (Helga has none, refuses to speak to him) but have no patience with such public washing of dirty linen. Couldn't wait to shake dust of the place off my feet.

MINDEN, LOUISIANA. (Nov. 29-Dec. 13, 1946) Temple Methodist Church. Rev. Billy Lee Garr, minister.
Sunday morning, while preaching on God's Perfect Love, heard sound like high-balling express train, followed by crashing, splintering uproar, screams and shouting. A tornado touched down, taking out a block of houses and reducing to kindling Grace African Methodist Episcopal Church, across the street from our meeting. Eight dead, including pastor ... as he was preaching! Fifty injured. Why them? Why especially them – the poor and the discriminated against? And why during worship?

The tragedy at Minden troubled Jimmy for weeks. He would start up from his sleep, heart pounding. He would relive that moment of silence when the hellish roaring had stopped and the groans and screaming had not yet begun. He had run with others across the street. No part of the church remained standing. Men, women and children ran from the wreckage like ants from a scuffed nest: hysterical, moaning, dazed, unaware that legs were broken and bodies bleeding. Some, crazed with anxiety, crawled over the debris, calling out for children, wives, husbands.

Searching in the rubble for the trapped, Jimmy came upon the pastor of the church, his chest crushed like an eggshell. He recognized the ebony mask of his face; he'd seen it night after night among the segregated in the balcony. Now, white with plaster dust, he seemed a ghost. The police and ambulances had come whooping and he was ordered away. Numbed, he wandered the streets, weeping. In his hotel room before the mirror he begrudged his wholeness.

MOBILE, ALABAMA. (March 3-18, 1950) Rev. Winston Burton, pastor.
Arrived to find no advertising on church and pastor asleep at home mid-afternoon. He'd confused dates; wasn't expecting us for two weeks. Showed him correspondence. "Isn't that awful of me? Sorry." The man's a fool. Couldn't afford layover of two weeks in hotel so insisted campaign go ahead. Used the opportunity to practise new "positive" approach. Tired of bludgeoning people with God's judgment. Last straw for Helga. She thinks Galileans are "negative, narrow-minded idiots."

There were perhaps twenty in the sanctuary on the opening night as Jimmy moved to the pulpit.

"What does the word gospel mean?" he began. "It means Good News. Jesus didn't come to drape crepe on our lives. The message when he was born was, 'Behold I bring you tidings of *great joy!*' The music that burst through the heavens wasn't a dirge but an anthem. It was the birth of a baby, not the funeral of good times.

"Let's get away from this idea that Christianity is a gloomy thing. Let us no longer be misled by these religionists who go about as studiously sad as an undertaker, their faces as doleful as a basset hound's. We've all met them: the Noble Order of Mote-removers and Neighbor-judgers – those self-appointed guardians of public morality, those inspectors of warts and carbuncles, their noses in everybody's business and with unsought advice for all. From all such, Dear Lord, deliver us!"

Afterward, in the hotel room, Helga paid him the first compliment in months. "Good," she said. "I was glad to hear you give a shot to that gloomy bunch of ass-draggers."

As a result of the meeting in Mobile, Alabama, Jimmy Coulter received an invitation to conduct a city-wide tent campaign in Los Angeles. He could hardly restrain his excitement. Helga threw into the air the deck of cards with which she was playing solitaire and shouted, "California, here we come!" Jimmy didn't sleep that night, and spent much of the following day on the telephone. He called TG Wheeler, who was pastor of a church in Raleigh, North Carolina. By his own admission, TG couldn't "preach a lick," but he had built a strong church through his organizational skills.

"Tee, I'm building a team. There's no way I can handle it alone anymore. There are a dozen invitations for every one we can accept." Coulter's voice rose in excitement. "We've just been invited to conduct the Los Angeles campaign. It's a mammoth thing. A tent seating six thousand and –"

"A team? Like who?"

"Clark Costello as song leader. Billy Joe Harewood as advance-man."

"You're kidding!"

"And Helga, of course. Our own organist."

"What would I do?"

"Run the whole show. Public relations, finance, personal workers. There's a radio ministry in the works. Two hundred a week and your expenses ..."

"Tell you the truth, I been gettin' itchy to get out of here."

And so it was arranged. Overnight, Jimmy Coulter joined a small group of men who, because of their gift for preaching and their ability to put together an organization, were able to transcend denominational and doctrinal differences and conduct city-wide campaigns. At the time, they were not half a dozen in all of North America.

PART FIVE

38

HEAR DR. JIMMY COULTER HERE!
NIGHTLY 8 P.M.

In September of 1950 the tent was pitched at the center of a 20-acre fallow field, not far from the core of downtown Los Angeles and visible from the intersection of the Hollywood and Santa Anna freeways. Suspended from three poles, the great stretch of canvas flared to a rectangular circumference encompassing 5,694 folding chairs leased from Abbey Rents. A carpet of sawdust had been laid in the aisles, treated so that it wouldn't scuff into the air and trouble the evangelist who was allergic to sawdust. High on the tent poles were clusters of floodlights focused on a platform reaching from one side of the tent to the other. On it were easy chairs for the principals, and folding chairs on risers for the 200-voice choir. A rectangular, wood-frame pulpit covered with fluted red, white and blue cotton bunting was almost hidden by a spectacular arrangement of cut flowers.

On this, the closing night of the Greater Los Angeles Jimmy Coulter Campaign, the crowd had begun to gather early. Most parked near the tent, but old hands maneuvered close to the exits to avoid being trapped in the traffic jam that would follow the service. Some had arrived as early as five in the afternoon. They sat in the front rows, chatting or reading newspapers or Bibles, drinking from thermos bottles and eating a variety of foodstuffs from paper sacks. By 7:30 the tent was filled. Latecomers stood in rows along the canvas walls or sought vantage points in the entranceways.

Among the more than six thousand in attendance there were some known to the public, even a handful known to the police.

199

Some of the former wore dark glasses in order to be recognized. Three of these, a woman and two men, had made decisions for Christ as a result of the campaign. They were: Helene Marlowe, actress; Bobby Herman, College Football's Rookie of the Year; and Silver Harry Golden (born Silbert Hymie Goldenberg), "the Cecil B. de Mille of Porn Pix," found guilty on an obscenity charge the previous week by an Indianapolis court and free on $10,000 bail.

The white-robed choir climaxed their rendition of "Faith of Our Fathers" at a double-fortissimo roar, and at eight o'clock sharp the Coulter campaign team came from behind the platform with the briskness of a baseball team leaving the dugout. They mounted the platform and took their seats. Leading the group was Helga Coulter, blond and dazzlingly beautiful. She was followed by Clark Costello, dark of hair and eye and dressed with the sharpness of a racetrack tout; TG Wheeler, associate evangelist, his midriff thickening, his hair thinning; the Reverend Millard H. R. Howland, Jr., of the Los Angeles Evangelistic Center, in a yellow sports jacket and Roman collar; and finally the evangelist himself.

At thirty-three Jimmy Coulter's body was spare and erect. His stride bespoke vitality. His bearing communicated a man at home with himself and his surroundings. That immaturity in his features which had stayed through his twenties had gone. The face was strong, handsome. Beneath a cliff edge of dark eyebrows the intense blue eyes gleamed. The mouth had widened, the jaw was more prominent and thrust forward above neck muscles massive from ten years of preaching. In more youthful days he'd worn flashy jackets and flowered ties; on this night, the suit was of darkest blue and impeccably tailored. The tie was a regimental stripe against a television-blue shirt. Seated, he bowed his head and closed his eyes, frowning in concentration, almost as though turning his mesmerizing eyes inward to fix them on God.

Clark Costello went directly to the pulpit and blew into the microphone. The resulting roar halted all conversation and focused attention on the platform. He bared glistening teeth in a smile which never left his face.

"Good evening." The amplified voice was as robust and cheerful as the face. "Welcome to the Greater Los Angeles Jimmy Coulter Campaign. Is there anybody here in this magnificent Canvas Cathedral on this beautiful southern California Sunday evening who loves the Lord Jesus Christ?" There was a scattered response which tailed off and was followed by nervous laughter.

Costello cupped a hand to an ear. "Perhaps the mike isn't working," he said. He tapped it. "Seems okay. Let's try it again. Is there anybody here tonight loves Jesus?" The response boomed like a cannon's roar.

Feigning disappointment, he addressed himself to the pianist, a shy, young man from whose fingers arpeggios flowed like sparks from a Roman candle. "Dick," he said, "Dick Jones, ladies and gentlemen, our piano virtuoso!" Applause. "Dick, do you think it's possible that the *smog* here in L.A. ...." He put a hand to his mouth as though guilty of a horrendous gaffe. "Oh, my! I said a naughty word – smog! *A four-letter word!*" He waited for the laughter to die. "I can't help wondering whether the ... magnificent ... crystal-clear ... sun-kissed ... God-blessed atmosphere here in Los Angeles hasn't given everybody laryngitis."

He turned suddenly resolute. "We'll try it one more time. Are you ready? Is there anyone in this magnificent audience of more than six thousand people, here or in the great overflow audience outside ... is there anyone here ...."

He broke off, feigning trepidation. "I'm almost afraid to ask," he confessed amid much laughter and clearing of throats. "All right now, this time is for real: Anybody here loves the Lord Jesus Christ, say Amen."

The roar seemed to belly the taut canvas of the tent. It burst from confinement, rolled across the acres of parked cars and was heard half a mile away. Costello stood silent until the happy, self-congratulation of the crowd had subsided. "That," he said, "is more like it. Turn in your song book to page sixteen: *Shall We Gather at the River?* Will you all please stand ...."

Jimmy Coulter scanned the audience, seeking to assess its mood. His chin was slightly elevated and he held a serene smile. He knew that, at the angle from which the photographers were shooting, his face would have an ascetic quality, a handsome spirituality. He was aware how important his face was to his success, regarded it as part of his stock in trade, and could examine it in the mirror with more objectivity and less conceit than most men. It was for this same reason that he chose his clothes in consultation with a Wilshire Boulevard tailor. It was why he took time to sit in the sun and carried a sunlamp in his luggage. In the privacy of his hotel room he wore a baseball cap–his hair tended to mound too high and the cap shaped the contours. Jimmy Coulter knew that his followers wanted him to incarnate their preconceptions and he sought to meet those expectations.

The crowd before him was more a cross-section of the community than had been "the Lord's despised few" when he'd begun his ministry. Fundamentalism was finding, if not respectability, broader acceptance. It now encompassed the wealthy with the poor, the intellectual with the illiterate, management with labor. There were more young in attendance, and more men. In previous years, the media had turned its attention to religion and had brought to world attention such figures as Bishop Fulton Sheen, Norman Vincent Peale and Billy Graham. Consequently, the presence on this night of so many photographers stirred an excitement in Jimmy Coulter.

They were clearly not the familiar amateurs, mincing self-consciously to the area below the platform to pop their flashbulbs. These were professionals. It was evident in the way they prowled about, in the way they suddenly froze, to draw a bead and shoot, and in the reflex ease with which they reloaded. He was intrigued. There had never before been so many of them at one of his services. He signaled to TG who came to kneel beside his chair.

"The photographers. What's up?"

"I been tryin' to figure it out."

"I count three," Jimmy said.

"There's one more shootin' the overflow. Maybe they heard about Helene Marlowe."

"There's a reporter with Bobby Herman. See what's up."

Clark Costello's voice broke in. "In a few minutes Dr. Coulter will be bringing you his special message for tonight, 'America's Last Chance For Greatness.' It's a subject that has been burdening him for days. But now, before Reverend Howland leads us in prayer, and the great white-robed choir–two hundred voices strong–joins me to sing, 'How Great Thou Art,' and just before everybody's Miss America, Helga Nostrand Coulter's thrilling testimony to God's saving grace–which you'll be happy to know is now available on long-playing Clarion label records and can be purchased at the literature table at the close of the service–here is Dr. Coulter with a word about our radio ministry."

As Jimmy strode to the pulpit, the front rows of personal

202

workers rose applauding. The crowd followed, retreating row by row toward the rear like a wave moving to an invisible shore. Coulter waited for the applause to die. He'd publicly forbidden the taking of pictures during his sermons but would now give the photographers the opportunity to get the shots they needed. He raised his hands above his head in response to the applause. There was an immediate blaze of shuddering light. As the applause continued, he picked out people he knew, pointing at them and saying their names. Each gesture was illuminated. Enough. He stepped back, bowed his head and closed his eyes. Dozens of pale-blue circles dotted his vision.

"Ladies and gentlemen," he said, gathering assurance as his voice filled the tent and drew the crowd into a unit. "In the name of the Lord Jesus Christ I bid you welcome." He went on to make an appeal for the funds needed to sustain the network of radio stations now numbering twenty-seven in the United States, Canada and Quito, Ecuador. The ushers passed envelopes down the rows. Each had on its face a blank check. He'd only returned to his seat when TG was back.

"They're from the *Journal*," he said. "There's two reporters. One's doing a feature, the other a news story."

"But why?"

"They don't know. Their instructions were to do a saturation job on the Coulter meeting."

Helga was at her special microphone which she had positioned to one side of the platform and specially lit. ("I'm not a preacher, and I don't want to look like one. And I want them to be able to *see* me.") She'd recently taken to wearing floor-length gowns of white chiffon, the decolletage just short of indecorous, with great, pleated sleeves so that when she raised her arms she appeared from a distance like an angel about to take flight.

"We live in an age that worships youth and beauty," she was saying. "It's the emphasis today – in movies, in magazines, in advertising. We even paint the dead with cosmetics so they look like they're in the bloom of health. Everybody's worried about their face and figure. I know a woman in Hollywood who's afraid to smile for fear she'll show a wrinkle." She paused. "That's so silly it makes me smile." Whereupon, she broke into the broadest of smiles, her eyes sparkling, her perfect teeth gleaming.

"I'm often asked whether I regret having participated in the

Miss America Pageant. They say to me, 'Isn't it little more than the worship of beauty? Aren't you required to display yourself for the world to see?' My answer to questions like that is, 'No, I don't regret it.'" She gave the crowd a sly smile and added, "I might, if I hadn't won." There was laughter and applause.

"You remember the parable of the talents?" she continued. "To each of us, God gives various gifts: for the arts, for teaching, for business – and that most important talent of all, the talent of the homemaker. In his wisdom – and I say it humbly – he gave me the gift of song, and ..." She stretched out her arms and did a slow pirouette, "... and other things." The crowd responded with laughter and cheers.

"The important thing, my dear friends, is what we *do* with our talents. What does the Bible say? *For what have you that you did not receive?* Whatever we have, it's a gift from God, and unless we dedicate it to him, it is in the end, as the Preacher says in Ecclesiastes, 'Vanity, vanity. All is vanity ....'"

She took her seat beside Jimmy. He leaned close. "Helga, I asked you to stop all that whirling about. It's cheap."

She appeared to be gazing at him fondly. "You do your job, I'll do mine."

"You make it look like a burlesque show."

She smiled at him sweetly. "How would you know, darling?" she whispered. "Been sneaking off by yourself?" A photographer crouched before them, focusing. She looked out at the audience, broadening her smile. "They love it."

The final crescendo of the choir's anthem had barely died when Coulter was at the pulpit. He brought the crowd to its feet with his outstretched arms. "Bow your heads." His lips touched the microphone; his voice was alive with intensity. "Lord, grant two things: Grant me the power to send my message straight to the heart of every man and woman here, and grant each of them an open mind and a receptive heart. Amen."

He waited for the people to settle in their seats. When absolute silence came, he began:

"We stand at the crossroads of the centuries. Who can doubt that future generations will regard this as the most momentous time in all history. Every border between the Communist and the Western world bristles with bayonets. The military trigger their earthquakes. The arms race intensifies. The destructive potential mounts like a mushrooming cloud. The world stands in doubt and indecision, asking, 'What will tomorrow bring?' It is not unreasonable to wonder if there will *be* a tomorrow."

Swiftly, with staccato sentences, he painted a picture of world conditions. "In the face of all this, how do we respond? Do we say, 'Look what the world has come to!' or do we say instead, '*Look what has come to the world!*'?"

The thousands had become one. All eyes were fixed on him. No one stirred. He stretched out an arm, a finger pointing. It seemed directed at each face in the crowd.

"We are like the priests in the temple to whom Judas came after he had betrayed Jesus. His face twisted with remorse, he hurled the thirty pieces of silver to the floor, and turning to the priests, cried out, 'I have sinned in that I have betrayed innocent blood.'

"And what was the response of the men who had bribed him to do the deed? They turned their backs and walked away. 'What is that to us?' they said. 'See thou to that! That's your business, not ours.'

"And have we not done the same?" he whispered.

"When Hitler and Mussolini began to tell the world their dreams, we said, 'What is that to us?'–and soon their dreams became our nightmare.

"When the underfed nations of the world began to cry out for a more equal ration, we said, 'What is that to us?'–and soon we were all being rationed.

"When the Japanese attacked China, we said, 'What is that to us?'–and soon our sons were dying with the Chinese in the Pacific.

"When the Soviets laughed God out of court and appointed themselves champions of the underprivileged, we said, 'What is that to us?'–and now we are beginning to see that it may be a matter of life or death to us!

"Jesus commanded us to love our neighbor, and for a long time we thought this was a pleasant religious option. We are beginning to realize that it is an imperative. Today it is *love thy neighbor or else!* In a world that has become a neighborhood but not a brotherhood, no injustice anywhere can be dismissed by saying, 'That's their funeral,' for it is likely to be ours too!"

He prowled back and forth on the platform as TG paid out and pulled in his microphone cord. He entreated, he cajoled, he thundered, sometimes whispering, occasionally hammering a fist on the pulpit, pleading with arms outstretched and perspiration coursing down his face. After forty minutes, he came to the conclusion.

"You ask me, perhaps, what can you do. What can *any* individual do in a world caught in the grip of great forces?" His voice became almost conversational. "Last year there was a convocation of one hundred thousand people in the Los Angeles Coliseum. Suddenly, every light went out. Before anyone could panic, a voice boomed over the loudspeakers. 'Don't be alarmed. We turned out the lights for a purpose. Do this: each one of you get a match. If you don't have one, borrow one.'

"When the noise subsided, the voice came again, 'When I give you the signal, light your match and hold it up.' The voice rang out, 'Light your match!'

"At first, a few flickering fireflies in that great bowl of blackness. Then the bowl became a jewel box of light. Suddenly, it burst into a great blaze of light, seeming by contrast brighter than the light of day. Then, slowly, the light flickered, pinpointed out and died. The crowd sat silent in the darkness.

"In the silence, the voice came. 'What did you do? You lit one match. One flickering, short-lived match – nothing in this great sea of darkness. But when all of us did the same, it became a light brighter than the noonday sun.'

"Then, in the words of Jesus, the voice went on, 'Even so, let your light shine before men, that they may see your good works and glorify your Father which is in Heaven!'"

Some three hundred responded to the invitation. Afterward, he and Helga posed for dozens of pictures with Marlowe and Herman, and with Bill Virden, an enforcer with the California Mafia who had been among the converts. Jimmy talked until midnight with one of the reporters.

Monday's *Journal* and all twenty-four papers in the Hoffman chain carried a front-page story of the campaign. As well, the *Journal* committed the Section page and two inside pages to pictures, color stories, biographical sketches, and first-person testimonies by Virden, Marlowe and Herman. Silver Harry Golden announced that he would approach Helga, seeking to cast her in the role of Mary Magdalene in a film he'd been inspired to make.

Display ads were rushed into the newspapers. Radio time was bought to announce that the campaign would be extended. On the

Monday night, fifteen hundred were turned away. Duplicate services were required the following Sunday.

The campaign became "the place to go." Sundry celebrities, from film stars to businessmen to politicians, dropped by. The media jammed the press tables and roamed the aisles. Jimmy was besieged by reporters and followed everywhere by camera crews.

The campaign ran for eight weeks. Some 350,000 attended; 5,324 decisions for Christ were recorded. Overnight, Jimmy Coulter became a legend.

39

Jimmy Coulter had read of men suddenly thrust into the spotlight of worldwide fame and destroyed by it. He was certain that when celebrity came to him (he seldom doubted that it would) he would be able to avoid the perils. But he was not prepared for the onslaught of public attention that followed the Los Angeles campaign, nor had he anticipated the changes it would make in his daily life.

"Privacy ends," he wrote his mother. "Freedom disappears. You become an icon: gazed upon, touched, revered and, yes, hated. You go into the street and a crowd materializes. You are transported from place to place by others. You pick up a paper or a magazine and there you are – pictured, quoted, discussed. You are sought after by the famous and by the bizarre. You get hundreds of letters; some beg for money, some threaten your life, some plead for your prayers. You have to delegate the answering of your telephone; it rings incessantly. Everyone wants something: your attention, your approval, your presence. And the press! They never leave you alone. They intrude, they clamor, they lie in wait."

At first he'd welcomed it. For over ten years he'd barnstormed the nation, living from a suitcase, staying in hotel rooms that stank of stale cigarette smoke and countless predecessors, traveling in broken-down automobiles in the early years.

He'd made new friends every two weeks, then said good-bye to them. He'd pushed lazy or unimaginative pastors and committees, trying to infuse them with his own energy. He'd been so poor he was ashamed of his clothes. A number of times he'd had to ask for an advance against the love offering. He'd endured bad acoustics and squealing amplifiers and crying babies and airless auditoriums.

He'd preached when he was running a fever or queasy from bad food or dizzy from exhaustion or empty in spirit; and worst of all, at those times when his mind was fuzzy and his thoughts wouldn't take form and his sentences kept tripping over each other.

But this was in the early years. Fellow evangelists spoke of it as "hard scrabble," and rather than begrudge it he embraced it. It was God preparing you. It was doing your apprenticeship. For a time, his favorite verse of scripture was, *I have learned, in whatsoever state I am, therewith to be content.*

There were rewards in the new life – his picture on the covers of *Life*, *Time*, *Newsweek*, *U.S. News and World Report*, *Atlantic Monthly* and *Paris Match*. He was invited to join Sam Snead, Bob Hope and Bing Crosby for eighteen holes of golf. He was interviewed on national television by Jack Paar and Dave Garroway; and CBS hoped he could be Protestantism's answer to Bishop Sheen.

Invitations to conduct campaigns poured in from around the world. London promised the Harringay Arena, with a closing rally in Wembley Stadium. New York City offered Madison Square Gardens. Vancouver would settle for a date in 1954 in the new British Empire Stadium. Would he address the student body at the Massachusetts Institute of Technology, the World Council of Churches in Geneva? Would he accept a Doctor of Divinity degree from Lafayette College?

With celebrity came Midas' touch. A letter from a lawyer in Los Angeles informed him that he had been bequeathed a house in Malibu by a woman converted in his L.A. campaign. Overnight, there was a market for everything he said: long-playing records of his sermons and Helga's songs, a radio network that reached around the world and the beginnings of a television ministry. Letters flooded his new headquarters in Burbank, most containing money to pay for broadcast time. He began a syndicated newspaper column – ghost written by a teacher seconded from the Moody Bible Institute. He set aside a few hours each morning to write books, which sold in the hundreds of thousands. The love offerings on the closing nights of his campaigns ran into thousands of dollars. Criticism led him to put himself and Helga on salary and to incorporate the Jimmy Coulter Evangelistic Association.

He tried to control his time but found it impossible. There was so much to occupy him, so many people to see, so little time to spare. He found himself living on the edge of exhaustion. He

40

Each year Yale University brought in a prominent preacher to speak in the chapel and make himself available to the students. In the winter of 1955 Jimmy Coulter had accepted the invitation as a break from campaigning, and each morning took pleasure in donning a black gown and his Doctor of Divinity hood to preach. The chapel was filled with students sitting on the floor and crowding beyond the doorways. Afternoons were spent in personal interviews.

Jimmy Coulter was especially looking forward to an appointment with Roger Whitton. A senior, Whitton was the outstanding student in the graduating class, an honors student in political science, captain of the debating team, and since his sophomore year, quarterback of the university's Ivy League championship team. He was the sixth of his family in an unbroken line of Yale graduates, the only son of a wealthy Boston family.

Whitton had a relaxed manner, and Coulter liked him immediately. After a few minutes of conversation, he said, "You wanted to talk to me."

"Yes," Whitton said, shifting in his chair and growing serious. "I guess the best place to begin is to tell you that I was raised a Presbyterian but it didn't take. If you were to ask me where I am today, I'd have to say I'm an atheist. I think religion's important, but I've never been able to get satisfactory answers to my questions. I've been listening to you this week and you seem to be getting at something entirely different. It interests me."

They talked for two hours: at first fencing, trying to score debating points; later vehemently, occasionally verging on anger. Whitton was a skilled opponent and he pressed Jimmy beyond

211

his usual responses in similar confrontations. Toward the end, Whitton's combativeness started to recede. He began to listen rather than debate.

The telephone interrupted, reminding Coulter he was due to meet Helga for a faculty reception in his honor.

"I'm afraid I've got to break," he said. "Sorry."

As Whitton rose he put out a hand. "I want to thank you, Dr. Coulter. You've made me realize it isn't a matter of having all the answers but of whether I'm ready to commit myself." He managed a smile. "I'm not sure I am . . . . Anyway, I'm going to think about it . . . Seriously. Thanks. Thanks a lot."

Alone, Jimmy was depressed. There had been a moment of elation – he'd vanquished the captain of the Yale debating team. He'd made his case with a facility acquired in hundreds of such conversations, made it with reasonable arguments, convincing arguments, but arguments which he knew no longer convinced him. In the heat of the discussion he believed them – even as he was never troubled by doubt while preaching – but Whitton's questions were the questions he himself had been troubled by all his life. He would put them aside – there were more pressing problems. When they arose, he would cover them over with prayer and devotions. But at unexpected moments they would reappear – sometimes as a flicker, at other times consuming as a flame.

He realized that Roger Whitton might go from their discussion to pray, as he had at the same age. It was obvious that Whitton hadn't come merely to engage in academic dispute; he was searching for meaning in his life. He'd recognized that the cost was the commitment of himself. He hadn't realized how great that cost could be.

Jimmy Coulter knew. George Bernard Shaw's words came to mind: "It's not that Christianity has been tried and found wanting; it has been found difficult and not tried."

It broke on him: What right did he have to intrude in Roger Whitton's life, possibly to alter the course of it? And by what right did he stand night after night before tens of thousands, urging them to give all to God when he was not prepared to do so himself?

Neither Helga nor Jimmy spoke as he maneuvered the rented car out of New Haven and onto the throughway to New York City.

Helga would be catching a plane home, while he remained in the city to meet with the committee planning the Manhattan campaign. After a while Helga stopped working on her fingernails and began to make conversation, but Jimmy's thoughts were elsewhere.

"I asked you," she said testily, "whether you'd have enjoyed it more if some of your interviews had been with girl students."

He glanced across at her. He could see she was in a foul mood. "No."

"No what?" she snapped. "No, you wouldn't have enjoyed it more or, no, you didn't enjoy it at all?"

"It's pretty obvious that *you* didn't enjoy yourself. I didn't think you would. I was surprised you wanted to come along."

She was out to bait him. "What makes you so sure I didn't enjoy myself? There was lots to do. I don't have the hots for God the way you do, you know."

His thoughts were back at the university with Roger Whitton. With his mind and advantages, were there any limits to what he might achieve?

"As a matter of fact," Helga was saying, "I enjoyed myself very much. It was very nice, all those men. Why wouldn't I enjoy myself? It would have suited me just fine if we'd stayed on longer." After a few minutes, she added, "I'm a normal woman, you know."

His tone conveyed infinite patience. "Yes, Helga, you're a normal woman."

"Apart from that incredible ego of yours, what makes you think I'm going to be content to wait forever for you?" Jimmy fixed his eyes on the road. He wasn't going to be drawn into a quarrel. "Well, how long has it been?" she asked.

"How long has what been?"

"Since we made love, for Christ sake!"

"Helga," he said, "haven't we been over that enough?"

"I'll tell you how long: twice in eighteen months."

A road repair crew, lights flashing, had halted traffic. They waited, the engine idling. He was remembering the morning almost two years earlier when Helga had come home, her face black with anger, to announce that she was pregnant.

Jimmy felt a rush of joy. "Are you sure?"

"Would I say I was if I wasn't?" She flung herself into a chair, not troubling to remove her coat, and sat staring off glumly. "You realize what it'll mean? I'll be stuck here at home." She was silent for a moment, then blurted out, "Stretch marks! It makes me furious. Furious! *Furious!*"

Jimmy had taken Helga's pregnancy as an answer to prayer. Marriage had radically altered the pattern of his life. He longed for the days when he'd been able to be alone, when he was free to fill his mind with God and preaching. He and Helga were together night and day. On the road they lived in hotel rooms. At home they seldom entertained and seldom went out to dinner. Because their lives were public, they guarded the time between campaigns.

Jimmy had become profoundly weary of the smiling, gracious lady who was in private a narcissistic shrew. He was weary of her self-love, weary of her insatiable need for the adulation of strangers. When they were alone, Helga heaped scorn on the people who attended their meetings, mimicking with malicious skill the women who served on committees. Sometimes Jimmy would rise to preach filled with rage, struggling to remove Helga from his mind and to establish a rapport with the audience.

With Helga two months pregnant, he'd dropped her off at a private hospital in Chicago "for a check-up," continuing on to Toronto to visit his mother. They were at breakfast when the bad news came. He returned from the phone, his eyes blank with pain. "She's lost the baby."

He went to the basement, pacing in the darkness, praying, questioning. After a while, his mother brought a steaming mug of tea and they went to sit in the kitchen. It was she who put in his mind the thought that Helga had had an abortion.

"I didn't say she *did*. All I said was, it doesn't make sense. You tell me she's been having no trouble. Then she goes into this private hospital for a check-up and loses the baby. Why in Chicago and not in Wheaton? Why this Dr. Magruder rather than her own doctor? That's all I'm saying ... I should mind my own business."

His hurt needed a target. "Yes, you should. You don't like her."

"Don't be ridiculous."

"You haven't since day one."

"All right then!" Lizzie flared. "How often has she been in my home in all the years you've been married?"

He let it drop and the following day drove to Wheaton. It was late when he pulled into the driveway. The house was dark. Helga was in bed. He lay, his hands behind his head, watching the light from passing cars traversing the ceiling. He thought she was asleep but she suddenly said, "I'm sorry we lost the baby." He made no response.

After breakfast the next day, he asked her why she had gone to a hospital for a check-up. Had Dr. Cameron referred her to the Magruder hospital? And if he'd wanted her in hospital, why not in town where he could look in on her?

She was patient with him at first, responding as one might to a slow-witted child. But as he continued, her lips compressed and she made an exaggerated sigh.

"Jimmy, everybody around here knows me. I'm tired of being fawned over. Doris Green told me about Dr. Magruder and... Look, can we drop it, for Christ sake!"

"You didn't miscarry, did you?"

She glared at him. "Your mother put that in your head, didn't she? She just can't stand not having her big son – her preacher son – at her beck and call."

"You had an abortion."

Each word was accented equally: "No, I did not have an abortion."

"Helga, why go on with the charade? You didn't want the baby. You've been impossible ever since you learned you were pregnant. And when does this famous miscarriage happen? – conveniently on the day after we close in Moline, when you know I'm going to Toronto."

She turned on him and began to shout. "All *right*! No, I didn't have a miscarriage! Yes, I had an abortion! Is that what you want to hear? Okay, you've heard it. Are you happy now?"

He was seeing only her mouth: the red lips contorted, the spittle spraying ... "Did they let you see it?" he asked. "Our child? Or shall we always think of him as a blob of bloody mucous at the bottom of a pail?"

"My body is my own," she said quietly. "If you want children so much, why don't you adopt them?"

As the traffic toward New York City picked up speed, Helga's voice cut into his thoughts. "Well, why do you think I broke our lunch date at the Faculty Club?"

"Okay," he said, his mind far away, "why did you break it?"

"Because something better came up." She laughed coarsely. "Hey! That's good: something better came up." She continued to laugh in a taunting manner.

"Are you trying to tell me something?"

"I don't know," she said lightly. "Am I?"

"Helga, I'm in no mood to play games. Are you telling me that ..." He drew back from finishing the sentence.

"Say it plainly, Jimmy. Am I telling you what?"

"That you went to bed with somebody this afternoon?"

"What a thing to say!" Her voice was mocking. "*I* said I went to bed with somebody this afternoon? *I* said no such thing. You know I wouldn't do anything like that."

He decided not to pursue it. At the airport, as he parked in the area reserved for rented cars, she said, "Not even with someone in the department of history," and got out of the car.

41

It was close to midnight when Jimmy Coulter entered the lobby of the Waldorf Astoria Hotel in New York City. He had been out walking, and wore a hat and horn-rimmed glasses, and had turned up the collar of his topcoat to avoid recognition. A man coming from the bar bumped into him and turned, full of apology.

"Sorry, friend. Sorry 'bout that. Scuse me."

Coulter said, "Leo McGeer!"

McGeer peered at Jimmy, eyes blinking, unsteady on his feet. Then he recognized him. "Jimmy! For goodness sake!"

A woman was with him. Her makeup was overdone and her black hair had an orange cast. Studying Coulter, her eyebrows rose and her mouth dropped. "Jesus H. Christ!" she said. "Jimmy Coulter!"

McGeer turned on her, going off balance as he did. "Will you shut up! Just shut up, will you?"

"What'd I do? I know it's him. I've seen him on the TV."

Jimmy wanted to extricate himself. "I'm just on my way to bed." He put a hand on McGeer's arm. "Take care."

Leo McGeer drunk and whoring! In his room, Coulter felt a pang of desolation. He had been close to despair all day, needing to talk to someone, someone with whom he could be candid, who would understand the irresolution in his mind and the questions that had been renewed by his conversation with Roger Whitton. It couldn't be any of his associates or anyone who might judge him or betray his confidence. He thought of how McGeer had helped him find the way in his early years.

At 2:30 there was a knocking at his door. It persisted. He went to the door but didn't open it. "Yes?"

217

"It's me. Leo."

He shepherded McGeer to a chair. He was lurching on his feet, but years of training enabled him to control his slurring speech. He told how he'd learned the room number by tipping a bellboy. "They all know you're here," he said with a wink, "but nobody's talkin'—if you know what I mean." He rambled on, offering an elaborate explanation for his being in New York City. Jimmy, trying to adjust to what was happening, said little.

After an extended silence, McGeer said, "You're wonderin' what gives. Right?"

"No," Jimmy said. "It's none of my business."

McGeer loosened his tie and undid his collar. "If you're thinking about Barb, don't. There's been nothin' there since the year we were married."

Jimmy was thinking about Helga and the professor in the department of history at Yale.

"I'm in the ministry, I'm a preacher, so I shouldn't take a drink. Right?" McGeer was saying. "Okay, okay. I know that. I've been a preacher since I was six, remember. Six!"

The thought silenced him for a moment. Then he sat back in the chair. "You're not saying much."

"Tell you the truth, Leo—I don't know what to say. I'm trying to get my bearings."

"It's very simple. Just blowin' off a little steam. Everybody blows off a little steam once in a while. Right?" He fixed his eyes on Jimmy. "Except you?"

"I'm not your judge, Leo."

McGeer looked about. "You wouldn't have anythin' to drink? No, of course you wouldn't." Again, he focused his gaze on Jimmy. "How's it going, Jimmy boy?"

Desperate to relieve his mind, Coulter said, "I've been having trouble with that old problem of doubt. In fact, I've been thinking of those talks we used to have."

McGeer looked at him owlishly, his head bobbing forward. "Still worryin' about doubt?" He was silent, letting it register. "You know somethin', you're a lucky guy. You don't know how lucky. No, I mean it—worryin' about what you believe and don't believe. With me, believin' in God is like believin' in the timestables. Know what I mean? When I was still in diapers I was tellin' everybody what to believe." He laughed. "Didn't have the

218

foggiest notion what it was all about." His eyes glazed as the memory revived. "Six years old. My mother used to sit behind me on the platform, and if I couldn't remember the sermon she made me memorize, she beat the shit out of me when we got back to the hotel ... Sorry, shouldn't have said that. Not about my mother, I mean my language. What was I? A fuckin' puppet, that's what I was. Oops! Sorry!"

Finally, Coulter broached the question. "Then why do you stay in the ministry? Why don't you get out?"

McGeer jerked his head, snapping it upright. "Good question. Why don't I quit? Granted, I should. But why should I? What would I do? It's all I know. And I'm good at it. Right? And who'm I hurtin'?" His head went down. "The way I see it, religion owes me. I'm not takin' anythin' I haven't paid for ... In church every night of my life until I was in my teens." He looked up at Jimmy, near tears. "D'you have any idea what it was like? Didn't go to school. No friends. Never played on a team ..." He reined in his emotions. "The way I see it, religion owes me."

He sagged, as though the pressure had gone from him, leaving him deflated. "Anyway, what'm I s'posed to do – sell used cars?"

42

During the winter of 1955 the snows had been especially heavy in the Alps and on the upland pastures of the Lombardy plains in northern Italy. Spring came swiftly and settled in with warm, drenching rains. The runoff spilled from the alpine passes to become the Po river, and quickly accumulating, rushed eastward seeking the Adriatic. The embankments ruptured at a number of places but not sufficiently to ease the mounting pressure. Just west of Ferrara, swollen, gray and heavy with silt, the river breached its containment, debouching a wall of water that went racing through the valley with a sound of thunder, inundating towns and villages and farmland, carrying everything with it, and as it slowed, depositing a sodden alluvium in a great spreading fan of mud and debris.

Jimmy Coulter, with Michael Cardinal Maloney of the Archdiocese of New York and the Most Reverend Jesse Angus Schaeffer, President of the National Council of Churches, were flown from Washington to Milan and then by helicopter to the scene of the flood. They had come as emissaries of President Adam Scott and as representatives of the church.

As their helicopter set down, a brazen sun was glowing in a cloudless sky and there was little wind. The crest of the flood, roaring down the valley, had dumped its debris in a cul-de-sac. Hundreds of dead were heaped in a tangle of bodies, twisted and pinioned by each other and by the uprooted trees and boulders borne with them in the waters.

The three men were soon enveloped in the stench of rotting flesh. They talked with officials and rescue workers, and preceded by a jostling circle of reporters and photographers, moved on to a five-square-mile area where the flood waters had run off, leaving a flat plain of silt.

The dead lay strewn about like discarded toys, half buried in the mud. They came upon the face of an old man – all that was visible. It was as though a death mask had been placed on a table. The eye sockets, the gaping mouth, even the nostrils, were filled with silt. The long hair lay in sodden ropes.

Numbed, they went on, seeing here a hand thrust through the surface, the fingers clutched and rigid; seeing there the breasts and swollen belly of a woman arched in a frozen agony. It was as though an enormous cleaver had sliced off portions of bodies and laid them randomly on a dun-colored table. Survivors wandered about, their eyes dull as the sediment. Some sat in the muck, keening. Others wailed or sobbed in a dissonant chorus. A few knelt before Cardinal Maloney, pressing forward to put their lips to his hands or clothing; others reached out toward Reverend Schaeffer in his clericals. They took Jimmy Coulter to be an official, held out their hands to him and then turned away.

At midnight Jimmy Coulter sat alone on the shore of the Adriatic. The villa was silent, the night warm, lit only by the stars and one bare bulb that illuminated the path to the shore. In the darkness, waves seemed to rear like great phalanxes of black horses, thundering in, shaking their crested heads and collapsing on the beach. He saw again those pitiful figures, turning in their desperation to Maloney and Schaeffer but not to him. It was as well; he had nothing to give them.

There was no sound other than the cannonading of the sea and a soft sibilance as shallow rills of water ran up on the sand. He felt an urge to walk into the water until he was lost in its depths. The urge grew so strong that another part of his brain took alarm and thrust him to his feet, turning him back to the villa.

He'd been sitting in the darkness of his room when the telephone rang. At first, Jimmy hadn't recognized the voice, thick with fatigue and without intonation. Adam Scott asked about the devastation but made no comment. As they talked it was obvious that he hadn't called for counsel, but simply to hear the voice of a friend, a voice that wouldn't make demands, that wouldn't press him in one direction or another.

"Sorry I've rambled on so," he said dispiritedly. "You might remember me in your prayers tonight ..."

Coulter put down the phone and paced in the darkness of his room. Here is a man whose responsibilities, particularly at the moment, are awesome. He turns to someone he believes can help him. And what is he given? Empty words.

What had Jesus said? *If your children asked you for bread would you give them a stone?*

43

---

progress report–wedger

Clyde:

Having spent the morning with Helga Nostrand Coulter, my view of her husband has changed. I begin to wonder if he may not one day be canonized as a Christian martyr. His lady-love to put it plainly, is a pain in the posterior.

To begin, she kept me waiting in her living room for an hour and ten minutes while, it's my guess, she was busy fabricating the façade she presents to the public. When she made her appearance–and she enters as though onto a stage–it was something to behold: not a hair out of place; skin akin to those on air-brushed color photos of society matrons. In the filtered light of the room, in a caftan of ornamented silk that must have set her husband back a love offering or two, she was a knockout.

Without a word of apology for being late, she looked at her wristwatch, mentioned that her time was limited and told me to proceed. First, however, she wanted to know if I had seen her on the platform. I confessed I hadn't but was looking forward to the Toronto opportunity. She was visibly disappointed. I tried to draw her out about her early years but she wasn't interested–"That's all been done." I asked about her conversion experience (this whole born-again thing is still a mystery to me), but she seemed bored. Nor would she go into detail about how she and Coulter met. "You seem obsessed with the past."

She brightened when I concentrated on her and the increasing role she was playing in the campaign services. Had she ever wanted to preach? No, women shouldn't preach–but she does

223

want to extend "her ministry." She sees it as "holding a conversation with the congregation in an intimate manner, touching people where they live." She feels that life has given her unique experiences, among them the opportunity to meet "most of the great men and women of our time." She wants to talk about these people in a kind of Chatty Kathy fashion, using them to illustrate Bible truths. Sounds to me like name-dropping for Jesus.

In a word, I found her cold, self-centered and ambitious. As far as I could see, her interest in things spiritual is nonexistent.

Far more intriguing was a conversation I had at dinner with Karl Buehl and Tony Rodriguez. Buehl is city editor at the Journal. It may be ancient history to you but I hadn't known that Mr. Hoffman became a citizen of the United States by a special act of Congress. Apparently, William Ralston Hunt, who founded what is now the Hoffman Press, lost his marbles late in life and became paranoid. Built himself this Rhine castle in the Sierras, complete with a moat. (There was a joke at the time that he even stocked it with piranha!) Killed himself by putting his head in the bowl of an imported Italian toilet, encircling it with his arms and continuing to do so until he was dead. There were years of litigation over the estate and finally the courts ordered it sold. Hoffman bought it. But a non-American is not permitted to own a newspaper, so Congress passed a bill making him a citizen of the United States, *retroactively*. This led to problems in Canada– a similar law obtains there–but the Chief's friend, Mackenzie King, solved that.

Tony tells me, incidentally, that Mr. Hoffman's wife is twenty-four years his junior and leads him a merry chase. Fancies herself an actress and hangs out with a group of Hollywood swingers of all three sexes. (Could explain the Chief's interest in the Rimmington episode.) The scuttlebutt is he'd love to dump her but won't because of California's community property laws.

Tony also gave me an intriguing lead on a mysterious four-month disappearance by Coulter back in the fifties. I'll fill you in on my return Wednesday. It will necessitate a trip to England.

Jenny

44

He had been on the Isle of Wight for almost a month, living in an old cottage with foot-thick whitewashed walls, low ceilings and a thatched roof that was home to families of mice. The cottage had only two rooms, but there was a fireplace in the main room, and the kitchen had a woodstove and enough pots and dishes for simple living. Coulter had arranged to rent it through Jay Conant, his lawyer, and was using Conant's name so that he wouldn't be betrayed by the initials on his luggage. The cottage was on the north coast about five miles from Caithness, a hamlet of about forty people who subsisted mainly by sheepherding and fishing. There was little likelihood of his being recognized; no one in the town had television and the newspaper most circulated was a thin country weekly which carried only local news. He had grown a beard, not for purposes of anonymity but because there seemed no point in shaving.

He had come to Caithness after the three days at Ravenna during which he'd become increasingly depressed and withdrawn. Cardinal Maloney and Dr. Schaeffer had returned to Washington and he'd gone on alone to London to lay over at the Savoy Hotel until word came that the arrangement had been made at Caithness.

He'd chosen Caithness because it was where Mr. Rimmington had been born and raised and where his body had been shipped when he died. On the first day, he walked to the cemetery – having seen it as he was being driven from town in a dilapidated trap along the sheep track that served as a road. He had no trouble finding the grave. Most of the markers were old, the legend on many of them erased by time and the sea air. Mr. Rimmington's was a small bronze plaque fixed to a marble slab and was almost grown over by weeds.

Howard Llewellyn
RIMMINGTON
1889-1932
Not much happened

Sitting in the weeds beside it, remembering, there were no tears
or sadness. Biting on the pulpy end of a stalk of timothy – as he'd
so often done in imitation of his mentor – he wondered if perhaps
he'd come because Mr. Rimmington more than anyone else had
given direction to his life when he needed it. It was Mr. Rimmington who had stimulated his interest in words, in books, in writing;
in grass and tree and beast and field, and in man and God. How
often when life was cruel he'd remembered Billy Miles. Could it be
that Mr. Rimmington's doubts were also a part of his legacy?

Each morning he rose at dawn and walked the countryside, usually skirting the chalk cliffs that tumbled untidily to the Solent. It
was poor land, mostly hard clay. The long grasses were sere and
brittle in the December cold. He'd bought warm outer clothing in
London, but when the wind blew from either of the northern
quarters he was often bone-chilled. There were days when he was
glad for the beard. There were other days when there was no wind;
ghostly, with a fog that isolated him in a gray sphere and made him
take care when he walked. The damp penetrated his clothing and
crept under doorsills and around windows into the cottage. There
were sawed logs stacked at the back. Each morning he split some,
and kept the fireplace roaring and the stove ruby red and an iron
kettle on the boil.

A nondescript dog, a collie of sorts, joined him the second day
and met him each morning. It would trot on ahead, checking over
its shoulder if he stopped, and when he sat would sit near him. For
all his calling to it, it wouldn't approach close enough to be patted.
Nor at the end of the walk would it go with him into the cottage.
He named it Rimmy.

Jimmy was no cook and subsisted mostly on eggs and a side of
bacon and porridge and sometimes stews – which reminded him of
his childhood. He bathed standing in a copper washtub drawn close
to the stove, rinsing by sluicing the water over his head and down
his body.

Three weeks after he arrived, a two-wheel cart drawn by a
shaggy draft-horse creaked to the gate, and Mr. Rheese, who ran

226

the general store in Caithness, helped him carry in a wooden box. It was from Fortnum and Mason's in London and was filled with expensive jams and biscuits and dried fruits and hams and canned foods, all nested in excelsior. A note indicated that the sender was Jay Conant. Included were copies of the *Times* and the Manchester *Guardian* and the European edition of the *Herald-Tribune*. He twisted them into slender faggots, avoiding even a headline, and put them in the fire.

There were no books in the cottage and no radio. He had expected to be lonely but he wasn't. He had thought he might brood through the days and into the night but he didn't. Rather, he was often filled with an expanding sense of well-being. He began to talk to himself, sometimes upbraiding himself for not using the time, but wasn't responsive to the accusations. With a slight smile he'd speak aloud Scarlett O'Hara's words: "I'll think about it tomorrow."

He'd committed himself to go up to London to spend Christmas at the Savoy Hotel. In the hired car, on roads heavy with holiday traffic, he broke from the euphoria. Here was the real world; it could no longer be thrust away. Everything was being jeopardized by the contradictions in his life. He dare not continue with the accumulated tension which at times almost incapacitated him, manifesting itself in alarming pains in his chest and arms and back. Little wonder: he was being torn between mind and heart, pulled one way by his obligations and another by his desires. Others might stand in envy, taking him to have everything, yet here he was at the pinnacle of his life, at the height of his powers, desperate and confused.

On his return from London he would use the isolation and the solitude to think and pray things through.

PART SIX

The Present

45

Jimmy Coulter came to Washington this week: the propounder of
the laws of God mingling with the fabricators of the laws of men,
God and Mammon in confrontation. It was no contest.

Coulter was here to launch what will be, by declaration of the
Congress, an annual Salute America Week, seven days of un-
abashed patriotism coincident with the heady days of spring.
Who better to inaugurate the event? Jimmy Coulter, now into his
sixties, has come to symbolize the homely virtues to which
Americans pay lip service on great public occasions. Then, too,
he was the nominee of President Adam Scott, a choice confirmed by unanimous vote of Congress.

His appearance was, of course, a media event. Coulter is a
Madison Avenue dream realized, being photogenic, larger than
life and eminently quotable. It was also a political event, although
Coulter, aware of Billy Graham's Gethsemane after his too close
relationship with Richard Nixon, eschewed any word or act that
might be judged partisan.

What is this fascination that evangelist Jimmy Coulter—and Billy
Graham before him—has for presidents and lesser politicians?
Graham was a close friend of Dwight Eisenhower (although not of
John Kennedy) and especially of Lyndon Johnson and Richard
Nixon. On Johnson's last night in office, Graham was his White
House guest. He went with Johnson to the inauguration cere-
mony. After the oath had been administered to Richard Nixon, he

a copy next

led in prayer. And when Nixon arrived at the White House to take up his tenancy, Graham greeted him on the portico and stayed the night. In more recent years, Jimmy Coulter has taken over as the familiar at the executive mansion.

Coulter arrived in Washington Friday evening aboard a jet dispatched to convey him from his home in California. He was preceded down the stairway by his wife, a former Miss America, and was greeted by Vice President Ethan Roberts.

The Coulters spent the night at the White House in the bedroom directly above the president's. Coulter must know the room well: he jokes about "staying at the White House Hilton whenever I'm in Washington."

I studied Jimmy Coulter the following morning at the Congressional Prayer Breakfast, a barbaric custom which, depending on who the guest speaker is, brings forth a handful or a host of the nation's political brass at the ungodly hour of seven A.M. to backslap and *bon-mot* each other until such time as the speaker is introduced and it becomes appropriate to render unto God rather than Caesar.

I've attended a number of these rituals without discerning any improvement in the ethics or moral sensibility of the members. It should be recorded, however, that Senator _____ (in Christian charity, he will go unnamed) who has spent at least half of his life in Washington dozing (seated or standing) did manage to stay awake through Dr. Coulter's 20-minute peroration. If ever a move is made to beatify the famed evangelist on the ground of undoubted miracles, this accomplishment alone should withstand the scrutiny of the most hostile Devil's Advocate.

Off to the Burning Tree Country Club for a morning round of golf with the president. I can report that Coulter, who is known to be a "sports nut," hooks his woods, swings like a rusty gate, but putts as though there is a magnet in the cup. As he holed-out on the eighteenth–as might any celebrity who knows the value of a souvenir–he inscribed his name on the ball and tossed it into the crowd, quipping, "As the Apostle Paul said, 'I have finished the course!'"

b copy next

At noon, a press conference. Dr. Coulter fielded twenty-one questions. I kept score: seven on the world situation–it was seen as endangered by Godless communism; five on the state of the nation–it was seen as endangered by secularism; four on the state of Christianity–it was seen as endangered by liberalism; two on the state of the economy–it was seen as endangered by the loss of that old-fashioned Calvinist ethic of an honest day's work for a fair day's pay; one on the status of women–it was seen as endangered by the withdrawal of too many women from child-bearing and homemaking; and one on television program-ing, which was seen as endangered by too much violence and an increasing sexuality.

In summary: Dr. Coulter sees all of our institutions as under fire but is nonetheless encouraged, believing that America's tradi-tional faith in God will enable her to persevere. You may sleep soundly tonight, citizen.

I wandered among the crowd at the Jefferson Memorial for the mass public rally held there. For a full forty minutes, fifty thou-sand Americans stood or sat on the approaches to the monu-ment, mesmerized by the preacher's words.

What did he say? He reiterated the denunciations of the Old Testament prophet, Amos, applying them to the United States; and followed this with a penny lecture on the evils of contempo-rary American life, those evils being drinking, sexual promiscuity, drugs, me-firstism and general godlessness. No mention was made, however, of the sins of big government, of warmongers at the Pentagon, of covert plotters at the CIA, of the exploiters of minorities, of the creators of acid rain, of the fabricators of unsafe cars, of the despoilers of natural resources, of shoddy housing contractors or, indeed, of any of those corporate sins which, in this city, stand as natural targets for thunderbolts.

He was given a standing ovation, which, to one observer, seemed curious. If in the name of God you have been truly denounced, shouldn't you want to crucify rather than clap?

That aside, a Jimmy Coulter mass meeting is something unique. There is no ambience in all the world to compare with it.

c copy next

The atmosphere pulses with an excitement usually found only at a major sports event. It is an emotional compost of anticipation, aspiration, reverence and guilt. The skeptics are there with the zealots and the ecstatics. Some are there to confirm their biases, the sick in hope of touching the hem of the garment, the world weary and heavy laden hoping for rest. There are many of the meek and lowly of heart, finding themselves by identifying with the dazzling man on the platform. And there are the misfits who, at long-postponed last, have found the one glory place where they *belong*!

Through Jimmy Coulter lives are changed—let no one deny it—some so radically as to seem new. Families are united, or sometimes split asunder. Alcoholics come to sobriety. Crimes are confessed to. Minds teetering near the brink may tumble over the edge into madness. Visions are seen, some more brilliantly delineated than the psychedelic's. The young may have their feet set on paths of service that will lead them to the ends of the earth.

All this happens, and more. Not necessarily with any permanence. When the magic leaves town, the prosaic begins to recoup its lost ground. Studies show that a year later the numbers added to church rolls are few. Vows are forgotten. The daily grind of Christian service discourages the faint of heart. The light flickers out, and for some the darkness is the darker. Congregations fall into schism as the newly anointed insist that all march to their drummer's beat.

Things are better, things are worse, things are much the same.

Is a Coulter campaign worth the energy and the money spent? The answer is yes or no depending on the yardstick used. Its greatest benefit would seem to be the providing of a booster shot for those who are already Christian. But the campaign does raise for consideration the central questions of life, even if it deals with them in a puerile fashion. It causes many to scrutinize their own lives, and it exposes thousands to the glories of the King James English of the Bible.

Beyond that, an old-fashioned evangelistic campaign perpetu-

d copy next

ates one of the great frontier traditions of the nation. With the passing of Jimmy Coulter and Billy Graham, the probability is that the phenomenon will go from the scene. In this, the evangelistic campaign of America's earlier years is not unlike the traveling circus of the same era. When the circus came to town— brassy, spangled and heart-stopping—it was the event of the season. Under the big top, wonder and excitement passed from heart to heart until all were joined in a single emotion and all became children again. You were certain you would never forget the skills, the beauty and the daring you had witnessed.

But you did. The ordinary returned, and the collective thrill that had run the spine like a xylophone mallet faded. Today, transferred to television, the circus from time to time thrills, but it is a pale shadow of the old. In the same way, the stark preachments and the raw emotions of the old-fashioned evangelistic campaign do not survive the tiny screen. Television evangelism is a gelded thing.

At Jimmy Coulter's press conference he announced that in two weeks he would be returning to his home city of Toronto for a campaign. "We have to keep in touch with our roots," he said.

Having followed the world's most renowned evangelist through the day that launched Salute America Week, one is convinced that his roots are indeed in Canada. But not in Jerusalem.

46

"Do I remember him? Of course I remember him. I might forget
Cary Grant or Alfred Hitchcock, but not Jimmy Coulter!"

Archibald Hemmings, formerly desk clerk at London's Savoy
Hotel, was well into his seventies, and as Jenny Wedger climbed
the stairs to his lodgings on the third floor of a row-house on
Balaclava Lane, she worried that he might be senile. It was soon
evident that he wasn't. He spoke rapidly and in the direct manner of
the aged who have decided to have done with unnecessary civility.

"There isn't anybody worth mentioning who hasn't stayed at
the Savoy," he said. "Prime Ministers, movie stars, royalty ... we
had them all. Still do, I suppose. Many of them I can't remember,
but I'm not likely to forget Jimmy Coulter. I was given the sack
because of him."

Jenny was content to let Hemmings proceed at his own pace. It
had taken her three days to find him: hours of looking at microfilm
in the morgues at the *Mirror* and the *Express*, finally to come upon
a bit of booty, a brief story from December 1955, noting that Dr.
Jimmy Coulter was in the city, was staying at the Savoy and had
refused to talk to the press; then the better part of a day at the
hotel, walking on eggs with people sticky about the privacy of their
guests. Only two of them had been at the hotel more than twenty
years. Neither would respond to her queries, but one yielded
enough to suggest she have a chat with Archie Hemmings.

"You say you were sacked because of Jimmy Coulter," Jenny
asked Hemmings. "Whatever for?"

"Because I gave a tip to a journalist friend of mine at the
Express, Patrick Greene, that Dr. Coulter was in the hotel." He

laughed with a wheezing sound. "We used to pass the word along. A little extra to play the pools, if you follow my meaning."

"Do you recall anything unusual about Dr. Coulter's visit?"

"Depends on what you consider unusual. Like registering under another name?"

"He registered under a false name?"

"Dr. Coulter didn't. You couldn't in those days. You had to turn in your passport. Somebody else registered but Dr. Coulter moved in. Wearing a beard, but I recognized him. Not much went on I didn't know about."

"Do you remember anything else?"

"Just that it was Christmas. And that he was in the hotel two days and never went out."

"Did he have any visitors?"

Hemmings' eyebrows arched and a wide smile rearranged the network of wrinkles. "Not in the usual sense," he said, and chuckled.

"I don't understand?"

He gave Jenny a solemn wink and lowered his voice. "Not much that went on I didn't know about, if you follow my meaning."

Jenny took a five-pound note from her handbag, folded it and placed it under an ashtray on the coffee table between them. "A little extra to play the pools," she said.

"He had a lady friend in the adjoining room."

Jenny felt excitement stir. "You're sure about that?"

Hemmings peered reproachfully at her over the top of his glasses.

"I didn't mean I don't believe you, but how do you know?"

"Not many secrets in a hotel," Hemmings said, his moment of pique passing, "especially on Christmas Day when things are quiet. His bed wasn't slept in. The maid turned it down, she told me, and that's the way it was in the morning. And room service ... Didn't order a thing all the time he was in the hotel." A twinkle came into his eye. "On the other hand, the lady in the adjoining room ordered service for two – breakfast, lunch and dinner. Except there was never anyone but her in the room when the waiter laid out the table."

"The rooms connected?"

"Dr. Coulter's was a suite but, yes, they connected."

Jenny took a breath and held it. "You don't happen to recall the name of the woman?"

Hemmings squinted in thought and the wrinkles polarized as iron filings about a magnet. After a moment, he shook his head and said "Sorry."

"There's no way I could take a look at the registration book?"

"From twenty years ago? They've got dozens of them over twenty years. They're in storage."

Jenny looked about her. It was obvious that Hemmings lived not far from poverty. She decided to risk offending him. "Mr. Hemmings," she said, "you've been very helpful and I appreciate it. The story is an important one to me. I've come here from Canada to follow it up. It would be worth fifty pounds to me to learn the lady's name. Is there any way that could be arranged?"

Hemmings gave a prolonged wink. "Come see me around tea time tomorrow."

She offered to take Paddy Greene to dinner but he would have none of that and took her instead to Hobley's, a pub on Fleet Street. It was chaotic with talk and laughter and redolent with the scent of beer. They had to put their heads close to be heard.

"So you've been to see old Hemmie," Paddy shouted. "I'm afraid I was the cause of him getting the sack. He tipped me off that your Mr. C. was in the hotel and I marched right over and knocked on the door of his suite. Pretty brash in those days. Got short shrift. The management heard about it and fired poor Hemmie. Tell him hello."

"In the item you did, you said that Mr. C. had come from the Isle of Wight. Did you look into what he was doing there?"

"Wanted to, but couldn't convince the desk."

"How did you find out he went to the Isle of Wight?"

"He'd hired a car. Anglia Car-Hire, if memory serves. They had all the data, of course. Driver's license. Destination. I checked with their office in Portsmouth. He'd taken the ferry to Wight. I don't know where from there. It's my guess he was on a holiday. You think it was more than that?"

"I really don't know at this point."

Paddy grinned at her. "Dr. Jimmy Coulter comes to England for some unknown reason twenty years ago, and here you are at this

238

late date looking into it." His smile broadened. "You've no intention of telling me what you're onto, have you?"

Jenny smiled at him.

"Ah well," Paddy Greene said. "Drink up."

Archibald Hemmings heard Jenny on the stairs and called out, "Come in. Come in."

"I'll need another fifty pounds," he said. "It cost me the first fifty to get my friend to do it."

And to think I was afraid he might take offense if I offered him money, Jenny thought, going into her purse.

Hemmings squinted at a piece of paper. "The woman's name is Arla Todd. The address she gave is Beverly Hills, California."

47

At midnight, the quarrel with Helga finally spent, Jimmy Coulter slumped in an armchair in the darkness of his study, legs thrust out before him, chin on his chest, depleted. In her bedroom Helga lay face down, sobbing into the bedspread. After a while she went to the bathroom to gulp five grains of valium. In her room at the far end of the house, Juanita whispered into the telephone, from time to time casting frightened glances at the door. Off somewhere, forgotten, a television set sent hollow laughter through the house.

It had begun at dinner. Helga had come to the table in a foul mood, having nurtured real and imaginary grievances throughout the day. With the Toronto campaign less than a week away, Jimmy's days were full. He was home only for dinner, if then, and gone in the mornings before she was up.

Helga's day had begun badly. There had been a letter for Jimmy from Honolulu and for half an hour she debated whether to open it. But then she thought: why not? Kathryn had stuck her nose in after promising not to. The way Julie had taken to her was enough to make you sick.

Rather than leave the letter on the silver tray in the entrance hall, she gave it to Jimmy as they went in to dinner. He scanned it and put it in a pocket. When Juanita removed the soup bowls and went to the kitchen, Helga asked, "Well? What's with that sister of yours?"

"You know. You've read the letter."

Juanita entered, served them and left. The door to the kitchen had only swung closed when Helga said, "The nerve calling me Miss Candy-Floss! I've had enough! She can stay out of our lives." She poked at her food, then pushed it away. "That filthy mouth of hers. You said yourself she was a tramp."

"Helga, just stop it! Stop it right now!"

He was drum-tight with tension. He had spent the past two hours with TG. Reports had been coming from some of the staff of persistent queries by Hoffman Press reporters, of prying into the financial structure of the Association. And there had been that long list of questions about his beliefs. What could have prompted *that*? He scented danger. He had refused to talk to that woman from the *Tribune* and had considered telling Helga not to see her, but had finally said nothing.

"A tramp," Helga was saying, "that's what she is. An easy lay. A street-corner whore. She was once, she is now."

"You of all people to talk about a filthy mouth," he said.

"I say what I think. If it offends your precious lily-white ears, that's too goddam bad. No wonder you've never told the children who their mother is."

"What difference does it make now?" he said, wanting to drop it. "Haven't they turned out all right?"

But she wasn't prepared to be mollified. "Never mind their mother," she harangued. "We know about her. What about their father? Who was he? Some sailor with the Chinese clap, for all we know. I'll bet she laid anybody with the price of a drink."

He thrust his chair from the table with a violence that overturned an elaborate floral centerpiece, sending water cascading to the carpet. He went out onto the balcony. It was growing dark. Combers from a distant storm were crashing on the shore. Helga followed him, her voice filled with venom.

"Don't you walk out on me," she shouted. "I wanted to tell the children from the beginning, but no, wait a while, you said. That while never came, and now I'm being drawn into your lies. What else could I do when Julie brought it up? But don't expect me to keep on lying for you. It's your mess. You didn't have the guts to tell them about that slut of a sister of yours."

All the years of estrangement were surfacing. "The Reverend Mr. Holy Joe," she screamed. "Thou shalt not lie. Thou shalt not bear false witness. Tells everybody else how to live but not so hot at it himself. Oh, you're something! You really are."

He spun on her. "I said I was wrong, didn't I? I should have told them. I admit it. I'm sorry."

"He was wrong," she mocked. "He admits it. Twenty-four years late the Great Procrastinator admits it. Somebody mark it down – it's a first." She stepped in close and lifted her face to his.

"So what are you expecting, Mr. Goody-two-shoes–a medal? Somebody to pat you on your pretty little head and say, 'There's a good boy! He was wrong and he's sorry.'"

He searched back for something with which to wound. "There'd have been no need to adopt anyone's children," he said, his voice cold with malevolence, "if you hadn't murdered your own."

Now it was loosed: the resentment that had lain like a fearsome, hibernating beast through the long winter of their alienation. All the dormant memories swarmed like loathsome slugs from a rotten carcass: the visit to Dr. Magruder's hospital, and later, the operation to make further visits unnecessary. Nor had she sought to hide it but had brazenly confessed it, laying the responsibility at his feet. Hadn't she warned him that there would be no children until she was ready? Would *he* be willing to do what he was asking of her – to change his life, to tie himself down, to sit at home while she was off gadding about the world? To have his body ballooned, stretched, scarred? Easy for the man to talk!

Now that the slumbering rage was awake, he found himself lusting to rend and tear and wound. With practiced skill he chose the words. "Perhaps it's good we didn't have children. They might have been like their mother in her utter absorption with herself. It's better they were never born. Their mother would have held it against them that they usurped her precious time and flawed her precious beauty. Don't tell me it's easy for the man, that the man doesn't bear the pain and suffer the stretch marks ... *You didn't bear them either!* 'Scrape the life off the wall of my womb, Dr. Magruder. Suck the budding brain and the beating heart and the tissue that will be arms and legs and fingers and toes. Suck it out of my body and dump it dead in a pail. It will mar my beauty. It will rob me of the spotlight!'" He spat out the final words. "It might require me to be a real woman."

He turned and went down the stairs to his study, every nerve vibrating, every muscle aching, his skull ready to explode ... and filled with self-loathing. He had vowed that the words would never be spoken, but the need to wound had been greater. Over the years they had quarreled often, but the boundaries had never been breached. Now the last tenuous connections between them were gone. A numbness stole through him like the onset of an anesthetic. He stood against a wall of book shelves, his forehead on his arms, his brow depressing a row of books. He didn't hear Helga on the stairway, and when she spoke her voice startled him.

"Too selfish to be a real woman, was I?" Her words were measured but her voice was quivering. "Wouldn't let a baby rob me of the spotlight? Well, did you? Why do you think Jonathan won't talk to you? You were so busy being the great Jimmy Coulter you didn't have time to be a father! How often I watched him as a little boy trying to have you to himself, all to himself for just an hour. For a baseball game. For a camping trip. But you? You were so in love with your work—no, goddammit, *not* God's work, *your* work!—seeing this senator or that president or this broadcaster or that reporter. What about you as a father?" Her voice vibrated with passion. "Don't you *dare* lay it all on me!"

Later, having gone through the house looking for her, he found her sitting in the darkness by the pool. There was no moon and no wind, but the sound of the surf was loud and at first she didn't hear his question.

"I said, what was I supposed to do," he shouted, "leave the ministry?"

"I left mine."

He laughed in disbelief. "You're not serious?"

"Deadly serious."

"Helga, come on! I mean ..."

"What you mean is: what you were doing was too important to be interrupted and what I was doing wasn't."

"Well, if it comes down to that—yes. That's exactly what I mean."

"Talk about wanting the spotlight! Who were you when we met—just a nobody. And suddenly all that publicity. *My* publicity. Wasn't that why you married me?" She chuckled humorlessly. "How many campaigns did Jimmy Coulter get back then, and how many, Jimmy Calder?" She laughed mockingly, then kept the laughter going.

"How long are you going to keep up that insane cackling?"

She made as though quoting from a newspaper. "Helga Nostrand, Miss America, lost a slipper on the way to the altar to marry Canadian evangelist, Jimmy Calder ..." Her laughter took on a mocking gaiety.

He had sought her out at the pool, needing to justify himself, but now his rage flooded back. "How long ago was that?" he asked. "I've been trying to think of something as dated as an aging beauty queen. Oh, my! Mirror, mirror on the wall ..."

"You are sweet."

"Sweets for the sweet."

"If that's what you followed me here to say, you've said it. Now will you please leave me alone?"

"You can twist it any way you like," he said. "I did the best I could. My work is on the road. You knew that when you married me. You knew that when we got the children. My ministry takes me all over the world and there's nothing I can do about it."

"That is so much shit and you know it."

"Helga ..."

"You make me want to throw up with that kind of talk. You know and I know that you're a goddam hypocrite. Jimmy Coulter, the man of God! Bullshit! You're an actor: Jimmy Coulter playing the Reverend Dr. James Coulter. You run a gospel roadshow, a three-ring circus featuring the Father, the Son and the Holy Ghost. C'mon, Jimmy, you can fool all the people, but you can't fool me. I'm not blind. Do you think I've forgotten the way you used to be? How long is it since you've prayed? I mean the way you used to. All of us tiptoeing around so we wouldn't disturb the great man at prayer. So holy you were a royal pain in the ass, but at least you were honest. What happened to that Jimmy Coulter?"

He was glad for the darkness. The blood had drained from his face.

"I watch you, you know. God, what an actor you'd have made! The gestures, the divine light in the eye, the noble, uplifted face .... I watch you with those poor jerks in the palm of your hand, manipulating them. You even get caught up in your own words. You just love it ... And you have the nerve to talk about *me* wanting the limelight. God!"

"I notice you speak well of him when there are cameras or reporters around."

He heard the clink of glass and knew she was at the table pouring a drink. She came to stand in front of him. Her voice was quiet now, but husky with intensity.

"I watched you last week at that prayer breakfast. You quoted that text where Jesus says, 'Woe unto you when all men speak well of you!' I look around and I think, Christ! – the room is full of congressmen applauding. There's the Governor of New York. You're introduced by the Vice President of the United States on behalf of the goddam President. And in your sermon you quote this big-shot scientist and that famous writer ... all friends of yours. Name-dropping as often as a pigeon shits. And I say to myself, 'Woe unto you, Jimmy Coulter ... all men *do* speak well of you.' Jesus gets crucified. You get the keys to the city."

"It's a different time," he said lamely. "It takes a different approach today."

There was vitriol in her voice. "Yeah ... and nine commandments instead of ten."

"What's that supposed to mean?"

"Whatever happened to, 'Thou shalt not commit adultery'?"

"Helga," he said, "you're drunk."

"I'll spell it out for you." Her voice hissed with fury. "I'm talking about Arla Todd. As *Time* magazine might put it: 'Great and good friend of the Reverend Jimmy Coulter, internationally famous Holy Joe.'"

"She *is* a good friend."

"Isn't she though!" She drew close and he caught the scents of alcohol and perfume. "What a dummy I was! That time at Yale when I rubbed your nose in it and you didn't seem to care–I should have known. Then you get back from that so-called retreat. Gone four months and you don't want any part of me. I let it ride. You were struggling with something. To think of all those years when I thought I was married to you and you were married to God! *Jesus Christ Almighty!*" She broke off, catching her breath. "Then a few months ago I figured there were a few questions that needed answers, and not getting any from you I hired somebody who specializes in getting them. They tell me you're very good at covering your tracks. TG registers two adjoining rooms, only he doesn't use his. I must ask him how he enjoys pimping for Jesus."

He turned from her and went down the beach. She followed, dogging his steps, shouting over the thunder of the waves, abandoning a shoe in the sand. Finally, to escape her, he waded into the ocean and stood braced against the waves, taking each assault as it broke over him.

After a while her fury burned itself out. She called in a hoarse voice: "You may as well come out. I'll stay here until you do. I have only one more thing to say."

He slogged slowly to the shore, his hair plastered to his head, his teeth chattering, his clothes sodden and hanging. Looking past her to the house, warm with light, and beyond it to the dark hills, he said, "What is it?"

Her voice was without intonation. "You will break off your affair with Arla Todd once and forever or I'll announce at your first press conference in Toronto that I'm suing for divorce on the ground of adultery."

She turned and went toward the house. A wave ran up the beach, washed over his shoes and filched the sand from beneath them.

48

Clyde:
Since getting back from London I have been troubled by the fact
that the evidence about Jimmy Coulter and the woman, Arla
Todd, shacked up at the Savoy is based on little more than back-
stairs gossip. It seems to me that if we assert that the two of
them had a rendezvous at the hotel we would be getting danger-
ously close to criminal libel. Consequently, I asked Tony Rodriguez to see if he could find Todd. I had to give him reasons, of
course. Herewith his reply.

Jenny:
No trouble finding the Todd woman, but to date I haven't been
able to establish any cozy relationship between her and Coulter.
The lady owns an attractive house at 630 Walden Drive, Beverly
Hills, and according to the neighbors (WASPS all) lives a quiet
life. She's the owner of a children's boutique called TODDlers on
Wilshire Boulevard, which, as you may know, is in the sky-high
rent district. Decided on one of the famous Rodriguez shot-in-the-
dark gambits and phoned her at her home. All confused servility,
I identified myself as a clerk at Robinson's and said I had a gift
to be delivered to her—ordered, so I said, by telephone by a Mr.
J. Coulter. Dolt that I am, I had failed to get his address for billing,
and would she save my neck with the accounting dep't by giving
it to me. Looks like I'm not ready for an Academy Award nomina-
tion yet: she said she didn't know anyone named Coulter and
that there must be some mistake. Tried to draw her out but no

luck. However, something slightly offbeat in her reaction. Will check further.

Tony

Decided I should follow up myself. Called Tony off and flew to L.A. Checked out Todd's boutique and learned that it was started with a loan of $20,000 from the Bank of America, the loan guaranteed by the legal firm of Irving, Haight, Conant and Stonebaugh, who, Tony tells me, are Coulter's legal counsel.

Todd is a handsome woman. Dark hair with an auburn cast. Green eyes. Not as well preserved as Helga Coulter but then Mrs. C. seems to me more confection than woman. Introduced myself and asked could we have a word privately. Led me to a room you wouldn't believe: wall-to-wall stuffed animals of every species, size and color. Felt I was in a mad taxidermist's fantasy.

Cool lady. Does she know Dr. Coulter? No evasion. Yes, known him for years. Converted in his campaign in Stone Mills, New York. What does she think of him? Wonderful man. Doing an enormous amount of good. Started pressing her on specifics but got nowhere. I could see she was getting ready to see me to the door, so I put it bluntly: Did she remember where she spent the Christmas of 1955? 1955! How could she possibly! Told her it was my information she was at the Savoy in London, and that was the end of that. Graciously but firmly: "Good afternoon, Miss Wedger."

She reacted to my questions without the flicker of an eye. It should be noted, however, that she avoided direct replies to the important ones. Nevertheless, it seems to me that if I'm expected to include the Todd angle in my story, we should all be aware that we could be in real trouble if Coulter or Todd should decide to sue. That's a decision I leave to you.

Jenny

PS: Let me add, purely as a matter of interest—it won't be in the story, of course—that one is driven by the facts to a fascinating conclusion. We were able to establish that Coulter interrupted his stay on the Isle of Wight only once—to go to London to see Arla

248

Todd. It is not unreasonable, therefore, to assume that seeing Todd was more than a mere roll in the hay. Bearing in mind that the two have known each other for about forty years, an inevitable question arises: is it possible that they have had a thing going throughout Coulter's entire career? A further question stems from what I'm sure you would call "woman's arithmetic." The Coulter twins were born September 26, 1956. What then is one to make of the fact that that's exactly nine months after Christmas 1955? Add to that the fact that Jonathan and Julie Coulter bear a familial resemblance to their father but not to Mrs. C. And note further that both Julie and Todd have auburn hair (which, admittedly, could be tinting) and green eyes.

49

Hugh Hoffman put the pages of the memorandum together and tapped them on the top of the desk, continuing to do so absently, his eyes looking off, glittering.

"So," he said, "'America's Conscience,' as *People* magazine called him only last week, is not only a hypocrite, he's an adulterer and has children out of wedlock." He paused to scribble a note on a pad and then looked up at Clyde Rogers sitting opposite. "First rate!" he said. "Absolutely first rate. Curiosity and persistence – far more important in a reporter than education or style."

The two men were in Hoffman's Los Angeles office, Rogers being in the city for a conference of senior editors. He'd debated whether to show Jenny's note to Hoffman but had decided that the possibility of a libel suit demanded it. And he was still ill at ease about the revelations of Coulter's personal life.

"Coulter opens in Toronto when?" Hoffman was asking. "Next Sunday, isn't it?"

"Yes."

"Everything's in order? You've settled on the lead piece for the series?"

"As we originally planned, I think – the Macdonald-Reimer story. It gives the background against which the others can be played."

Hoffman did a couple of drumrolls on the desktop. "Possibly," he said, "possibly. I would have thought that, particularly with this" – he tapped the memorandum before him – "you would want to begin with the Wedger story. It'll make news and create maximum interest in the remainder of the series."

Rogers shifted in his chair, obviously uneasy. He scratched his head, unconsciously patting the thinning strands back into place. Hoffman looked at him closely. "You're not still troubled about the material dealing with Coulter's relationship with the Todd woman?"

"I wouldn't say troubled ..."

Hoffman's face donned its mask. "Precisely what is it that's bothering you, Clyde?"

Rogers drew a deep breath and expelled it through pursed lips. "Don't misunderstand me. If Coulter no longer believes what he's preaching, fair game. It's a legitimate news story. But his personal life ... We don't normally report on the extramarital activities of public figures."

He paused, then continued with reluctance. "Beyond that, regardless of what you or I may think of Coulter's message and his methods, I'm convinced that, on balance, he's good for the community." He coughed slightly onto the back of a hand. "As you know, I've got five kids. There are so few positive influences these days that I find myself reluctant to denigrate those we have."

Hoffman took a cigar from the humidor on his desk, and having performed his ritual, lit it. "I would remind you, Clyde, that it is the responsibility of the press to print the news, not to judge it or to try to measure in advance what its effects will be. We are not censors, we are chroniclers. The newspaper business is predicated on the people's right to know. What they do with that knowledge is not our responsibility."

Rogers replied with spirit. "You say it's our obligation to print the news, not to judge it. In theory, yes. But the fact is: we make judgments on the news every day. We're all familiar, for instance, with the drinking habits or the womanizing of, say, certain members of the government, but we don't print it. Not unless it gets way out of line and affects the man's ability to do his job. It was no secret that John Kennedy was quite a swordsman, but it didn't get written about until after his death. In reporting on him as president, it was irrelevant. The same applies in Coulter's case."

Hoffman fixed him with his unblinking gaze. "You don't see the difference between a John Kennedy and a Jimmy Coulter in the matter of personal morality?"

"No fundamental difference. They're both public figures."

Hoffman snorted. "The difference, as I have pointed out to you, Clyde, is that Coulter isn't a politician, he's a preacher. He prates about God's word but he doesn't believe it. He denounces adultery, yet he's been having an affair with this Todd woman for God knows how long. He goes on about the sanctity of marriage, and his own kids are born out of wedlock. The man is a monumental hypocrite."

There was a glint of perspiration on Rogers' brow. "But the piece is libelous. If Coulter sues, we couldn't make our case. The same with the Todd woman."

"Surely you've run it past your lawyers?"

"Their view is we shouldn't carry it as is. They're a little unhappy about the material on Coulter's beliefs but ... well, you know how lawyers are. I'd be prepared to take our chances. But not with the stuff on Todd. As Jenny points out, we make our case on the ground of hearsay and circumstantial evidence. I don't think we'd have a leg to stand on."

Hoffman had begun his drumrolls again. "Don't you frequently carry stories your lawyers tell you won't stand up in court?"

"Yes, of course."

"By what reasoning?"

"That the story is in the public interest and that, in all probability, the person libeled isn't going to sue."

"Because he wouldn't want to submit to public questioning under oath?"

"Well ... yes."

"Don't both of these reasons obtain with Coulter?" When Rogers didn't immediately respond, Hoffman said, "Do they not?" Still Rogers didn't reply. Hoffman's face was flushed. He banged a fist on his desk and bellowed, "Damn it all, Clyde, what's gotten into you?"

Rogers' head came up. "I'm not prepared to carry the story in its present form."

Hoffman stared at him for a moment. Then he pressed a button on his intercom panel.

"Yes, Mr. Hoffman?"

"Come in, please, and bring your notebook."

His secretary appeared, nodded to Clyde and took a seat. "Internal memorandum to Clyde Rogers," Hoffman dictated. "May this memorandum serve to absolve you, Clyde, and editorial staff members Jenny Wedger and Anthony Rodriguez, of any legal responsibility growing out of the publication of the series on Dr.

Jimmy Coulter in the Toronto *Tribune* or in any or all Hoffman Press newspapers. The decision to proceed is entirely and solely mine."

As the secretary left, Hoffman, his voice silky soft, said, "Any other problem?"

Clyde Rogers' deferential manner had gone. "Mr. Hoffman," he said, "in all my years working with you, I haven't encountered anything like what has happened in doing the Coulter series. You seem to have lost your objectivity. You have interfered in my editorial function. From the beginning, you have seemed bent on destroying Coulter: in the pursuit of the homosexual angle, in your involvement in looking into Coulter's financial affairs, in his personal life ... I don't know why – and it's none of my business – but it has made my job very difficult. Almost intolerable."

Rogers set himself for the blast. He was prepared for the dismissal he presumed would come, but Hoffman sat quietly. When he spoke, he seemed entirely in control.

"Clyde, let me posit a situation. If you were working on a story on Vito Giordino, the Mafia boss, and your staff turned up certain unsavory facts about his personal life – some sexual aberration, perhaps – plus the fact that he's hiding income, and that he's a bigamist, what would you do? Would you not follow up the story with all the resources available?"

Rogers yielded a grudging "Yes" and was about to continue when Hoffman pressed on.

"Yet, in Coulter's case, you're reluctant to." He paused, puffing on his cigar, looking at the ceiling. "When we first discussed the Coulter series, I asked if you were a religious man. You said, joking, 'No, I'm an Anglican.' I know you're not a Coulter follower, but I think you'll agree that you're in the same camp. Well, I'm not. I'm opposed to Coulter's ministry. And, Clyde, I've discovered an odd thing: this makes me suspect. It makes me one of the bad guys. Whereas, while most people may not agree with everything that Coulter believes or with the methods he employs, he is perceived as being on the side of God and is therefore one of the good guys. I've had some experience with evangelists. Most of them are relatively ignorant men with narrow minds and narrow interests. They know almost nothing of the human psyche and little of the effects of guilt in the human spirit. But that doesn't deter these self-appointed spokesmen for God Almighty. They are like the old-time medicine men. They live off people's fears. They're quacks, practising spiritual medicine without a license, offering remedies they neither understand nor have bothered to examine. They're not evil men in the usual sense, not men of ill-will, not malicious – indeed, they may be eminently likable – but in their zeal to 'do good' they often do great and lasting harm. They exploit guilt and fear. They twist the mind. They sometimes do good – at least temporarily – but it happens by chance. I think such men are – to use your phrase, Clyde – on balance, *bad* for the society. And if through my newspapers I can portray them accurately, I've fulfilled my responsibility as a publisher."

Clyde Rogers looked at his boss, pursestring frown drawn tight. Hoffman waited a moment, then said with a smile, "Well ... who are you with – the good guys or the bad guys?"

50

On the morning after the quarrel with Helga, Jimmy Coulter went to Arla Todd's house by a simple subterfuge: driving to his office, parking in the allotted slot, then passing through the building and into the taxi waiting at the rear. He walked the final two blocks to Arla's house, checking to see that he wasn't followed, and slipped through the back door.

They made love and he told her of Helga's ultimatum. She got up, slipped into a housecoat and went to the kitchen to prepare coffee. He dressed and followed. Neither said anything while she went about setting out cream and sugar and he shrugged into his jacket and adjusted the knot in his tie.

"Will she do what she threatened to do?" Arla asked.

"I don't know. She might."

"Does she have somebody else?"

"I doubt it. Nobody important to her, anyway."

"Maybe that's why she gave you the ultimatum. It sounds to me like she still loves you."

"Helga?"

"In her own way."

"Helga loves Helga."

"Not the children? Not you?"

"We're part of her. She looks in the mirror and she sees not only herself but the children and me. If I'm not there the picture isn't complete. *She's* not complete."

Arla filled two mugs with coffee and put them on the table. "I'm not your everyday, garden-variety narcissist," she said, "but I too look in the mirror. What will I see there next time? Me alone?" She sat down. "That was a dirty trick. I was giving you my own kind of ultimatum."

255

He sat opposite her. She was staring vacantly into her cup. "You know, I've been in love with you as long as I can remember, and yet in all those years I've never really had you for more than a few hours at a time. She's had it all. She's had you. She's had the children. And now she's going to take away even the little I've had." She gave a short, humorless laugh. "What was it Jesus said? *To him that hath it shall be given, and from him that hath not it shall be taken away, even that which he seemeth to have.*" She smiled wanly. "Pretty smart fella, Jesus."

He reached across the table and took her hands in his. "Darling, try to understand. We've been talking about what's in the mirror. Well, in mine there are tens of thousands of people, people who look to me, who trust me. What will it do to them if I let them down?"

She made no response, and when he saw that she wasn't about to, he went on.

"Try to understand: I'm not just me, I'm an organization. I'm a hundred-million-dollar-a-year business from which thousands of people get their livelihood. There are television and radio and motion picture contracts – they can't simply be torn up. There's a college, with teachers and a student body and an enormous debt. There's a publishing house. There are missionaries on the field ... I wish it weren't so, but the whole thing's like a pyramid on its apex, and that apex rests on me."

"Then you've already made up your mind."

"No, Arla, I haven't."

"But you have. You just explained it – you don't have any choice. Wasn't that what you were saying?" When he didn't answer, she said, "Maybe you do, maybe you don't. There's one thing sure – I don't."

"I'm trying to work it out."

"You could," she said, "stop being your brother's keeper."

A thin thread of silence grew between them that neither seemed ready to break. Finally, Arla sighed heavily. "If wishes were horses ..."

"Where would you ride?"

"To London."

"To see the Queen?"

"To the Savoy Hotel ... that Christmas so many years ago. The one real chance we had."

He put his fingertips beneath her chin and raised her face so that she was looking at him. "You talk as though it's all over."

"Isn't it?"

"Of course it isn't. There have been other times when we thought we'd never see each other again." Restless, he got up and went to the window.

Arla said: "I think we both knew that if we were going to make the break it had to be then. Not having seen each other for more than ten years. Knowing that our marriages were hopeless. Realizing there could never be anybody else ..." She raised her eyes to look at him. "Jimmy ..."

He turned to face her.

"You were ready to quit the ministry then, weren't you?"

His answer was almost a whisper. "Yes."

"Why didn't you? You've never told me." She hesitated, not sure she should go on, but knowing this might be their last time together. "When you went to the cottage on the Isle of Wight, you were so torn up. That boy at Yale – you were worried that you might have misled him. The flood in Italy. All the dead. The sadness. You were wondering how God could let it happen."

"You couldn't see all that and not wonder about God."

He sat opposite her again, slowly rotating his cup. "I was praying one night, and suddenly I knew that my problem wasn't doubt. It was disobedience. Doubt was my excuse for not doing what God was asking me to do. If you can get rid of God by doubting him, then he has no claim on you. You're free to do what you want."

She reached out and took his hands in hers. "I don't understand. What was God asking you to do that you weren't doing? You'd given him your life. Everything."

His voice was dispirited. "I'd given him nothing."

"Jimmy, love, what had you held back?"

"Myself."

She sighed with resignation. "I really don't understand."

He got out of his chair and went to the window again, looking out, his eyes unfocused.

"Remember the story of Jesus being tempted in the wilderness? Israel is occupied country. Jesus is a young man of thirty. He's begun to realize that he has extraordinary powers: Leadership qualities. A knowledge of human behavior. The power to perform miracles.

"The Jews are expecting the Messiah to come and deliver them. He goes into the desert to think. To pray. Is it possible that *he* is the Messiah?

"Then come the temptations: Turn these stones into bread. Use your powers to meet the physical needs of the people.

"Go to Jerusalem and leap from the top of the Temple – God will bear you up. Perform a miracle in the most public place. The people will rally to you.

"Then, the third temptation: The Devil taketh him up into an exceeding high mountain and sheweth him all the kingdoms of the world, and the glory of them; And saith unto him, All these things will I give thee, if thou wilt fall down and worship me. In simple English – compromise! Your message is too hard. You are challenging the authorities. Compromise ... and the world can be yours."

She wondered if he had finished, but he cleared his throat and went on.

"That's what the struggle was about on the Isle of Wight – was I willing to give up everything?" His voice had fallen so low it was almost inaudible. "I'm afraid I settled for the kingdoms and the glory. ..."

He returned to the table, his face somber. She wanted to ease the moment for him but didn't know what to say. It seemed he wouldn't go on, but then he said, "From that time on ... gradually, imperceptibly, my faith slipped away. I found it harder to believe. Now, I don't even pray."

She studied him, her face troubled. "Are you telling me that you don't believe in God anymore?"

"I'm sorry. But what could I do? I couldn't quit." His voice was infinitely weary. "I'm afraid I don't have it in me to be a saint, to turn my back on the world ..."

After a moment she said, "Look at me."

He raised his eyes. "Jimmy ... If you couldn't give it up back then, can you today?"

51

That afternoon as Jimmy Coulter turned in at the Malibu Community, the security guard signaled to him. "There's someone here with an envelope for you, sir." A man, his face flushed with excitement, came to the car and said ingratiatingly, "It's an honor to meet you, Dr. Coulter. I watch you all the time on TV." He handed him a brown manilla envelope. "Don't worry, sir," he said, laughing nervously, "it's not a subpoena. It's a hand delivery from Mr. Hoffman of the *Journal.*"

In his study he felt some apprehension as he ripped open the envelope. Within was a manuscript and a handwritten note:

My dear Dr. Coulter:
You will find attached a photocopy of an article, one of a five-part series on you and your ministry scheduled to be run in the Toronto Tribune and to be released internationally through the Hoffman Press coincident with the opening of your Toronto campaign. Four of the pieces might be described as run-of-the-mill. The fifth (attached) has been written by Jenny Wedger, a member of the Tribune staff, and documents what appear to be a number of extraordinary facts.

It is, as you know, a rule in publishing that the subject of an article not be apprised of the contents before it is printed. I have decided, however, to break the rule in this instance because (a) the allegations in the article will have widespread ramifications, and (b) it seems to me that special consideration should be given you in light of your former association with the Tribune.

If you have any questions, or wish to discuss the matter, I

shall be home over the weekend. The telephone number is
454-1029.

Hugh Hoffman

lead copy – coulter   wedger

The Reverend Dr. Jimmy Coulter, the man who has led thousands of men and women to faith in God in forty-five countries
of the world, secretly quit the ministry for four months because
he no longer believed in God or in the gospel he preached.

In the winter of 1955-56, unknown to any but his family and
closest associates, the preeminent mass evangelist of our time
struggled to salvage what he could from a faith that had gone
adrift and a belief in God that had foundered on the rock of
doubt. It seems that struggle was in vain.

An investigation by a team of *Tribune* reporters reveals further
that, during part of this period of withdrawal from the ministry, he
was accompanied by Arla Adelaide Todd of Beverly Hills, California, a divorcee and a close friend of the evangelist's. At one
point, Dr. Coulter and Ms. Todd occupied adjoining suites at the
Savoy, a posh hotel in London.

Neither Coulter nor any spokesman for the Jimmy Coulter
Evangelistic Association, a multi-million-dollar conglomerate
based on the evangelist's worldwide following, will say so much
as "No comment" when questioned. TG Wheeler, Coulter's associate evangelist and his closest confidante, told the *Tribune* by
telephone from Santa Monica, California, "Look, those are the
kind of rumors you don't dignify with a reply." He then hung up.
Numerous attempts to contact other highly placed members at
Association headquarters have been unsuccessful.

The most important piece of evidence relating to Coulter's loss
of faith is a five-page letter in his handwriting written to his son
four years ago. It is reproduced elsewhere on this page. The
letter makes it clear that:

— Jimmy Coulter no longer accepts the Bible as the Word of
God;

a copy next

— Jimmy Coulter no longer believes that Jesus Christ is the Son of God; and

— Jimmy Coulter denies the existence of the God revealed in the Old and New Testaments of the Holy Bible.

Despite his loss of faith more than twenty years ago, Jimmy Coulter has continued to preach, and beginning today is expected to draw capacity crowds to Toronto's Canadian National Exhibition stadium. A majority of those who will attend subscribe to the doctrines repudiated by him in the letter.

Here is the evidence of Jimmy Coulter's defection:

Wherever the famed evangelist preaches, reports of his meetings are carried in the press. However, a search of the *Tribune*'s files, along with those of the Hoffman Press, the Associated Press, United Press International, Reuters International and The Canadian Press, reveals not one report of any public appearance by Coulter anywhere in the world in the period between November 30, 1955, and March 20, 1956.

An examination of the program log of WJV-TV, Roanoke, West Virginia (which has carried every Coulter program since his television ministry began), shows that each of the programs provided to the station by Coulter Enterprises during the "missing" period was a repeat of an earlier program.

A similar examination of the log of OKAY/Radio, Atlanta, Georgia, which carries Coulter's weekly radio show, reveals that during the same period the programs supplied were replays of earlier broadcasts.

The evangelist's syndicated newspaper column, "Coulter's Counsel," did contain original material. However, it is common knowledge that the column is not written by the evangelist himself but by one of his aides.

Where was the world-renowned preacher during the four months when he was missing?

On November 19, 1955, Coulter left Yale University, New Haven, Connecticut, where he had addressed the student body, and drove to New York City in a Chevrolet Impala leased from Hertz Rent-a-Car. The following Monday he flew to Washington,

b copy next

261

D.C., aboard Eastern Airlines, flight 127, where he was met at the airport by limousine (S-24) leased by the Department of State, and driven to the White House where he spent the night.

The next day, in the company of His Eminence, Michael Cardinal Maloney, Bishop of the Archdiocese of New York, and the Most Reverend Jesse Angus Schaeffer, President of the National Council of Churches, he flew to Italy aboard Air Force One as a special Presidential emissary, part of a combined church and government program of relief set up to assist survivors of the disastrous flooding of the Po river valley. He spent three days at the scene. Newspaper reports show that he was visibly shaken by the devastation in which almost 1,500 lives were lost.

Instead of returning to Washington with other members of his party, Dr. Coulter flew to London, registering at the Savoy Hotel.

Monday, November 27, he rented a Jaguar XK-E sedan from Anglia Car-Hire, 42 Bedford Place, London CW1, and drove to Portsmouth, a city on the south coast of England, taking a ferry to the Isle of Wight. There he lived alone for four months in a rented house on the outskirts of the town of Caithness, an isolated sheep-farming community on the north coast of the island. Arrangements to rent the house were made by the Beverly Hills law firm of Irving, Haight, Conant and Stonebaugh, and payment was made by them. The firm acts as legal counsel to Coulter Enterprises. During his stay on the island, Coulter grew a beard.

The evangelist broke his stay on the island only once, to go to London, registering at the Savoy Hotel on December 23 and checking out at 6:45 P.M. Christmas Day.

The *Tribune* has learned that Ms. Arla Todd was also registered at the Savoy, having checked in December 20. Ms. Todd and Dr. Coulter occupied adjoining suites on the fourth floor of the hotel.

Ms. Todd and the evangelist are friends of many years. They met in 1939 when Dr. Coulter conducted a campaign in Stone Mills, New York. Ms. Todd subsequently moved to Los Angeles where, at age twenty-two, she married Allan Raymond Jackson, a radio time salesman. They were divorced three years later on grounds of incompatibility. Ms. Todd owns and operates a chil-

c copy next

dren's boutique called TODDlers on fashionable Wilshire Boulevard in Beverly Hills. The business was financed at its inception with a loan of $20,000 from the Bank of America, the loan being secured with collateral provided by the law firm of Irving, Haight, Conant and Stonebaugh, Coulter's legal counsel. The loan has since been repaid and Ms. Todd's boutique is a successful enterprise, grossing approximately $500,000 last year.

Dr. Coulter's stay on the Isle of Wight ended March 20, 1956, when he returned to London. The following morning he departed Heathrow airport on British Airways and flew New York City to Los Angeles on American Airlines. By all the evidence, he had not seen his wife, Helga Nostrand Coulter, or any member of his immediate family or any of the staff of Coulter Enterprises for a period of almost four months.

During that period he had canceled campaigns in Des Moines, Iowa, and Albuquerque, New Mexico. A scheduled address to the World Council of Churches annual meeting in Bern, Switzerland, was also canceled. The reason given in each instance was that Dr. Coulter was suffering from "a minor but persistent respiratory infection." Dr. A. R. F. Gaines, the Coulters' family doctor in Los Angeles, would not comment, but Dr. Gaines' former receptionist, Alice P. Ross, says that Dr. Gaines had not been consulted by Dr. Coulter at any time during the period in question.

Coulter returned to the ministry April 20, 1956, conducting a 15-day campaign in Salt Lake City, Utah. By all reports, the meetings were successful in both attendance and results, the only departure being that the evangelist refused all requests for interviews.

For purposes of analysis, the *Tribune* obtained transcripts of Dr. Coulter's sermons over the past twenty-five years and submitted them to Dr. R. Louis Griswold, professor of homiletics at Princeton Theological Seminary, New Jersey. Dr. Griswold reports that there are significant differences in Coulter's preaching before and after his four-month absence from the pulpit.

"There is," Dr. Griswold states, "clear evidence that the spontaneity evident in Dr. Coulter's earlier sermons is absent. Since the Salt Lake City campaign, the text is almost identical in each

d copy next

instance. Apart from topical references, it is as though the sermons have been delivered from a written text or from memory."

In effect, Dr. Griswold is asserting that for twenty-five years Jimmy Coulter has been delivering his sermons almost by rote.

When the Reverend Leo Francis McGeer of Toronto's First Church of the Galilean (retired), the man responsible for Coulter's conversion, was asked about the evangelist's friendship with Ms. Arla Todd, he said: "I've known Dr. Coulter since his Toronto days and he's straight as a string. You're implying that Dr. Coulter is involved in something like the famous Aimee Semple McPherson disappearance of the twenties. I'm sure he wouldn't be a part of anything like that."

There are parallels to the mysterious disappearance of Aimee Semple McPherson, the internationally famous pentecostal evangelist of the early decades of the twentieth century. Like Coulter, she was born in Canada (Ingersoll, Ontario) but soon moved to California. Twice married, she traveled the United States and Canada, speaking to great crowds. In 1918 she settled in Los Angeles, and in 1923 opened the Angelus Temple, preaching to thousands and conducting a nationwide radio broadcast. In May 1926, while swimming in the Pacific Ocean, she disappeared, reappearing a few weeks later with a bizarre story of having been kidnapped. Reporters traced her movements to a motel near Tucson, Arizona, where she had been living with a male member of her congregation. She was later tried on charges of fraud but was acquitted. She died from an overdose of sleeping pills in 1944.

The *Tribune* is not suggesting that the similarities between Aimee Semple McPherson and the Reverend Jimmy Coulter are more than coincidental, but a number of questions do remain.

If, as the evidence suggests, Dr. Coulter lost his faith, did he find it again? If he did, why does he refuse to respond to questions sent to him by registered mail? His continuing silence suggests that he has merely returned to the highly lucrative gospel circuit and may well be perpetrating a fraud.

The public, to whom Dr. Coulter looks for support, has a right to know.

52

Hugh Hoffman's was an enormous, squat house which appeared to have worked its way up the slope of an upthrust slab of mountain to pause at the edge. Viewed from the valley, it seemed frozen in mid-leap from the peak. Surrounded by cypress and pine and eucalyptus and skirted by a high, sculptured hedge of holly, the house was invisible from the road. There, massive wrought-iron gates hung open but seemed to forbid rather than to welcome. As Jimmy Coulter turned his car into the driveway, a uniformed guard snapped a salute and raised a hinged barrier to pass him through. Welcome to East Berlin, he thought sourly.

He had decided to waste no time on pleasantries. He knew it would be useless to ask that the article be killed, but had to make the request. He could apply to the courts for an injunction prohibiting or delaying publication, arguing that the article was misleading, injurious and defamatory, but he knew that Hoffman would have anticipated such an action and would already have satisfied himself as to his legal position.

As he mounted the steps, Hugh Hoffman met him with an outstretched hand. After the dazzling sunlight, the house was gloomy, with oak-paneled walls and dark beamed ceilings, and tomb-cold from air-conditioning. In the living room, he was led to a wide wall of window, there to look into the valley and off beyond the rows of retreating inferior hills to the ocean. He managed to pick out his own house – a minuscule, dun-colored interlocking of rectangles on the shoreline.

"Bought it in 1960," Hoffman was saying. "It was built by Edward G. Robinson, the movie actor – or so the real estate agent claimed. How do you like the view?"

Coulter was slow to answer. "I was thinking of your office in Toronto," he said. "You like to look down on things."

Hoffman made a small tilt of his head. "I hadn't thought of that." He pointed to an easy chair. "Club soda on the rocks, if memory serves."

When Jimmy said "Nothing, thanks," Hoffman asked to be excused if he finished the Scotch already poured. Lowering himself into a chair, he began to question Coulter about plans for the Toronto campaign.

"Mr. Hoffman," Jimmy interrupted, "we both know this isn't a social call. I read the article. I gather you'd like to discuss it."

"Excuse me," Hoffman said with excessive politeness, "my note said that if *you* wished to discuss it ..."

"Let's not fence. If you hadn't wanted my reaction you wouldn't have sent it to me. I'll get right to the point: Is there anything I can do to have it killed? If there isn't, please say so now."

Hoffman lit a cigar. "You haven't taken issue with the facts," he said softly. "I take it you have no quarrel with what our reporter has written?"

"Any discussion of her allegations can best take place in a court of law."

"Then let me give you my position. I'm satisfied she has her facts right and that the entire Jimmy Coulter enterprise is based on what I would call misrepresentation." His eyes didn't waver as Jimmy looked at him. "Others might call it fraud. However, there is always the possibility that the story might be wrong in some of the details. I wanted to give you the opportunity to correct the record."

"You haven't answered my question. Is there anything I can do to have the article killed? It could do immense harm."

"I'm afraid not," Hoffman said. "You're a public figure. You hold a public trust."

"As do you as a publisher."

Hoffman nodded. "Agreed. And I intend to fulfill it. It seems to me you have only two options: to resign from the ministry or to make your position clear to the public. In either case, I'm prepared to print any statement you wish to make."

Jimmy looked at him levelly. "The Lord giveth, the Lord taketh away."

"I don't follow."

"The last time we met, you claimed that you made me. Now you want to break me."

"Nonsense. I'm merely doing my job. It seems to me that, for your part, simple honesty would —"

Anger drove Coulter to his feet. "Who are you to talk about honesty? On the basis of a personal letter and a series of presumptions, you have the gall to judge me!"

"You *did* write the letter, did you not?"

"To my son. Privately. Years ago. How did it get into your hands — one of the Watergate burglars?"

Hoffman remained in his chair, sipping his drink. "If I believe the public is being misled, it's my duty to say so. Would you expect me to do anything else?"

"I'd expect you to be sure of your facts before you appoint yourself guardian of the public's well-being."

Hoffman turned his palms upward as though to say, how much more reasonable can I be. "If what our reporter says is untrue," he said evenly, "I'm offering you the opportunity to state your case in your own words."

Coulter turned to look out of the window. "And in the meantime, open Pandora's box."

After a moment he returned to his chair. "There's something I don't understand. Why do you want to destroy me?"

Hoffman smiled thinly. "Why in the world would I want to do that?"

"I don't know. But look at the facts. Here you are, the publisher of a great chain of newspapers, personally involved in a story. Why was the article sent to you? Was it because you ordered it written? And why did you personally send it to me? That's not standard practice. I've been in the business, remember."

Hoffman's voice was laced with scorn. "Yes, you've been in the business. You wrote sports, I believe. Perhaps out of that vast experience you can answer your own question."

"Perhaps I can," Jimmy said. He sat forward in his chair, elbows on his knees, looking directly into Hoffman's eyes. "When you and I talked in your office in Toronto, it was obvious you were bitter about religion. Something to do with your childhood, your father. You hold some kind of grudge, and you've turned it on me."

"The preacher as psychoanalyst," Hoffman sneered.

Having nothing to lose, Coulter decided to bait his antagonist. "What happened," he asked, "did you feel called to the ministry and found you didn't have what it takes?"

"Such puerile nonsense!"

"So you decided to come at it another way. I've heard that when you came to the *Tribune* you were going to change the world – and what a power the *Tribune* was in those early years. Then the day came when you were rich and owned a string of newspapers, but somewhere along the line the reformer's passion had run out. Your newspapers are fat but they're empty. Your editorials thunder and denounce, but nobody who matters is listening."

Hoffman's skin was the color of clay and his lips were compressed. "Is the sermon over? Can we get back to the business at hand? If the *Tribune* story is inaccurate, or if you want to state your case, I've offered you the space. What more can I do?"

Jimmy Coulter got out of his chair. "You can go to hell," he said. He strode across the room and down the hall to the front door.

On his way down the mountain his concentration wavered. On a hairpin turn the car strayed onto the shoulder, spun about, and came to a stop on the edge of the canyon facing uphill. A cloud of dust overtook him. He sat for a moment, shaken, tasting fear as passing motorists hooted.

At home, he strode through the house, and shedding a trail of clothes on the patio, dove into the pool. In the deep end, hanging upright in the water, he heard Helga call from her bedroom window in a peevish, parental voice: "Jimmy, for goodness sake! Juanita's in her room."

He stopped treading water, let himself go limp, and sank until his face was immersed. How total the silence. How undemanding the water. How beguiling the gleaming underside of the surface. He hung suspended, his mind out of focus. Then he surfaced, tilted his head back and lay horizontal, his face awash, his eyelids shut against the sun. It occurred to him to pray, but he didn't.

Helga's voice broke in from the balcony. "Do you hear me? You're to phone Gillie Whittier in Toronto. The doctor says your mother's dying."

53

Jimmy opened the door slowly and peered into the semi-darkness of the room. The smell flared his nostrils: an acrid layering of stale sweat, cheap perfume and death. A primal terror stirred in him as it always did when death was about, an irrational fear that he would inhale the death essence. For reasons he had never understood, he thought of death as noxious. On the deck fronting his home he would sometimes find a dead bird – as lovely a creature as a scarlet tanager or a hummingbird, its neck broken against the window. He would use a piece of facial tissue to pick it up, washing his hands afterward. He had often thought himself fortunate that his ministry was itinerant so he didn't have to perform that inevitable part of a pastor's work – visiting the dying and burying the dead.

His mother lay in the middle of the bed, her skeletal form delineated by the thin bedsheet, her head back, her mouth agape. Her breathing was shallow: an arid bubbling followed by a soft hiss and then silence, a silence so prolonged that he sometimes wondered if the next inhalation would come. He closed the door and went on tiptoe to look down at her: at the skull face, the hair matted on the pillow, the pale, ridged, toothless gums, the furred tongue humped at the back of the throat. His eyes moved down to the bony chest and the fleshless arms, the skin yellowed and crepe-like and spattered with liver spots.

The stench of her breath reached him. He went to the window and raised it. Cold air ballooned the curtains. He pushed at the window, trying to lower it. It resisted, and then suddenly eased to bang shut. The skeleton stirred. The throat made dry, clicking sounds. Perhaps if he remained still she wouldn't awaken and he would be able to go out and tell Gillie Whittier and the nurse that she wouldn't rouse. But slowly the blue-veined eyelids parted and the yellow eyeballs came to focus on his face.

"Hello, Mom," he said softly.

Seconds passed. The puckered mouth struggled to form words. "Is that you, Jimmy?"

"Yes, Mom. It's me."

"My dear wee Jimmy," she said and lifted a hand toward him.

He took it, squeezing it gently. The skin was afire with fever. He felt the hand drawing him. There was no avoiding it. He went to his knees by the bed and put his face beside hers.

"My dear wee Jimmy..."

It took all his resolve to remain as he was. The heat against his cheek and the combined odors of unwashed hair, body scent and the sickly-sweet perfume were overwhelming. His face, pressed into the fetid pillow, was distorted in a grimace.

"Jimmy, Jimmy... I've been waiting for you. Did they tell you I've been waiting for you?"

"I'm here now."

"I thought you'd never come." Her tears ran hot against his cheek. "But you're here now. You're here now..."

After a moment, she was asleep. Carefully, he disengaged himself, wiped the wetness from his face with the back of a hand and went to sit in the chair by the bed. The only sounds were the rasp of her breathing and the murmur of voices from the living room. In the gloom, memories crowded forward.

He remembered staying late at the *Tribune* on a pay night, and after the paper had been put to bed, being drawn into a game of banker. Two hours later he was ahead thirty-two dollars – almost two weeks' salary. He had changed the money into dollar bills, and when he got home had gone to Lizzie's room and turned on the light. As she awoke, he threw the bills into the air. They fell like autumn leaves, tumbling, swooping.

"Mom! Thirty-two dollars! I won it!"

"Gambling?"

"Playing banker." He reached into a pocket. "With my pay check – nearly fifty dollars!"

She got out of bed in her nightgown and gathered up the money. When the last bill had been retrieved, she counted them. "We'll put it away for a rainy day." As he followed her, wanting to claim the money for himself, she went to the kitchen and stuffed the bills into a china teapot on the top shelf. Then she checked the money in his pay envelope against the company statement and gave him his usual three-dollar allowance.

He remembered, too, the dream of the little boy in the outsize suit, and knew that he was that boy who, before he was grown, had become "the man of the house" from the day his father left. Why had he so swiftly made his father's role his own? His youth may have been stolen, but why had he so willingly surrendered it?

The darkness deepened. He recalled the wasteland of his teens: the dark sense of unworthiness, the inchoate longings, the fear of rejection that immobilized him in the presence of girls. His friends off on dates, he would sit alone in the shifting darkness of the Kum-C theater watching the gray, two-dimensional image of Jean Parker, dreaming the lovelorn's dream. No girl that he admired could possibly find anything likable in him.

There had been a few abortive forays into sexuality: gauche, sweaty fumblings with buttons and necklines and brassieres, fingers inching between clenched thighs to the damp triangle of silk. And afterward, guilt. Why? Was it the shriveling counsel of the priests as he reached puberty? Was it his mother's frown at any allusion to sex? Or the memory of her on her knees before his father, clutching at him, pleading with him?

His entire life, he thought, had been a maneuvering to avoid rejection, to ensure a pat on the top of the head and a "Well done, Jimmy." He had hidden his needs and subverted his appetites to win approval. He had sought praise before pleasure. How cleverly he'd fabricated the requisite Jimmy Coulter; holding up before the world this clever, clear-eyed, unselfish, ingratiating mannequin. And having gained the approval he sought, he despised it, knowing he was undeserving of it and that it had been won with a life-long lie ....

Lizzie's lips were moving. Something was seeking to surface. A word came breathily from her throat – "Jesus ..."

Ah yes, Jesus!

He sat with her through the evening. She mostly slept, rousing from her torpor as the time approached for the injection. They talked only briefly, the conversation breaking off as her eyes went to the clock to see if it was time for the nurse to come with the demerol. At two in the morning he lay down on the sofa in the

271

living room. Dawn was graying when the nurse shook him awake to tell him that his mother was dead. He went to the bathroom and washed his face, then entered the bedroom and closed the door. His mother's hands were crossed on her chest and her hair was arranged on the pillow. On the bureau he saw a picture of her as a young woman: laughing, vivacious, her head thrown back, her eyes sparkling ...

So this is how it ends, he thought. An addict counting the minutes to the next fix, a bag of bones in a yellow, shriveled skin, longing to slip into the black envelope of unconsciousness.

An ambulance came, and two cheerful young men took away the body. He wrote a Death Notice and dictated it to the papers. He called an undertaker who, on hearing his name, became obsequious and immediately fell into the jargon of the born again. The nurse, in street clothes and carrying a small suitcase, broached the matter of her bill. He wrote a check. Gillie Whittier approached.

"Could I have a word with you, Dr. Coulter?"

"Of course Gillie."

"I shouldn't be botherin' you, knowin' how you're feelin' and all, but before you go would you mind puttin' away the bed. It's the sittin' room, you know – the room where she was."

"Of course. Where would you like it?"

"There's a locker in the basement. I've took off the sheets. I'm sorry, but there's no man about, you know."

"Gillie, I want to thank you for your kindness to my mother."

"Don't be thankin' me, Dr. Coulter. It was a privilege. She was a saint, your mother. She's with Jesus now, praise God."

"I'll put away the bed," he said.

He rolled up the mattress and was surprised to find it warm. He stood with his arms about it for a few minutes, and the tears that hadn't come, came.

54

Helga opened the door of her hotel suite, expecting it to be the valet returning her dry cleaning. Instead, she saw a woman and was immediately wary. It was not uncommon for women to discover Jimmy Coulter's suite number and appear unannounced. But the woman before her appeared unlike the "Jesus groupies," as Helga called them. She was dressed in an expensive-looking navy-blue silk suit, the scarlet scarf at the neck enhancing the fairness of her skin.

"Yes?"

"I'm Arla Todd," the woman said. "May I speak to you?"

Helga felt a rush of anger and was conscious of blood flooding her face and neck. "I'm on my way out."

"It will only take a few minutes."

"What do you want? Does my husband know you're here?"

Arla shook her head. "No. I came from Los Angeles to see you. May I come in?"

"You haven't told me what you want."

"Mrs. Coulter, I have something very important to tell you. I can't say it out here."

Helga picked up her gloves from the hall table and pulling them on, stepped aside. "Now, what is it?" she asked, closing the door.

Arla felt an artery pulsing in her neck. "First," she said, "I want to be sure I have things straight—"

"If you're here to try to talk me into anything, forget it. Say what you have to and get out." She shook her head in astonishment. "Jesus! You've got a nerve."

"First, I'd like to—"

"Before you say anything, I've got something to say to you. I don't know how long my husband has been dangling you on a string, but let me tell you this: there's no way he'll ever marry you. He's already married – no, not just to me, to his work. Your lover boy is a preacher, and preachers don't leave their wives. It's bad for business."

She looked at the other woman disdainfully. "How come you've stuck with him all these years? And don't tell me it's because he loves you."

"How come you've stuck with him all these years knowing he *doesn't* love you?"

"He stays with me and I stay with him for the reason a lot of people stay together. It's not cloud nine but it's a hell of a lot better than the alternative. You settle for what you can have."

"That's why I'm here. I'm prepared to settle for less. As you say, it's better than the alternative."

"You don't have an alternative."

"Oh, but I do."

"No, old girl, you don't!" Helga said flatly. "You two will break it off or I'll blow the whole thing up in your face."

She fixed Arla with her eyes. They were hard and cold. "You realize he'll be out of the ministry. Can you survive that? Maybe you could, but if you think he could, you're wrong. His friends are in the church. His life is in the church. Has been for forty years. He's Jimmy Coulter, for Christ sake! What would he do with himself?"

"People are more tolerant today. I'm not sure divorce would –"

Helga laughed scornfully. "Some local preacher might get away with it, but not Jimmy Coulter. And Jimmy divorce me for *you*! Who are you? – a slut he keeps on a string. What can you do for him?"

"Give him what you don't – love, consideration ..."

"Consideration!" Helga tugged viciously at her gloves, smoothing the fingers. "How much consideration do you get from him? Comes around for a little nookie, then by-by, baby." She laughed cruelly. "Maybe not even that. Maybe he can't do it anymore."

"You wouldn't know, of course," Arla said. "Too bad. All that carefully tended beauty wasted.... I almost feel sorry for you."

"You feel sorry for *me*! I'll make the two of you wish you'd never met."

"Maybe you can, but what'll happen to you? The aging beauty

queen who couldn't keep her husband. And what would you do without the spotlight? And the children? What will they think of you if you deliberately destroy their father?"

Helga looked at her, a sneer on her lips. "Got it all figured out. Well, let me tell you something: he'll never quit. No way! Never!"

"You're wrong," Arla said, but her voice lacked conviction.

Helga read the other woman's vulnerability. "You said Jimmy doesn't know you're here?"

"There's no need for him to know. We can settle –"

"We'll settle nothing!" Helga snapped. She put her hand on the doorknob. "I've got things to do."

"Then you're prepared to carry out your threat?"

"You're goddam right I am. You two will break it up or I'll –"

"No, you won't."

Helga hooted, "*You're* going to stop me?"

Arla's heart was beating wildly. "The children ... Julie and Jonathan. They're mine."

"You're a liar."

"You can check it out."

Helga's face turned paper white. "You're lying. They're Kathryn's. We adopted them from Kathryn ..."

"Kathryn brought them to you, but they're mine. They were born at Good Samaritan Hospital in Los Angeles. September 26, 1956. Jimmy's their father."

Helga cast about, looking for something with which to strike. She wanted to fly at the woman standing there: to punch and kick and tear and maim. She let out a screech of rage. "All those years! The lies! The rotten, stinking lies!" She went to the door and flung it open. It banged against the wall. A mirror fell to the floor and shattered. "Out!" she screamed. "Get out!"

55

The item in the Death Notices stated that the funeral would be private but that friends might call at the Funeral Chapel between the hours of seven and nine Friday evening. Hundreds came to queue in the street, and admitted in batches, milled about in the Slumber Room, there to sign the Book of Remembrance, to whisper with friends and to crane about in hope of a glimpse of Jimmy or Helga Coulter – some to appropriate a souvenir bloom from among the dozens of floral tributes. Most were merely curious but others were sad and sought out Julie, who was representing the family, to recount tearfully the times of trouble when Lizzie had given them courage.

At 9:30 the doors were locked and the family came from a nearby room to join Julie. Helga led the way, her face and blond hair framed by a black silk scarf, so arranged as to suggest a nun's covering. Following on, pale and strained, was Kathryn, and behind her Herb, Jr., and his wife Constancia. Gillie Whittier remained with the family, as did Leo McGeer.

Each in turn went to stand by the casket. Kathryn, having hung back, went last, and for a long time stood looking at her mother, her face a mask. Then she reached out and put a hand on Lizzie's crossed hands and was shaken by great, silent sobs. Julie went to her and led her to a chair in a corner.

McGeer, bent and walking with a cane, moved about the room with a word of comfort for all, making the point with each that he'd been "Mrs. Coulter's spiritual father."

Jimmy, who had been brought to a rear door in a limousine, joined the group. McGeer went to him, took his hand and squeezed it. Jimmy controlled the urge to thrust him away.

276

Julie came to him and they embraced. Her resolution crumbled and she gave way to tears, clinging to him. He held her close until she was in control of herself and then went on to speak to the others. Helga maneuvered to remain at the opposite side of the room.

The manager of the chapel oozed into the room, caught at Jimmy's sleeve and asked in his oleaginous manner if he could see him in his office. "A few details." Jimmy went with him, and after ten minutes was glad to escape. As he returned through the Selection Room with its display of caskets, he saw in the semi-darkness a figure peering through the crack in the double doors to where the family was gathered.

He called out, "Jon ..."

Jonathan started, turned, and seeing his father, stared at him for a moment and then looked away.

"Hello, son," he said. "I'm glad you came."

Jonathan, affecting casualness, drifted off to the far end of the room, running a hand along the polished surface of the caskets as he went. Jimmy sought to bridge the gap. "Are you coming in?"

Jonathan didn't respond, apparently engrossed in raising and lowering the brass handle on one of the caskets.

"Come in with me. Your grandmother loved you very much."

Jonathan snapped closed the lid of the casket. "Why don't you just leave me alone?"

Jimmy went to him and they faced each other. "Jon, this is childish. We're grown men."

Jonathan said nothing, rubbing the polished wood with apparent concentration.

"Is it because I was a lousy father?"

"That was years ago. To hell with it."

"Then what's the problem?"

Jonathan looked at him. "You," he said. "All your lies ..."

"Jon ..."

Jonathan put his hands on the casket and leaned forward. "Have you ever given a moment's thought to what it's like to be Jimmy Coulter's son? Has it ever dawned on you that to many people you're a figure of ridicule? When I was a kid in school, it got so I'd flinch when I was introduced to somebody. In university, I'd be in my room studying and some of the guys would go by in the hall and bang on the door and yell, 'Hallelujah, brother! Keep those cards and letters coming!' There you'd be on TV, pointing that long finger of yours and shouting about God and sin. With everybody hooting. I defended you I don't know how many times. Okay, you're my father! Then what do I get? – a letter telling me you don't believe a word you're saying. *Christ!*"

They stood face to face, their eyes fixed on each other's. Then Jonathan turned away, his anger spent.

After a while, Coulter said, "The *Tribune* has a copy of the letter."

"Great! How did they get it?"

"I thought you might know."

Jonathan puzzled for a moment. "I do ... The son of bitch!"

"It'll be in Sunday's paper."

"Ah well," Jonathan said lightly. "You'll think of something." He walked away, flipping closed each casket as he passed.

56

All was in readiness. The year of planning and the weeks of work by more than five thousand volunteers had come to fruition and the Canadian National Exhibition stadium was filled to capacity with fifty thousand in the stands and other thousands milling about outside. Eight thousand cars crowded the parking areas on the lakefront and in the exhibition grounds. Two hundred chartered buses, their signs testifying that they had made runs from cities and towns throughout Ontario and from as far away as Michigan, Pennsylvania and New York State, were ranged in tidy rows in a nearby lot. Latecomers – some clutching infants or handbags, or hauling stumbling children by the arm – ran from the parking lots or the streetcar terminal only to find the entranceways barred.

Within the stadium, the speakers' platform was a blue carpeted rectangle against the emerald green of the astroturf. It had been constructed on the infield of the baseball diamond and was festive with brimming baskets of cut flowers. Ranged in a semi-circle behind it was a choir of five thousand, each member dressed in white. One thousand ushers ranged the aisles. Three thousand personal workers, briefed and prayed over, moved to their posts with Bibles and decision cards. Delegations settled into their reserved sections, brandishing hand-lettered signs identifying their churches or communities.

At the western entrance, a marching band of five hundred uniformed young people stood awaiting the signal that would send them in quick-step onto the playing field to form the living words CHRIST IS THE ANSWER while rendering a medley of Christian martial airs.

To record the proceedings for subsequent broadcast, mobile television cameramen were spotted about the perimeter of the field, with fixed cameras perched on metal scaffolds on each side of the platform. At the westernmost end, above the scoreboard, a videoamplification screen flickered with gargantuan close-ups.

The day itself was an answer to prayer: brilliant with sunlight, the blue skies broken only by an occasional contrail–frosted spider strands against the heavens. A breeze off the lake moderated the 85-degree temperature and caused the dozens of Canadian, American and Christian flags to stand out bravely.

Behold the day that the Lord hath made!

At 9:50 that morning two dozen *Tribune* delivery vans, nosed behind each other like elephants at a circus, entered the grounds and dumped stacks of bundled newspapers before the stadium. There were ready buyers. Firstcomers had lined up at dawn and now stretched from each entrance like tentacles. Newsboys hawked papers to them. As the hours passed and the crowds grew, they were beleaguered by clots of eager customers, reaching toward them with impatient hands even as they sought to make change. Few waited until they were in their seats to read, but stood where they were, contending with the wind as they perused the pages in silence.

Jimmy Coulter had moved from his suite at the Royal York Hotel the night before. Near midnight he and TG Wheeler had descended on the freight elevator, slipped unobserved from a door leading to the laneway in back of the hotel and had been driven some five miles to the suburban Inn on the Park. They knew that early next morning the Sunday *Tribune* would be on the streets, that within minutes every radio station in the city would have the story on the air, and that they would be besieged if their whereabouts were known.

Coulter hadn't slept all night and had spent the morning in his pajama bottoms, pacing the deep pile carpet, occasionally going to the window to peer across the city to the light towers of the CNE stadium, just visible against the lake. At ten, a copy of the *Tribune* was slipped beneath the door of his suite. He studied it and then put it on the coffee table, face down. He went to the radio and switched it on, only immediately to turn it off.

At noon, remembering the three-hour time difference, he called Arla. There was no answer at her home. A clerk at the boutique said she was out but was expected back after lunch.

He had finished showering and was in his shorts when TG came by. "Better step on it. The limo'll be here in half an hour."

"I'll be ready."

TG studied him closely. "You don't look all that great. Are you okay?"

Jimmy nodded and went to the bathroom to shave. The razor trembled in his hand. TG came to the open door to slouch against the frame, looking at the floor. The silence hung heavy.

"Have you listened to the radio?"

"No."

"It's murder. I talked to Billy Joe at the hotel. Absolute chaos. The press is like to break his door down. The phones! He's ready to hide out in the bathroom. I talked to the stadium. They're turnin' them away by the thousands. The American networks are there. The wire services. The BBC ... I told Costello to have a word with the personal workers and the choir. And not to worry – you'll explain when you get there."

Coulter rinsed his face and dried it. In the bedroom, he found a shirt and put it on, slipping a tie under the collar and beginning to knot it. TG shuffled about the room, tracing a pattern on the carpet with the toe of a shoe.

Finally, not looking up, he said, "You told me Hoffman was going to work you over, but nothin' like what's in the paper...."

"Tee ..."

"I told you, I don't want to hear about it. Right now we've got the stadium. That out of the way, we'll talk. Cool it, Jimmy. I want your word you won't do anything foolish. We go right ahead as usual. You don't say a thing. Okay? Right?"

"Tee, I can't do that."

TG waved his hands before his face as though warding off a swarm of insects. "Hold it! Later. Right now we got a service to go to. We ride it out."

As dawn had begun to lighten the sky Jimmy Coulter had settled it. He knew he could stand before the crowd and picture the accusations as an attempt to destroy him because of what he stood for. The world had always been the enemy of the church of God. It was trying to crucify him as it had crucified Christ. *Blessed are ye when men shall ... persecute you, and shall say all manner of evil against you falsely, for my sake.* He knew that if he marshaled all his skills he could win the day. They were his people. They would want to believe him.

But he put it from his mind. There would be no more lies. To go on would be to die; his spirit was already dead.

He thought he should make some notes on what to say to the crowd at the stadium but, at the writing desk, found himself unable to concentrate. He got up to pace the room. No problem. He always rose to the occasion. The moment would bring it out. Yet, the decision made, the heaviness remained lodged in his chest.

With tens of thousands waiting for his words, would he falter at the last moment? Could he trust himself? Yes – the charade must end. The truth might ruin him; it would also set him free.

There was a knock at the door. Julie stood in the hallway, her face pale. There was a folded newspaper under her arm.

"Julie! Come in."

But she remained where she was. When she spoke her voice was strained but unwavering.

"The story in the paper. Is it true?"

"Julie, darling, *please* come in." He reached for her hand. "We can't talk in the hallway."

She didn't take his hand. "Yes or no ... is it true?"

He sought the courage to say it flatly. "Julie ..."

"Daddy, three months ago I went to your room at the Harbour Castle. I asked you whether the things Jon was saying were true. You told me they weren't."

"No, darling, I didn't."

"Then you led me to believe they weren't. You lied to me. You've lied to all of us ..."

He went to put his arms around her but she eluded him and went down the hall. He followed. At the elevator he took her arms but she turned her face away. When the elevator door opened, she pulled free and was gone.

The black limousine rolled smoothly along Lakeshore Boulevard and passed through the Princes' Gates into the grounds. Policemen waved it past the boarded-up midway concessions and between a row of barricades to the lee of the stands at the eastern end of the field.

Jimmy Coulter stepped from the car into the sunlight and was

282

inundated by a rolling flood of song: thousands of voices swelling the majestic hymn, the amplified notes of the organ soaring above it, the rolling arpeggios of the piano sparkling within.

O God, our help in ages past,
Our hope for years to come.
Our shelter from the stormy blast
And our eternal home . . .

At the center of the platform, up on his toes, sports jacket open and flaring, Clark Costello was beating time with great sweeps of his arms, coaxing the last decibel of sound from the choir and congregation.

In the sunlight, Jimmy felt a momentary dizziness. His heart was pounding. A shiver of fear and apprehension ran through his body and he found himself wet with perspiration. It flashed through his mind that he was having a heart attack. TG drew near and whispered, "You okay?"

Jimmy sucked in a breath, expelled it and breathed deeply again. "I think so."

Under the shelter of thy throne
Thy saints have dwelt secure;
Sufficient is thine arm alone,
And our defense is sure.

"Better get in the car," TG said. "Here's the routine. At the end of the next verse, Clark introduces you and the car drives you to the speakers' platform. Helga and the others are there already. You go straight to the pulpit, do the welcome bit, make the appeal for the television money, then hand it back to Clark. He'll bring on the marching bands. Got it?" Jimmy nodded. His face was gray. "Remember now, we ride it out," TG said.

Time like an ever-rolling stream
Bears all its sons away;
They fly forgotten, like a dream
Dies at the opening day . . . .

The hymn climaxed in a crescendo that rolled across the lake to the islands and carried above the roar of traffic into the city. Costello lopped off the closing note with a chop of his hands, and the choir and congregation buzzed with self-congratulation as they settled into their seats. Costello went to the pulpit, his perpetual smile broadening.

"And now, ladies and gentlemen," he said, his voice communicating mounting excitement, "the man for our time! The man who has spoken to more people face to face than anyone in the history of the world. The man who more than anyone in this century has opened the hearts of his generation to the voice of God! Ladies and gentlemen – *Dr. Jimmy Coulter!*"

The limousine moved into sight, and picking up speed, swept down the center of the field toward the platform. There had been a scattering of applause as Costello ended the introduction, but it fell away to silence, a silence that seemed as substantial as the sound of the hymn which only moments earlier had echoed and resounded. The silence deepened, as only the participants on the platform continued to applaud, and as one by one, even they ceased.

The car eased to the side of the platform. Jimmy Coulter stepped out, pushed through a crowd of cameramen and went swiftly up the stairs, crossing to the pulpit. He caught a glimpse of Helga, hands clasped in her lap, her eyes down, her face composed. There came the whir of a plane taking off from the island airport, then it faded and the silence returned.

Putting his hands on the corners of the pulpit, Jimmy took a deep breath. "Friends ..."

His throat was constricted and the word came out hoarse, choked. He reached for the glass of water on the pulpit. As he put it to his lips, he heard the stentorian voice of a man in the crowd:

"Tell us the truth, Jimmy! The truth!"

"Amens" – like rifle fire from the bush in a guerrilla war. A whispering in the crowd – like a great sibilant hiss that rose and died as he stood there trying to gather himself.

At first the booing was like a hooting of owls. It multiplied and was soon the howl of a hurricane through a forest. The crowd was in tumult. Some shouted, "Shut up! Let him speak!" There was anger and scuffling and a flurry of fists. A balled-up songsheet came from somewhere, struck Jimmy on the temple and bounced away. A songbook came fluttering down from the choir. Others followed. Putting his lips to the microphone, he tried to be heard, but his words were lost in the uproar.

Head up, in a sheet-lightning storm of flashbulbs, Jimmy Coulter looked into the faces of the crowd as the tumult mounted. Then he turned, crossed the platform and went down the stairs.

He knew the limousine had returned to the end of the field and he walked toward it, a solitary figure in white against the green astroturf. Above him, a gargantuan close-up of his grim face flickered on the television screen.

He came to the end of the field. Workmen and hangers-on parted as he approached and watched in silence as he passed. He saw the car ahead. The driver had the door open and was standing beside it.

Spilling over the rim of the stadium came the amplified voice of Clark Costello. "Ladies and gentlemen," he pleaded, "may I have your attention? May I have your attention, please? Thank you. Thank you ... And now, someone I know you want to hear from, someone who is anxious to say a few words to you. Ladies and gentlemen – *Helga Nostrand Coulter!*"

The applause reached Jimmy as he stepped into the limousine. Then came Helga's voice, controlled, modulated: "My brothers and sisters ..."

Charles Templeton has earned distinction in an astonishing variety of careers.

Born in Toronto, Templeton was raised in Regina, Saskatchewan. Returning to Toronto in his late teens, he became sports cartoonist for the *Globe and Mail*, with his work syndicated in newspapers across Canada.

At the age of twenty-two he entered the ministry and during the next twenty years gained recognition as one of the most prominent churchmen in North America.

In 1959 Templeton left the ministry to join the Toronto *Star*. Within sixteen months he was appointed Executive Managing Editor. After a close attempt to win the leadership of the Liberal Party in Ontario, he returned to communications as Director of News and Public Affairs for the CTV Television Network. He then moved on to become Editor of *Maclean's* magazine in 1969.

Throughout his lifetime Templeton has seldom been out of the public eye. He appears regularly on national television and, with Pierre Berton, conducts a "Dialogue" daily on CKEY/Radio in Toronto. He has published two previous novels – *The Kidnapping of the President* and *Act of God* – which became international best-sellers, translated into many languages.